NIGHTBLADE'S END

RYAN KIRK

WATERSTONE
MEDIA

For my grandparents

1

—————

F our days had come and gone since the siege of Starfall ended. Only four days separated them from the destruction that had rendered an entire people homeless. It seemed so short a time, and yet the gulf between what life had once been and what it was now felt impassable, as though the Great Cycle had turned and torn the entire world apart. Asa knew her perspective was overly dramatic, but it felt true enough. Though she had only rarely called Starfall home, its destruction had torn a hole in her heart, an aching longing she felt every time she looked down on the ruins.

The rainstorm had put most of the fires out, but the flames that had buried themselves deep in the ruins of buildings continued to smoke, occasionally flaring up in bright but short-lived conflagrations. Asa found it hard to believe anything could still catch fire. So little remained. She'd never imagined a city could be so quickly wiped off the maps.

She heard, more than she sensed, the shuffle behind her. Koji had been healed, but his body remained stiff from disuse. He had been forced to rest for two days, and even though he'd been up and moving for the past few days, this was still the farthest he had walked since the battle that had nearly taken his life. The fact she could hear him before she sensed him was evidence enough of how weak he remained.

Returning to the ruins of Starfall had been his idea. They were camped with Lady Mari, less than a league away but still safely outside Starfall's crumbling walls. Asa had no desire to return, the memories of the battle too fresh in her mind, but Koji felt the trip necessary. He wanted closure. He wanted to understand what had happened, to give the devastation meaning. But Asa didn't think meaning could be found among the dead and desiccated buildings. Koji's hope was as empty as the buildings whose walls still stood.

She had no place better to be, though, and she didn't want to let Koji out of sight. He wasn't even strong enough to fight off a swarm of mosquitoes, and she refused to lose him too.

Together, the two of them picked through the ruins aimlessly, Asa mostly following silently as Koji searched for his answers.

Sometimes the intersections looked familiar, sparking memories she'd just as soon forget. She looked down streets she had run as the city burned, her only protection from the flaming arrows a small pot lid graciously given to her by a dayblade. The streets stood empty now, and the warm spring breeze carried dust and the smells of budding plants, burned wood, and battle. Death and life, mixed together in every breath she took. She wasn't particularly faithful, but if there was ever a symbol for the Great Cycle, Starfall had become it. The sun still rose and the world spun, no matter the events that shaped her life.

They turned another corner and Asa's memories

assaulted her with a nearly physical force. This was where she had come upon the old blade dying, his granddaughter wailing next to him as the blood seeped from his wounds.

Behind her, Koji must have noticed as she stiffened up. She sensed his hand go to the hilt of his sword, and she couldn't believe how slow the motion was. The thought of him protecting her was foolish, but reassuring. Koji would always be a protector, and she found that constancy to be something she could hold on to as the world shifted around her.

"What is it?" he asked.

She pointed at the corner where she had come upon the two blades. The old man's body had been moved. One of the first tasks the blades had set themselves to was clearing Starfall of the dead. There were still many bodies scattered about, locked tightly in places not easily accessed. Most had been gathered and given a proper pyre, though. "This was where I found Junko."

"The girl who's been following you around for the past few days?"

Asa nodded. She had rescued the young nightblade and escorted her out of Starfall during the siege. Since then, the girl had been an almost constant companion. They'd even argued about Junko coming with them on this small expedition. Asa understood the girl had no one else, but her presence was yet another responsibility Asa had no desire for. If Koji was willing to join her, she would have left camp that afternoon, never to return.

But Koji's will was as unbending as steel. At times, the quality was endearing. Today it drove her near the brink of violence. He believed in Mari. Asa had seen it in the moment he gave the lady his sword and bared his neck for a killing blow. She saw the dedication in the way his eyes tracked the lady and how his attention was distracted every time she was in sight. Koji wasn't in love, but his obsession was just as deep. He had found his duty, and Asa worried their paths might someday diverge.

They continued, wandering toward the gate Katashi's forces had broken through. As it came into sight, Asa fought down the memory of the wave of soldiers crashing against the thin line of nightblades tasked with holding that part of the advance until the other blades could escape. The fight had been one of the most intense she'd ever lived through. She recalled flashes of steel and fountains of blood, but little else.

She remembered her feelings, though, feelings she felt uncomfortable admitting even to herself. In the midst of that battle she had been calm, ready to give her life to save the blades. But now that the immediate threat was gone, her feeling of purpose had vanished as well. She didn't share Koji's belief.

Despite the ruin, she could feel the force of his optimism and hope. He stood in the skeleton of the city that had once been his home. His shoulders were back and his head was high.

They stood side by side, but leagues of difference separated them. Part of her wanted to share his sense of purpose, but most of her just wanted to put the conflict behind her. Like her mentor Daisuke, all she desired was a life untouched by the concerns of the world. The idea of joining the hermetic nightblade and his family grew into a strong desire at times, if only to escape this madness.

Koji's voice startled her. "What troubles you?"

She wrestled to find an answer close enough to the truth not to be a lie. "What was the point of all of this?"

His voice was reassuring. "We can rebuild."

Asa turned towards him, challenging his optimism. "Do you truly believe that?"

"I have to." His voice was confident, but a slight slump of his shoulders told the true story. Even his optimism, it seemed, could be damaged.

They returned to the heart of the ruins where the remains of the Hall of the Council stood, mostly as destroyed as any other building. Wisps of smoke still rose as something deep inside burned. Asa wondered if there was anything left in her that would burn, or if her fire was out for good.

She glanced at Koji. "Did you find your answers?"

He was silent as he looked over the hall. In all their time together, she had never seen despair cross his face, but it rested there now, his eyes moist as he beheld the once-beating heart of the blades.

He turned around before she could see a tear fall. When he did reply, his voice was determined. "We have to do better."

Just then, Asa felt a presence only a single street over. Koji must have felt the same. She saw him straighten and look in the direction of the presence. It was weak but moving.

Their first thought was the same. Was there a survivor they had somehow missed? As far as they knew, they were the only ones in the city today, and another soldier would have felt stronger to their gift. Asa ran, quickly passing Koji in his weakened condition.

When she turned the corner, she didn't see anyone. Asa took a moment to breathe deeply and center herself. The presence was weak and coming from a partially collapsed house. She walked slowly toward it as Koji followed a few paces behind, his labored breathing making it sound as though he had just run up a mountainside.

Asa jumped backward when the presence suddenly leaped out of the house at her. The action disoriented her on several levels. Survivors shouldn't move so quickly, nor should people who had such a weak energy.

Asa saw the glint of a short knife in the sunlight and stumbled, falling none too gently on her back as a figure darted out of the shadows.

In a glance Asa understood. The person was dirty, clothing hanging in rags off narrow shoulders. Ribs were clearly visible through the holes in the person's shirt, and the assailant's balance wobbled back and forth.

The thief clutched at a small parcel in his non-knife-wielding hand. With a few paces separating them, Asa felt no fear. A strong gust would blow this man right over.

Then the rags over the parcel slipped, and Asa caught a brief glimpse of what looked to be gold.

Asa was on her feet in a moment, and if she'd once had any concerns about her spirit still burning, they were quickly allayed as she reached for her swords. To imagine someone would so defile the places where blades had lived and died! She was sliding one of her swords out of its sheath when a hand locked firmly onto her wrist.

In the moment of confusion, the thief turned and ran away. It was more of a hobble than a run, and Asa's trained eye saw the way the thief favored his left leg. She'd catch him in a moment, no matter how close he got to the main gate.

"Let him go," Koji said.

"He stole from the blades." She tried to control herself, but her voice dripped venom.

"And?"

It wasn't the question so much as the resignation in his voice that broke her anger. She inclined her head toward his. At that moment, grief etched in the lines of his face, he looked like he had seen many more cycles than he had.

"The survivors gathered what was theirs days ago. That man was close to death from starvation. If it does him some good, who are we to deny him?"

Koji. A servant of the Kingdom, even to the end. He held not just to the letter of their oaths, but to the spirit. Her shame welled up in her, making her angry. She wanted to take out her aggression on something, or someone, but there was no one near. Why did he have to be so much better than her?

"Come, let's go back to the camp." Koji looked around and Asa had the distinct impression he was trying to memorize the scene. "There's nothing for us here anymore."

Away from the ruins of Starfall, in the camp that contained both the survivors of the siege and Lady Mari's army, the cool spring breeze carried pleasant scents that made Asa think of better times. As a young child, spring had never been her favorite season. Spring meant the beginning of the season of work. Life on the farm was always hard, but during winter the family spent most of their time inside. Winter was when Asa's father had taught her to read and write, his strong hands supporting hers as she first tried to write her name.

Spring meant endless days outside in the fields. Everyone in the family worked, and even though Asa was the youngest, she was no exception. One time she had run crying to her mother. Her hands had gotten so dirty, the mud so deeply ingrained, that scrubbing them did no good.

In her youth, she had thought her hands would be permanently stained.

The moon was out and bright tonight, shining through the cracks in the door of their tent. Asa held up her hands to the light, seeing they were almost as clean as a proper lady's. Despite the lack of dirt, her hands were still hard and calloused. As far as she'd come, some things remained the same.

Asa was tired. Her eyelids closed seemingly of their own will, opening again only after prolonged effort. Her body cried for sleep, but her racing mind prevented her from entering the world of dreams.

Next to her, Koji's loud snoring provided plenty of evidence of his inner peace. He always fell asleep quickly, and tonight was no exception. She fought the urge to trace the scars on his exposed torso with her fingers. Younger than her, his body had already been ravaged by a lifetime of fighting. But he shrugged it off as though it was nothing.

She envied him. Koji was a bit of a slow thinker, but once he made a decision, he stuck to it, following it to the end almost without question. She found it yet another endearing but frustrating trait, especially to one who doubted almost everything she did.

Asa eventually gave up. If she wasn't going to sleep, she might as well stretch her legs. There was no point lying in bed frustrated.

When she sat up, she noticed the flicker of firelight casting faint shadows against their tent. There was a lone silhouette cast by the flames, and Asa decided to see who else was up at this time of night. She quickly threw on her dark robes, welcoming their warmth as she stepped out into the chilly spring night.

Lady Mari sat at the fire, alone, surrounded by a handful

of her house guards at a respectful distance. From the lines of worry on her face, Asa guessed she had been sitting at the fire for a while.

Asa considered returning to the tent. Mari's gaze was locked on the flickering flames and she hadn't noticed Asa yet. The two of them hadn't really spoken except in passing since Mari had spared Koji's life. Approaching her felt awkward now, as if Koji's actions had erected a thick curtain between them.

Asa almost retreated, but the sad look on Mari's face drew her closer. The other woman was suffering, and although Asa wasn't sure how firm their relationship was, Mari didn't deserve to suffer alone.

Asa silently approached and sat down, recognized and unchallenged by the guards, but barely earning a nod from the lady.

Asa watched the stars as they crawled overhead, then stared deep into the fire as the flames danced over the logs and embers.

When Mari spoke, it made Asa jump a little on her seat.

"How is he?"

"Better. He has several days of recovery to go before he can possibly fight again, though. Dayblades come to him daily, which I think is starting to get to him. He wants to be out, helping you however he can."

She gave a soft laugh at that, edged with just a hint of bitterness. "He probably does more for me in hiding. His legend continues to grow with every telling. If he never fought again, his feats would still be whispered for generations. Some days I think that all I have to do is mention Koji's name and the Kingdom would be mine."

Asa knew what Mari meant. Everywhere they went, people were always whispering. Koji was possibly the strongest sword the world had seen in ages, and his deeds matched his skill. Still, the comment was surprisingly unguarded. Mari usually only spoke of leading her house lands. She never referenced the larger Kingdom. An innocent slip? Despite Asa's respect for Mari, she never forgot Mari was a lady of the court, raised in intrigues Asa had no interest in.

"The Kingdom—is that what you want?" Asa asked.

Mari's eyes sharpened as she focused on Asa. The gaze made Asa wonder just where the two of them sat. Were they friends, allies, or something else? She wasn't sure herself. Asa imagined Mari asking the same question.

Mari's eyes relaxed as they returned to the fire, her decision made. When she spoke, it was as one friend to another. "Sometimes. Only because I'm sure I could lead. My guidance would save lives, and prevent anything like this." She gestured toward the ruins of Starfall.

Asa allowed herself to be similarly unguarded. "Koji would agree."

"You don't?"

"I'm not certain any leader is up to the task of leading the Kingdom now." She knew she was treading on thin ice, but she didn't care to lie. If Koji's faith was justified, and Mari was worth following, Mari wouldn't punish those who spoke honestly.

Mari didn't, simply giving Asa a slight nod, the meaning uncertain.

Asa didn't want to travel down the paths of her thoughts, not when she'd come out here to escape them. To prevent Mari from digging further, she asked, "What keeps you up at night?"

Mari's voice was bitter. "Do you even need to ask?" She looked out over Starfall, symbol of so much failure.

Her expression softened and her shoulders sagged. "I am certain that I am the best leader for my house, but the challenges feel insurmountable. What if the army doesn't elect to serve me? What will the blades do now that their home is destroyed? Why should my people accept a woman as their ruler? Daily we receive messenger birds from the various nobles of my land, but I don't know how to reply. If I assert my claim, no doubt some will see a chance to seize power, tearing my house apart even further."

She sounded as though she'd continue, but she gathered herself. "I'm sorry, Asa. I know you have plenty to deal with now, but I'm not sure if I can do this."

Asa liked Mari. She wasn't sure the two of them would ever see eye to eye on much, but she respected the woman. The lady's strength and courage were unquestioned, and that counted for a lot in Asa's eyes.

Together they stared into the dying fire. Something about the flames entranced them both, and even Asa felt the effects of the flickering flame. She relaxed and spoke her mind. "I don't know the answers to the questions you have. But I do know this: when a sword is drawn, there is no room for doubt. The warrior who doubts their purpose dies. You face difficult decisions, but you can't turn back, even for a moment." She wondered if she was talking for Mari's benefit or her own. What was the point of fighting a losing battle?

"I am no warrior," Mari replied.

Asa stopped her. "You are as much as Koji or I. Your weapons may not be steel, but you grant death or life all the same. You drew your sword the moment you set us on this path."

They turned back to the fire, its warmth seeping through Asa's robes. Suddenly, she was hit by a wave of exhaustion.

She stood up, preparing to leave. She gave a short bow and turned to their tent.

"Asa?"

The nightblade could hear the change in Mari's voice. Mari spoke her name with an air of command. "Yes?"

"Thank you."

Asa gave Mari a short bow and headed back to her tent, wishing she could feel the same confidence those around her did.

ASA WATCHED as Jun healed Koji. Given Koji's status among the other blades, he merited visits every day from at least one dayblade. His body would have healed itself with time and rest, but there was an overwhelming feeling among the blades that their strength would be needed again soon. The strongest of them deserved the most healing.

The process was exhausting, both for the dayblades who healed and those whose bodies were being knit back together. After each healing, Koji sat and ate at least two bowls of rice and vegetables. Compared to what most people in the camp consumed, the meal was a feast fit for a king.

Asa had seen plenty of healings, but they never ceased to fascinate her. The powers of the dayblades were derived from the same source as the nightblades, and yet their skills were completely different. Only Kiyoshi, as far as she knew, had figured out how to tap into both sets of skills. Was that a worthy goal to chase? Or was it as pointless as so much else was?

Observing the healing, she knew she wasn't nearly skilled enough to try. She watched both with her eyes and her sense. To her vision, there was little to see. Koji lay on his bed, a light sweat on his forehead the only sign of his discomfort. Jun, the dayblade who had once saved Asa's own life, knelt next to him with his hand on Koji's chest. Except for the rising and falling of Koji's breath, the two of them were almost perfectly still.

Her sense painted a different scene, though. The energy around Koji was dancing in the peculiar pattern that it had since his last fight. The difference between Koji's aura and anyone else's was subtle, but Asa had spent enough time around him in the last few days to be certain that something about it was different.

Interlaced with that energy was Jun's. Dayblades manipulated the energy of others to hasten the healing process. Jun's work was intricate and fast, and Asa could only catch the faintest outlines of what he did. Her sense was trained to detect the swing of a sword, not the twitch of a finger.

Jun finished the healing. To Asa's sense, it was as though the older dayblade's energy slowly separated from Koji's, almost like two lovers stepping apart after a dance was over. Jun checked Koji over one last time to ensure he was well, then stood up. Even though the dayblade had seen over forty cycles, he moved with an easy and powerful grace. Asa wondered if Jun, too, had once been a nightblade. Kiyoshi couldn't be the only one to make the switch.

Jun's eyes met hers. Koji was sitting up and already reaching for his first bowl of rice. Jun looked towards the door, and Asa understood his meaning well enough. She bowed towards Jun. "Thank you for your time, master. Allow me to escort you out."

The deception, slim as it was, wasn't needed. Koji was attacking the bowl of rice with the same energy he fought opponents with.

Asa led the way out of the tent, then let Jun take the lead as he walked to a place where they wouldn't be overheard.

Jun didn't bother with formalities. His eyes looked sunken and hollow. As part of the cooperation with Mari's forces, the dayblades had been kept busy, healing not just other blades but regular soldiers who would accept their help. Asa didn't envy the burden the man was carrying.

"You've been with him since the battle?" he asked.

Asa nodded.

"Is it apparent to your sense that his energy has changed?"

"Barely, but yes. I lack the words to describe it, but he is different, even from other blades."

"Did you notice it before the battle?"

She shook her head. "It is difficult to say. As it is, I barely notice it unless we're very close, and only if I focus. It would have been easy to overlook before."

Jun sighed. "From my perspective, it is as obvious as the changing of the seasons. The other dayblades who have healed him have noted it also. It makes them uncomfortable, which is why I've visited the last three mornings."

Asa had wondered about that. Directly after the battle, Koji had been seen by whatever dayblade seemed available, but Jun had been the only one recently. Still, Asa didn't understand. "Why?"

Jun glanced at her, a momentary look of confusion on his face, quickly replaced by realization. "You can't feel it, can you?"

Asa didn't know what he was talking about.

"Asa, his energy isn't just different. The way he's interacting with it is different. He's manipulating the flow of energy around him."

Asa still didn't understand. She shook her head. "Isn't that what dayblades do?"

"Not like this. If I could do what he's doing, I would become a healer of legend. I can't manipulate energy that isn't mine or the person's I'm touching. This would be the equivalent of being able to heal someone while sitting on the other side of a city. What he's doing is subtle, and I suspect he isn't even aware of it, but he's pulling in the energy around him all the time."

"What does that even mean?" Asa said, worried. Was Jun saying Koji was sick?

Jun looked off into the distance, as though his answers might be found there. "I don't know. As far as I'm aware, nothing like this has ever happened. If there were any answers, they would have been in the library at Starfall, but that's gone now, too."

"Is he healthy?"

"Without doubt. Perhaps what we've noticed is the reason he's recovering so quickly. Perhaps it seems slow to you, but I can't overemphasize how close to death he came. The fact he's ready to fight again is remarkable. I don't mean to worry you, but I would ask that you be aware. If this ability is the source of his strength, perhaps it can be taught to others. If it's something else, well, close observation is the best we can ask for."

Asa agreed, and Jun went on his way. There were too many healings to perform in too little time.

She returned to the tent, where Koji had already started on his second bowl of rice. "What did Jun have to say?"

"That I'm to watch you, very closely," Asa replied.

A mischievous grin crossed Koji's face, and he looked even younger than he was. "No matter what?" With that, he started slipping out of his robe.

Tempted as she was, Asa was hoping to meet with the Council of the Blades today. If she was going to have any chance of catching them, she needed to leave earlier rather than later. She turned to leave, but Koji leaped toward her, mischief on his mind. Despite everything, he still had moments when he acted as though he was no older than a child.

Asa blocked one of his arms as he came to embrace her, twisted, and threw him down. He fell easily, but with a simple twist, he swept her legs out from under her, and she too fell toward the bed.

Frustrated that her plans were being delayed, Asa drove an elbow toward his face. Injured or not, she didn't like people interfering with her plans. She sensed his block coming and redirected her elbow. He deflected it with another hand, and before she knew what happened, they were trading blows.

The strikes ran the edge between playful and angry. She would attempt a strike, sense his block, then adjust her aim. He tried to stay in front of her attacks using his own sense. Four strikes passed in only a couple of heartbeats.

Then Asa sensed a block for a punch she hadn't even thrown yet. Instinctively, she switched limbs, driving her knee into his stomach. He flexed with the blow, absorbing it without difficulty, but she still saw she had hurt him. She pushed herself off, and the world seemed still for a moment.

Asa frowned, worried about what had just transpired.

Koji's grin slowly fell as he realized Asa wasn't playing anymore. "What?"

"I've never sensed anything that far in advance before. I hadn't even started to move when I sensed your block."

He didn't seem to think much of her problem. "It sounds like when I'm fighting at my best."

She shook her head, replaying the memory. "Koji, I'm not as strong as you."

"Nonsense." He tried to reach towards her, to give her some sort of comforting embrace.

Asa slapped his arm away and knelt down next to him. "This isn't about my pride. I'm serious. You're a much stronger swordsman, and what just happened was far beyond what I've ever been capable of."

Now his confusion was evident, too. "Have you been training?"

"No."

Lost in thought, she didn't sense the messenger until she was almost at the tent. It was a young nightblade Asa had seen around but didn't know firsthand.

Both of them turned as the blade entered without knocking. When she saw the state of the tent and Koji's loosely-hanging robes, she blushed and bowed deeply. "Apologies."

"Never mind," Asa growled. "What is it?"

"A bird has just arrived from our scouts. There's a significant force approaching, and Lady Mari summons both of you to prepare for battle."

2

T he rest of the morning became a battle of order against chaos. Messenger birds flew back and forth between scouts, Mari's forces, and the approaching force. After no small amount of confusion, Mari and her commanders learned that the unit approaching the ruins of Starfall was loyal to House Kita. Scouts reported they wore blue uniforms and carried banners emblazoned with the hammer and the sword, the ancient symbols of Mari's house.

Koji waited in a state of nervous agitation, pacing back and forth in his tent. Despite the arguments of the dayblades, he was certain he was ready to fight. He felt stronger than before, though he couldn't say why. His body ached, as though covered with bruises that he couldn't see, but he was confident that once he resumed training his strength and grace would return. If not for Asa's watchful eye, he'd probably have attempted regular training already.

The sun was high in the sky when Mari came to their tent. Koji recognized her energy without problem. It marked the first time she had visited since Koji offered her his sword to take his life. They hadn't spoken since, but his gaze rarely left her. He knew the purpose he intended to bend his life toward.

Koji bowed deeply to her. "My lady."

She returned the bow, less deep, as befitted nobility to their warriors. "Koji. It is good to see you well."

The simple statement lifted his spirits, his heart racing. "Thank you."

Asa, standing next to him, was less impressed. He wished that Asa saw Mari the way he did. Perhaps someday. She asked, "What do you need?"

The request wasn't out of place, and her tone was friendly, but the rudeness still grated against his sensibilities. Mari deserved the utmost respect.

Mari didn't seem to take any offense. "The leader of the approaching force is named General Fumio. According to his own hand, he is the leader of the First Expeditionary Force of House Kita. I know nothing of this, but he possesses my brother's seal and they fly our flag. I am inclined to believe him, and we are meeting under the flag of truce in the foothills. I'd like the two of you to assemble a team of trustworthy nightblades to escort me."

Koji almost jumped at Mari's bidding, but Asa's voice interrupted his automatic acceptance. "Are you certain that's wise? Our position is tenuous already."

"I have little choice. The blades are a part of my army, and there's no point hiding the fact. The blades and House Kita are tied together now. I'm wary of meetings, and without Takahiro near, you two are among the few I trust."

Mari left much unsaid. When she had last met under the flag of truce, she'd been betrayed by one of her generals and locked in a chest. Though her voice was calm, her eyes, darting furtively around the tent, betrayed her unease at the upcoming parley.

Koji focused on her last statement, though. Mari still trusted him, even after he'd confessed to killing her eldest brother. It wasn't quite forgiveness, but at that moment, he would have followed her through a hundred burning Starfalls.

Asa gave a small bow, acknowledging the task, and Mari left them to it.

Soon after, they gathered to approach the site of the meeting. Koji looked around, impressed by the variety of people Mari had assembled. Mari and two advisers were present, surrounded by a combination of soldiers wearing the blue uniforms of House Kita and nightblades wearing their traditional black robes. Jun, the sole dayblade, also acted as an adviser to Mari, and he wore the white clothing of a dayblade, matching Mari's own formal robes.

At present they held the advantage of the high ground, but they would soon sacrifice it. A warm western wind blew into their faces as they made their way down. The wind benefited the archers below, and Koji and the others shouldered shields in preparation for the worst. The weight was awkward and unfamiliar on his back, but the blades had recently experienced firsthand just how devastating the coordinated use of archers could be. They would never make the same mistake again. Strong as they were, they weren't invincible.

As they approached, Koji's senses were honed to a point. He felt honored to lead this guard, and if he needed to give his life to protect Mari's, he would without hesitation. Any fate was better than being dishonored in front of her.

His precautions turned out to be unnecessary. They approached without difficulty, and after a short time they were all seated under a small poled tent. Mari sipped some tea Jun had prepared as the general approached.

Koji took the measure of the man in an instant. General Fumio wasn't a nightblade, but he still carried himself as a warrior ought to. His posture and balance were nearly perfect, and as he walked Koji could see the scars that were evidence of a warrior's service. The general took in the varied assembly before him, his thoughts betrayed by only the smallest flicker of annoyance. "Lady Mari, your messages gave me some hint of what to expect, but it was not this. While it is good to see you, I have more questions than answers. Starfall is burned, nightblades form your honor guard, and your brother, whom I was supposed to meet, is not present."

Mari took another sip of her tea before speaking. Koji could guess how important this moment was to her. Her grip on the army above Starfall was solid for now, but they would vote on her within the next quarter-moon. If Fumio elected not to support her, she'd likely lose the soldiers above. But if she could win Fumio over, her grip on the army and her house would be greatly solidified. Koji wished he had some political skill he could lend Mari, but this challenge was hers alone.

Mari gave a brief account of the past moon, sticking only to the bare facts. She spoke of the siege of Starfall by Katashi's forces, her decision to rescue the blades, and her temporary control over the army. She didn't speak of the betrayals their house had suffered. "I am sorry, General Fumio. I sent birds to the other armies and to Stonekeep, but I wasn't aware your force even existed. If I had been, I would have notified you immediately. Which brings me to another question. What are you doing with your force?"

Fumio looked uncertain. "I'm afraid that is between your brother and me, my lady. My mission was secret."

"Hiromi is dead, general."

The shock on Fumio's face was genuine. Koji was no expert in people, but that much was plain. His teacup shook in his hand, which he steadied with a conscious effort. "What happened?"

"He was murdered, the victim of a conspiracy between Lord Katashi and General Kyo."

Mari's gaze was steely as she considered the general. Koji felt the tension in the air, picked up on by all the guards under the tent. No hand reached for a sword, they were all too disciplined for that, but he could sense the preparedness.

"I do not believe Kyo would be capable of such an act, my lady." There was an edge to Fumio's voice.

"Regardless, it is true. You have my word."

Fumio's eyes narrowed as he set down his teacup. "I've served side by side with General Kyo for over twenty cycles. Where is he? I will speak to him and get to the bottom of this. I will find the truth."

Mari's answer was direct. "I killed him in combat."

Koji leaped into motion almost before he realized what he was doing. He sensed Fumio going for his sword, trying to draw on Mari. The guards around the room shifted in response to the change in the general's balance. Koji acted without thought, darting towards the general, drawing his own blade, his sense giving him an edge on everyone in the tent.

The nightblade's sword was at Fumio's neck before his hand even got to his sword. Koji's voice was low. "Touch your weapon and sacrifice your life."

The general's eyes went wide, and hands went to swords

around the tent. They were moments away from a fight when Mari's voice interrupted. "Thank you, Koji, but that won't be necessary. General Fumio's doubt is reasonable. He's been a part of court intrigue long enough to suspect me."

Koji gave the general a long, hard stare before pulling away. He sheathed his sword in one quick motion and stepped back into the row of guards.

The silence between the two leaders practically crackled with tension, but Mari sipped patiently at her tea, eventually breaking the quiet. "I will provide what evidence I can. Kyo hired a young woman to impersonate me and who will testify to her crimes. If you honor the word of the blades, there are some who came to rescue me from Katashi's camp. And if you lend me your support, in time I will have Katashi's confession firsthand."

Fumio remained unconvinced. "Why would Kyo do such a thing?"

"I wish I knew. I loved my brother, but Hiromi ruled poorly. He was not prepared the way Juro was. Perhaps Kyo believed he acted to benefit the house. Or maybe it was a simple lust for power. That is a question I cannot answer."

Fumio sipped at his tea, more thoughtful than before. "What would you have of me?"

"Answers, first. What was your mission?"

The general paused before answering. "Hiromi believed there would be an opportunity to go north, cross the river, and flank Katashi's forces. It was a wishful plan, but I had my orders."

Mari nodded. "A strike force behind enemy lines. What was your objective?"

"Destroy the lands of House Amari and assassinate Lord Katashi if possible."

Mari looked beyond the tent towards the collection of soldiers in the distance. "With only that?"

Fumio looked pained. "They are elite soldiers, but yes. I argued against the plan."

They each took a sip of their tea. Mari seemed to be taking the measure of the general. "I plan to become the head of my house. I realize this goes against tradition, but the people must be kept safe. Will you join me?"

Fumio looked around at the assembled gathering. "Do I have a choice? Your blades are a potent force."

Mari's voice was stern. "You will always have a choice. Refuse, and your rank will be stripped down to private. You will still serve the house and the people, if that is your wish. Otherwise, you may retire. Accept my offer and we can prevent this war from causing even more destruction."

Fumio gazed at her for a long time. Finally, he gave a grim smile. "You remind me of Juro at times."

Mari gave Fumio a bow. "That is the greatest compliment I could receive. Thank you."

"I will bring my force up to your camp by the end of the day."

There was no more to be said. They finished their tea, bowed to one another, and left for their respective forces.

THE COUNCIL COULDN'T HAVE ASKED for better weather to hold their gathering. The sun shone brightly in the sky against tufts of wispy clouds. The cool air coming down from the snow-covered mountains swirled with the warm air from the plains below, creating a temperature that encouraged the weary warriors to bask in the sunlight.

Despite the nearly perfect weather, Koji felt uneasy. And Asa wasn't helping. Busy with other tasks, they hadn't had much time to speak since the parley yesterday, but when they did talk, Asa only wanted to discuss Koji's actions.

Koji couldn't understand. From his perspective, nothing noteworthy had occurred. But Asa was insistent.

"Koji, do you trust me?"

His pace didn't slow. If they made it to the gathering, this conversation would end. "Of course."

"Then why don't you believe me?"

"Because what you're saying makes no sense."

"Think, Koji! You were surrounded by other blades. Did anyone else have their sword out?"

Koji stopped and spun around. They already knew he was faster than most blades, so though he agreed she was right about the facts, her interpretation was beyond reason. She was pushing him to accept an answer to a question he didn't have.

Asa's frustration burst through. "I'm not the only one, Koji. You can ask the others. The blades are whispering about it."

Koji barely contained his own frustration. "What do you want from me, Asa?"

"For you to realize that you're stronger and faster than before. I wish you could have seen it from my perspective. I barely saw you move!"

He didn't have any answers for her. Little had changed in his mind, but she wanted more.

"What was it like?"

"Nothing seemed different. I've already told you that."

Asa looked as though she didn't believe him, but didn't push the issue.

Thankfully they came upon the gathering only a few moments later. Hajimi, the leader of the blades, had selected a location that acted as a natural amphitheater.

There was a small hillside overlooking a flat area suitable for speaking. The four surviving blades of the council sat near the base of the hill while the others sat higher. All concerned with the fate of the blades were welcome to attend. The space wasn't as convenient as their destroyed hall, but every blade should still be able to hear the debate.

Two facts caught Koji's attention. The first was just how few blades there were. Koji estimated there were several hundred present. There were those still out in the Kingdom, of course, but their numbers were greatly diminished. There was no doubting that. He suspected there were less than a thousand blades left in total, a thought that made him shudder.

The second fact was how few dayblades there were. Traditional wisdom held that dayblades were less common than nightblades because the skills were more difficult to learn. Koji had always heard it said there were about three nightblades for every dayblade. But here the number seemed closer to ten. He looked on a sea of black robes with only the occasional white robe. Had the dayblades been hit harder by the chaos in the land, or were the numbers he'd been raised with incorrect?

He and Asa took a seat on the hillside, about halfway up the slope, but he couldn't shake the feeling he was the center of attention.

Koji wished for the relative anonymity he had once enjoyed. He knew his strength. That was simply the truth of the situation. But he didn't believe his deeds deserved the recognition he received. His shame grew even more acute through the awareness of the crimes he had committed. He had helped burn the palace. He had killed the king and helped start this war. No matter what good he did, no matter how skilled he was, he wasn't sure his mistakes would ever wash away.

Before the meeting began, the two of them were joined by Junko, the young nightblade Asa had rescued from Starfall. She was often around and seized any moment she could to be next to her savior. The girl had been training daily since the siege, eager to prove herself to Asa. Asa, unfortunately, gave the girl little attention. Koji supposed she had other problems on her mind.

Hajimi stood up to address the crowd. Even from a distance, he looked as reduced as the gathering over which he presided. He had once looked strong, the sort of man one fought only if necessary. His eyes still blazed, but the muscle had fallen off his bones in the past couple of moons, and the dark bags under his eyes confirmed that he was getting no sleep.

His voice still carried over the gathered assembly. "Our home is gone, but our strength remains. We gather today to decide what direction our people will take. The floor is open to suggestions and thoughts."

Koji settled in for a long discussion. Typically, the council made their decisions and let the rest of the blades know. The rumor that had circulated was that Hajimi was uncomfortable making a decision without knowing the thoughts of the people. Koji found the idea detestable. At times like this, blades needed strong leadership, not a poll. There would be dozens, if not hundreds, of different ideas presented today, with no clear direction forthcoming. It was no way to lead.

One by one, blades stepped forward and spoke their minds, the assembly attentive and interested. Koji noticed a pattern after only a few speakers. Most everyone wanted to rebuild Starfall. They wanted to reclaim the past and the power they once possessed. There were suggestions of getting the lords to bend their knees to Hajimi, and one dayblade went so far as to suggest the next king be pulled from their own ranks, an idea as illegal as it was dangerous. But no one spoke against this line of thought with any authority.

Koji looked around the hillside. Most of the blades shifted back and forth uncomfortably. Those coming down were vocal, but Koji saw plenty of glances among the assembly. Most understood that the speakers were promoting a dream that could never come true, but no one had the courage to speak the truth. And the more speakers that advocated negotiating with the houses from a position of power, the more people seemed to believe this foolish delusion.

He felt sick, listening as the debate quickly became more and more foolish. The winds of change had come to sweep up the blades, and all they could think of was returning to the way things had been. The better past they spoke of seemed more imagination than reality, yet the illusion slowly won over many converts.

He couldn't allow it. The truth seemed so obvious. It hung over the gathering like a thick, suffocating blanket, but no one acknowledged it. He stood up to be recognized and heard the whispers grow in volume. Even Asa glanced up. She knew his mind and he felt her support. She was too self-interested to speak in front of the crowd, but knowing he had at least one supporter gave him the strength to speak with courage.

Hajimi formally recognized Koji as he came to the front. He swallowed hard as he searched for the right words. His instinct was to fight, an instinct honed over a lifetime of training. But agreement would get them farther.

"While I respect the voices who have come before me, I must disagree."

Koji wasn't sure if it was his imagination, but he felt as if large parts of the crowd were leaning forward to listen.

"There is a harsh truth we must acknowledge. Much of what I've heard today expresses a desire for the world to return to the way things once were. I understand this desire. I want my home back, and I want the respect that was once mine by virtue of these robes I've earned the right to wear. But the Great Cycle turns only in one direction. Look around you." He paused for emphasis and to find his next words.

"There should be thousands of us here. Each of us has lost friends and family, people we trained with and fought beside. Most of the people in the Kingdom want us dead. You all know this. We've all seen the fear and the hatred in the eyes of those we serve.

"Yes, there is strength here, the strength to change the course of the future. But not the strength to bend the Kingdom to our will."

Koji thought he heard some angry mutterings, but he wasn't deterred. "Our goal can't simply be to bring the past back to life. That's no better than an adult wishing for the responsibilities of a child. And we are not children. I am not wise enough to know exactly what should be done, but I do have one suggestion.

"For now, we follow Lady Mari. She is unconventional, but those of us who have met her and seen her in person have been impressed. She offers us shelter while the other lords plan sieges. Her house is rich in resources but poor in people. Without us, her lands would fall to the other lords. But together, we may yet bring balance to the Kingdom."

Koji thought about saying more, but his points had been

made. Speaking longer would be disrespectful. He bowed and took his seat. Even Asa looked thoughtful, and that was more of a compliment than he expected.

The speaker after Koji refuted many of the points he had made, but Koji could feel the change in attitude among the crowd. His voice had stopped the tyranny of the vocal minority. One by one, other speakers came down, each one essentially saying they agreed with Koji. Some differed in details, but there was one fact they all agreed on: their best chance of survival lay with Mari. The future was unknown, but their immediate steps seemed obvious.

When the council finally made its decision as the sun was setting, it was almost a bygone conclusion.

The blades would align with House Kita.

SEVERAL DAYS LATER, Mari's ambitions were put to yet another test, the vote of her army.

Koji and several other nightblades were asked to form Mari's escort for the event. As far as Koji knew, nothing like this had ever happened in the history of the Kingdom. He listened to Mari's arguments, but still wasn't sure he believed them. Leaders shouldn't turn to the people they led for support. Their duty was to lead, and the duty of others was to follow.

Mari had laughed when he told her this, and had asked if he thought that was the way the world worked.

"It is if you say so."

She had laughed even harder. Koji was pleased he could bring her some happiness, but was stung she thought so little of his outlook. "Koji, I'm sorry if I offend. The world would be a much easier place to live in if that was true. But do you think what is true of you is true of others? How many would follow simply because they thought it was their duty?"

Koji acknowledged her point. "But what if they decide you are not fit to lead them?"

"Then there's nothing I could do anyway. Any ruler who relies solely on fear or force is eventually overthrown. History has taught us that much. I couldn't use the blades in that way, either. I would have no choice but to step down."

Koji couldn't bring himself to accept the chance she was taking. "There has to be a better way."

She had won the argument that day, but Koji still didn't support Mari's ideas. They were strange and untested, with far too many questions. The risk of failure seemed too great to him. Koji had watched the way Mari fought for the votes of her soldiers. She had publicly revealed herself as the Lady in White, the rebel who had fed villages throughout the winter. She traveled with a nightblade escort wherever she went, both for protection and to remind the people that their fates under her leadership would be tied together.

But more than that, she was present. She led archery training, proving that though she was a woman, she wasn't without martial ability. Her skill with a bow surpassed all but the best in the army, and more than a few silver pieces had been lost by the men betting against her.

Mari attended every meeting the commanders held. Koji had escorted her during one and been impressed. She questioned the assumptions of the commanders, asked intelligent questions, and took the advice given. She openly acknowledged that she lacked the training necessary to be a general, but she was learning.

Mari ate meals with the men, spending most of the time listening to their concerns and complaints. At first, the men behaved awkwardly around her. After all, none of them had experience dining with royalty, much less female royalty. But over the course of a half moon, they had come to accept her.

There was still opposition, of course. A handful of the mid-level commanders couldn't bear the idea of taking orders from a woman. Under the current arrangement they held their positions, but if Mari did become the choice of the army, their rank would be in jeopardy. Unsurprisingly, some of their attitudes had trickled to the men who served under them. Koji didn't know how deep the attitudes ran, though. Among the blades, having a woman in command was well accepted. Blades were given authority matching their skills, regardless of sex, but the rest of the Kingdom didn't feel the same.

The army gathered on the same hillside the blades had met on several days before. Mari stood before them, prepared to address the crowd.

When everyone was settled and quiet, she began. Koji stood well behind her, per her instructions. She wanted him to be visible, but not so close that anyone believed she was taking orders from the blades.

"Gentlemen. Today we make history. Never before has the nobility of a house asked for the right to lead. I will not waste your time with fancy words. Most of you have seen me in battle. You've seen the way I lead, and in the past days, you have had your chance to ask questions of me. No doubt you have already made your decision. I know how unusual this circumstance is, and while I believe that I can lead this army and protect our people, I will not ask anyone to fight for me who does not want to. That is not my way."

With that, her speech, short as it was, was over. Koji had expected more.

She stepped back, and General Fumio stepped forward

to give the instructions for voting. Prior to the gathering of the army, every soldier had been asked to find a pebble. In front of them, where the Council of the Blades had sat days ago, was a small, covered structure. Inside were two baskets, one labeled with Mari's name. One at a time, every soldier would step quickly into the confined space and drop their pebble in a basket. Fumio would oversee. He was the only one everyone could agree to trust. Everyone's vote was otherwise private.

The process was simple enough. Before long, the men began lining up. Each vote only took a heartbeat or two, but it was still no small matter to get through thousands of votes.

Koji resisted the urge to use his sense to know what was happening inside the tent. For one, his duty was to protect Mari. His attention needed to be on her and the surroundings. Second, Mari had made the blades promise not to interfere in any way. He would uphold the promise.

Instead, Koji focused on the crowd, guessing their intentions from the way they held themselves. Mari stood proudly off to the side while people cast their votes. She gave a small bow of thanks to every soldier who walked through the voting tent, and after a while he wondered if it was starting to make her sore or dizzy.

The soldiers looked intrigued by the idea of voting. Most of them kept their faces neutral, but there was a spring in their step as they walked through the tent to make their voices heard.

Koji's sense wandered over the hillside, but he couldn't detect any threats. If someone did want to harm Mari, they weren't here. That much was a relief. Anytime someone tried to bring change to the world there would be those who fought against it. If Mari won here today, her battles would just be beginning. She would be the target of assassinations, political manipulations, and more. He believed in her, but he didn't envy her the responsibility she sought.

The sun had passed the midpoint when the final soldier walked through the tent and returned to his seat on the hillside. Fumio stepped out a moment later, for the first time since the voting began. His voice rang clear upon the hillside.

"No counting is needed. Lady Mari, this army is yours."

Koji watched Mari's reaction, muted as it was. She stepped forward, knelt, and bowed all the way to the ground. There were murmurs throughout the gathered soldiers. None of them had ever seen a lord or lady bow so deeply to anyone.

"Thank you," she stated simply as she rose. "Your confidence will not be misplaced."

With that, the assembly ended. Mari walked back towards her tent as the commanders began gathering their soldiers to resume the normal life of the camp. Even though a momentous occasion had just occurred, there was still guard duty to fill and food to cook.

Koji and Asa followed Mari. He was just about to congratulate her when a messenger reached them, out of breath. A look of fear radiated from his eyes. "My lady, I'm sorry, but we've just received a bird. The throne of your house has been claimed by another."

3

That evening, Mari and the leadership of House Kita sat around the fire. The flames provided needed comfort, a warmth to fight off the chill not just of the evening, but of the past day's events. The news from Stonekeep had frozen the hearts of her supporters. The effect had been particularly bleak after the excitement of the army declaring for Mari.

Despite the progress she'd made, her footing was now more treacherous than ever. She stood on the edge of a crumbling cliff, scrambling for safety.

Perhaps the worst consequence of the news was that it caused Mari to doubt herself. She never imagined she'd have to deal with another betrayal so quickly, and it made her question whether she should rule at all.

Strangely, Koji's presence at the fire kept her moving forward. Although she still felt a familiar surge of anger every time she looked at him, his support was vocal and passionate. His confidence in her gave her confidence in herself. If she had the loyalty of a warrior of his strength, she had the qualities necessary to lead her people. She had to believe that.

Mari had received a full report earlier that evening, and the news still stung every time her mind wandered toward the capital. The throne of their house lands had been claimed by Tatsuo, a noble adviser Mari had known personally since she was a child. He had always been close to the house, a fact that probably strengthened his claim.

The evening had been spent writing letters, sending birds and messengers to all the other nobles, announcing her own claim bolstered by the support of the army and the blades. Still, it would be days before she heard back and learned where the other nobles stood in this unexpected conflict. She wanted to believe they would support her by virtue of her blood. These lands had been ruled by House Kita for almost twenty generations. But she was becoming accustomed to the stabs of betrayal her house suffered.

If she had been in Stonekeep, she might have ordered Koji to assassinate Tatsuo. The traitor deserved no less, and although Mari detested assassination, her lands could not suffer through a civil conflict with the larger war on their doorstep. They needed unity, now more than ever. She didn't have time for gentler solutions.

Thankfully, being out in the foothills made that move less immediately feasible. Her distance from Stonekeep gave her some space to consider. She had the blades and the majority of the army. House Kita had other military units besides the ones with her, but they were smaller and scattered throughout the lands. By force alone she held the strongest claim.

Mari shook her head. She couldn't allow herself to think that she was in a battle for the throne. It was hers, and a traitor sought it. If she gave even the slightest credence to competing claims, it eroded her own authority. She was the Lady of House Kita.

The primary challenge was infiltrating Stonekeep itself. Tatsuo had control of the capital, his only claim to power. Mari had no desire to lead her army into a civil war, and Stonekeep was nearly impregnable. It was built into a mountainside, sitting atop a long, narrow path. Above it were terraced rice paddies that fed the city and were themselves protected from siege. If Tatsuo decided, he could hold the city indefinitely with no more than fifty soldiers. Mari's actions needed to be fast, subtle, and decisive.

Over the course of the early evening, she laid out her own strategy. Most of her plan remained unchanged. The situation in Stonekeep was only a small portion of the problems her house lands faced. She needed to unify the people by defeating Tatsuo, but she also needed to defend their lands from the invading armies of Lord Katashi.

The orders she gave tonight represented another test. She knew her followers would dislike the commands. But they had to accept Mari's orders. If she couldn't convince those closest to her to obey, what chance did she have?

Mari cleared her throat, and the attention around the campfire focused on her. Before she spoke, she looked at the assembly. Fumio was present. After the vote, one of her first commands had been to place him in charge of the whole combined armies. The choice had been a simple one. Not only was he the best qualified, but he was the highest-ranking general still alive.

Beside Fumio sat the best news Mari had gotten all day. Takahiro, the head of her guard, had finally returned just that afternoon. He had been away with a small contingent of blades, but had rushed back to Starfall as soon as he heard about the disaster. They had spoken briefly, but Mari had been pulled away by other responsibilities. She looked forward to spending more time catching up. Simply seeing him was enough to help her breathe more easily, though.

Next to Takahiro were the three blades Mari was closest to. Jun, the dayblade, had been with her since the beginning of her campaign. He was one of her oldest supporters. Koji and Asa sat side by side, completing her circle of support. She couldn't help but notice how closely the two of them leaned in toward one another.

Mari wasted no time with meaningless speeches. There was no pleasure in giving orders people detested, but if her people were to be safe, there was no other choice. "We need to act quickly to make sure our house doesn't fall apart. Our survival depends on our unity."

There were nods of agreement around the campfire. Of course, they'd all agree with her goals. They'd only argue with her methods. "Fumio, I'd like you to work with Jun. You'll take the army and whatever blades Jun can assemble. Lord Katashi's forces need to be driven back into their own lands. We need to secure our border and push them back across the river."

Her general seemed uncertain. "Wouldn't it be better to march the army to Stonekeep? It is the largest force in the land, and the sight alone should cause Tatsuo to abdicate."

Mari had predicted his argument. "No. Stonekeep is currently more important as a symbol than as a strategic location. Tatsuo will be dealt with, but not by an army. Our lands and people need relief, and that means driving Lord Katashi out."

Fumio nodded. She'd expected more of a fight from him, but his agreement stoked her confidence. Katashi was a problem. His forces had retreated after the siege of Starfall, but they hadn't fled back to their own lands. They had established a foothold in House Kita's lands and weren't likely to relinquish it without persuasion. If the birds they received were accurate, Katashi's forces were already spreading through the land again, taking what meager food stores existed after the brutal winter.

Koji's orders came next. "I want you to assemble a group of blades. Your unorthodox tactics delayed this war. Now I want you to help me win it. With all due respect to Fumio, if we simply try to match force with force, we're going to lose. Even if we win, the cost will be high. We're too heavily outnumbered. Attack their supply lines, kill their scouts, do whatever you can think of to break them."

Koji met her gaze. "I had hoped to be a part of your guard."

She had also predicted that was coming. Whatever debt of honor Koji thought he held had been centered firmly on protecting her. The sentiment was noble, but it wasn't particularly useful now. His skills were better used against her enemies.

"I understand, and I appreciate it." Her voice was calm, surprising even her. She hadn't forgiven Koji, but she thought she understood him. "I have special plans for my guard, Koji, and while your sword is useful guarding me, it will do my people far more good if you strike at Katashi."

He wouldn't like it, but he'd agree. Of all those gathered before her, his loyalty and obedience were strongest. Koji bowed, confirming her intuition. "Yes, my lady."

Mari turned to Asa, the only one left, and the one she was least certain about. "Asa, I would like you to become the head of my guard."

Both Asa and Takahiro seemed taken aback, and she saw the two of them glance uncertainly at each other. "My lady?" Asa asked.

"Yes?"

"Why?"

"Because blades have had female leaders for countless cycles. Because your swords are powerful weapons, and in the confined spaces of Stonekeep your skills will be invaluable. And because I need Takahiro to become my chief adviser. He can't fulfill both roles at once."

Takahiro was the one who realized her intention first. "You're planning on sneaking into Stonekeep, aren't you?"

Mari nodded. "I'm hoping to win Stonekeep through diplomacy, but if that isn't possible, yes, we will travel there with a group of blades."

Mari kept her eyes focused on the group. Asa and Koji were trading glances that made Mari certain they'd be arguing again tonight. She saw a distance between them that hadn't been there moments before. While they had a good deal in common, there was much they didn't, and they struggled against their differences of opinion. But they would both follow. They had to.

There were a hundred small details to take care of, but their campaign to save the Kingdom began tonight.

THEY WERE STILL about a league away, but the tall stone walls of Stonekeep already towered above them. The road they were on had been worn smooth, hundreds of cycles of travel evident with every step. The trail was relatively narrow, barely wide enough for two carts to pass. The path followed the side of a mountain, carved out over lifetimes of work. To their left was a solid wall of rock, water trickling down in places from the snow melt and springs high above. Where water was known to flow, small tunnels had been built under the path, allowing the water to pass underneath without soaking the path itself. To their right was a sheer drop, the valley floor already a hundred paces away and receding with each step. Birds flew off in the distance at eye level, floating in the air with ease on the sunny day.

The trail was steep, and only those used to the high mountain passes moved with any ease. The air was harder to breathe, and even Mari found herself struggling more than usual. She had been in the lowlands too long, it seemed. But she fared better than at least one of her companions. Next to her, Asa fought for breath, trying hard to hide her weakness in front of the others. There was no shame in it, though. Even the strongest lost their vigor if they weren't used to such heights.

Their journey caused Mari to remember the day her own father had been crowned the lord of their house, a moon after her grandfather passed away. She had only been a young child, but she remembered the bright procession that had crawled from the valley floor below to the city above. To this day, she wasn't sure she had ever seen a more impressive sight.

No such procession existed for her. They traveled small. Some of her honor guard were already in the city, making contacts and learning the mood of the people. Others were behind them. Mari traveled with only two. Asa was in her traveling robes, well-worn but thick fabric that protected her from the elements. Her swords were hidden on her back, and if past experience was any indication, she was carrying at least a half-dozen other weapons on her body. But none of them were visible.

On her other side was Takahiro. Of the three of them, he handled the thin air and steep trail the best. Some of the work he'd been doing with the blades had taken place in the mountains to the south, so his lungs were prepared for the strain of the hike. He was also out of uniform. The guard carried his sword on his hip, certain it wouldn't attract any attention.

If it wouldn't have raised questions, Mari would have preferred to travel only with Asa. She would have felt safe, and Asa wasn't quite as intense about protecting her as Takahiro was. The man constantly worried about her, fretting over one small detail or another. Asa let her do as she pleased. Perhaps Asa's gifts allowed her to feel more confident, or perhaps Takahiro hadn't quite outgrown the need to be protective. Takahiro would be a useful adviser, and would always be trusted, but Mari found his constant hovering exhausting at times.

Asa's breathing became labored once again. As had become their pattern, they stopped. She was no good to them if she was out of breath. While she recovered her strength, Takahiro and Mari spoke of their memories of Stonekeep and wondered what the city would be like today. Neither had been back for well over a cycle, even though both called it home. Asa's breathing steadied and they continued up without acknowledging the pause. Asa was too proud to thank them, and neither of them asked for recognition.

The sun had just passed the midpoint of the day when they reached the gates. Mari looked up at the massive doors, still amazed at what her house had built. The walls were several paces thick, the door heavy reinforced wood. Her eyes traveled up the steep path where several boulders sat behind a steel gate. In the event of a siege, if the door ever looked as though it would fall, the boulders would be released, blocking the entrance from invaders.

They passed the gate without problem. Mari and Asa kept their heads down, as they would be expected to. The guard told Takahiro he had his work cut out escorting two young women. Takahiro laughed and they were let through without challenge. Asa, being less used to the attitude toward women in the Kingdom, glared at the guard, but had enough sense to keep her head down, Mari noted.

Mari breathed easier when they had passed the gate. She'd expected more of a challenge, but now she was home.

The path beyond the gate was steep, narrow, and led in only one direction. As a child, Juro had explained the defenses to her. The path was the only way into the city. If they broke down the gate and made it through the boulders, any attacking army would then be forced into the narrow corridors where they could be picked off at leisure.

There was a reason why Stonekeep had never fallen. In fact, no one had even tried attacking. If Mari's memory was correct, the last time they'd even shut the gates was about a hundred and thirty cycles ago, and that had been due to a plague.

She breathed in the scents of the city. Everything was so familiar. How many times had she walked this very road? With the rest of her life consumed by chaos and challenging decisions, she took comfort in walking the paths of remembrance.

Her relief ended the moment they left the outer city and entered the flatter plain of the middle city. This was where the businesses operated and where the wealthier residents lived. The closer one came to the inner keep, the richer the households. Mari had expected to come upon a bustling and vibrant market, but she got a very different impression of her home today.

The mood felt downright somber. The stands were open, but sellers weren't shouting, weren't competing against one another. There were people buying, but not nearly as many as there should have been. The market was quiet and subdued. As Mari walked through, she saw grim faces and angry haggling. Even the smells of meat grilling over the open flame weren't enough to bring back Mari's pleasant memories.

She knew the winter had been rough, but of all places, Stonekeep should have been safe. It grew the vast majority of its own food and none of it had been in danger. Was morale that low, or was something else causing what she saw?

Mari resisted the urge to ask questions. She had pulled up her hood against the mountain wind and her head was bowed. She gained nothing by announcing her presence yet. They needed more information before they could plan their next move.

As they left the market, Mari was surprised to see "wanted" posters. From the sketches and descriptions, it sounded like some of the wanted were young men and women, some of the drawings making them look to be no more than children.

Mari noted the information but didn't react. There was obviously more going on than she expected, but there was no point speculating until she knew more. She followed Takahiro to the inn they had agreed to gather at, followed by Asa, who moved like a cat through the crowds.

The inn was run by an older man who was a strong supporter of House Kita. Impulsively, Mari pulled down her hood as she entered the common room. She looked around, noticing several people paying attention to the new arrivals. A step behind her, Asa whispered fiercely. "Put up your hood."

Mari complied. No one had gotten more than a brief glance, and she wasn't too worried, but it was wise to be careful. Takahiro spoke with the innkeeper, and a few moments later they found themselves in a comfortable, well-appointed room.

Mari wasted no time in turning on Takahiro. "What has happened?"

Takahiro's look was blank. "I know no more than you, my lady, but I agree. The city seems to have lost its spirit."

"I will be most interested in hearing what the other guards have to say."

Takahiro nodded. "I will make contact, my lady. Please, make yourself comfortable."

The former guard left and Mari walked over to the window, which had a view of the market. She shook her head, speaking only partly to herself and partly to Asa. "The walls might be the same, but this isn't the city I grew up in. This isn't my home."

TAKAHIRO RETURNED THAT EVENING, and the news didn't inspire confidence. The laws of the city and the land, the bedrock of their society, were gradually being overturned. Tatsuo understood well enough that the right to rule came primarily through the approval of the landowners and the nobles. His policies, one after another, benefited the ruling class. Mari and her family had always tried to balance the needs of the commoners with those of the landowners, a difficult but necessary dance. The nobility had always been content under Mari's father, but now they rejoiced.

The fact was problematic in more ways than one. If Tatsuo established himself firmly among the nobility, dislodging him might be more difficult than Mari had anticipated. She still awaited replies to the missives she'd sent days ago to the other nobles. Despite her strength, had she already been beaten? The thought terrified her, but she refused to give it credence.

The next afternoon, Mari asked Asa to escort her to the city center. There was an open council meeting scheduled. If tradition still held, it was an opportunity for people to air their grievances. Mari's father had felt the practice was one of the key ways the house held its people together. Everyone needed to know that their voices could be heard.

Asa walked silently behind her, and Mari wondered what the nightblade thought about. Asa rarely spoke unless spoken to, which was the opposite of most people who tended to surround nobility. Most days Mari appreciated the difference, but today she would have paid good money to know what was really going on in her companion's head.

They arrived at the courtyard, about a hundred paces long and thirty wide. People were gathered on benches on both sides. Mari recognized some of the faces, but not all. Some were present in order to be heard. Others watched, and still others schemed. From a glance, Mari felt as though she could tell who was who. For as much as the world changed, some parts of it, the parts she considered a pestilence, persisted.

Her father had been honest with his children. He wanted open council to be a time to judge the mood of the house lands. If it was within his power to right wrongs, he wanted the chance. But actions taken in public often returned to haunt them. Nobles and commoners alike used previous rulings to attempt to force their lord to acquiesce to ridiculous demands. The open council had been a mighty strain on her father.

When Tatsuo entered the courtyard, it was all Mari could do not to order Asa to kill him. She wasn't sure Asa would even obey such an order, but her desire was strong.

Everything aggravated her, from the way he walked to the way he sat at the head of the courtyard as though he was born to be there.

The first few plaintiffs were easily dealt with. A lord needed more seed for his land. A merchant wanted to open a second stall, as his first was too busy to support all his customers. Mari almost felt as though the scene in front of her was scripted. It very well might have been. It set the mood of the council, elevating Tatsuo's easy decisions.

The atmosphere changed when a poorly dressed man stood before Tatsuo. From his clothing, Mari assumed the man was a farmer. From the looks on the faces of Tatsuo and the council, it didn't appear like the man was supposed to be there.

The man began slowly. "My lord, I come before you today because food I have earned is being taken away from my family."

Tatsuo seemed bored. "Be more specific."

The farmer stuttered. "My lord, the agreement I reached with my master specified that one part out of every five would be for my family. When the master's men came last, we were only allowed to keep one part in ten. My family goes hungry, my lord, and I'd ask that you insist on the terms of the agreement. I'm certain a word from you would resolve this."

Tatsuo glanced lazily around the courtyard. "Do you have any evidence of this?"

"My word, my lord."

"Against a noble? Tell me, who is the master of your lands?"

"Yoshinori, my Lord."

Tatsuo scowled at the man. "Yoshinori is an honorable

man, and you dare to come here, trying to destroy his reputation?"

The farmer looked shocked. Mari had no trouble deciding if the farmer was telling the truth. His clothes were old and patched in places, but even more telling was the way they hung off his shoulders. He was hungry. She turned to Asa and whispered, "What do you sense in the farmer?"

"I do not think he is lying. His energy is very weak."

Asa's words confirmed Mari's belief. The farmer was likely in the right in this situation. Worse, his argument was true: a single letter from Tatsuo would solve the problem, and it was unlikely Yoshinori was going hungry.

But there was more, Mari suspected. Yoshinori's lands lay in the valley below Stonekeep. Given the proximity to the capital, he often played an important role in court affairs. It was easy to believe there was an agreement between Tatsuo and Yoshinori, an agreement which deprived the farmers of their crops and loaded the coffers of the two men.

With a new perspective, Mari watched Tatsuo. The lord dismissed the farmer. "Your complaint has no merit. I believe you were likely selected by the enemies of the house to weaken us. Leave now and you will not be imprisoned."

The farmer was at a loss for words. His jaw moved up and down, but no words came out. He recognized, suddenly, the danger his complaint had put him in. One part in ten wasn't enough, but it was more than his family would receive if he was imprisoned. He turned around and slunk out of the courtyard. Behind him, Tatsuo grinned.

The lord raised his voice so everyone, including the retreating farmer, could hear. "Mark this well, everyone. Our house is strong, and we will not be torn apart by those who seek our destruction."

Mari fought the desire to step down into the courtyard. There were still too many questions, and she couldn't allow more chaos. Her action, when she took it, needed to be decisive. After seeing Tatsuo in action, she knew just how decisive her action would be, too. He would be lucky to escape her wrath with his life.

She tore away from the audience, following the farmer with her eyes. Asa fell in silently behind her.

Mari found the farmer after he had taken only a few paces out of the courtyard. She put a hand on his shoulder to stop him and he jumped. She could feel how thin he was, so thin she worried that she might break his shoulder if she held on too strongly.

When he saw it wasn't a guard, he immediately relaxed. Mari allowed him to see her face. When he did, his eyes lit up. "Lady Mari."

Relief flooded the man's eyes and Mari experienced a wave of guilt. If she had made better decisions, perhaps this farmer's life wouldn't have come to this. "Say nothing of this. I will make things right, though."

Mari handed over a small bag of gold to the farmer. In all likelihood, it was more money than the farmer would make in cycles of work, but if Mari's plan came to fruition, it was only a very small part of what would be available to her. House Kita may lack people, but it didn't lack for gold.

The farmer started to get down on his knees, but Mari held him up easily. "No. Again, say nothing of this. Change is coming, but my presence must not be known."

She could almost sense the disapproval emanating from Asa as the farmer walked away. She answered the nightblade's unspoken challenge. "Perhaps that wasn't necessary, but dynasties have risen and fallen on less. He will not speak of me, but when I make my move, he will tell everyone what happened here today."

Asa didn't reply, but Mari didn't expect her to. "Come. It's time to take back my lands. Tatsuo will regret the pain he's brought to my people."

4

A sa hated cities. Because she was gifted with the sense, they pressed upon her mind like a never-ending nightmare, crushing her beneath the weight of so many people. Stonekeep was even worse than most. The space it was built in was small, so to accommodate more people, they had built upward. Buildings three or even four stories tall were common, packing people in like cows before a slaughter. There were too many people and far too little space.

She remembered the first time she visited a city. She had only seen a handful of cycles, and her parents had decided to celebrate a good harvest. They rarely visited cities, or even villages, for that matter. Their family stayed in their little corner of the world. Today, Asa understood it was because her father's untrained gift made him wary of crowds.

They didn't even make it to the city proper. By the time they were in the outskirts, Asa's head had felt like it was going to collapse in on itself. Her father, recognizing the signs he himself suffered from, turned them around, much to the disappointment of Asa's mother and brother. They had never spoken about what happened, but that must have been when her parents learned she was gifted as well.

There were limits to the sense. It differed from individual to individual, and although scholars had speculated endlessly on the topic, no one was quite sure if there was an absolute limit, or what factors set the limits for each individual. From a pragmatic standpoint, part of it was mental ability. At its most basic level, the sense brought in more information. The farther one's gift expanded, the more information it brought in. At some point, the mind couldn't handle any more. If a blade continued past that point, it was speculated, they either went mad or died. Of course, no one had returned from either destination to confirm the theories.

In cities, filled to breaking with lives and intentions, the amount of information brought in was too much to bear. In an empty field, Asa could let her sense wander for hundreds of paces without issue. Inside Stonekeep she didn't dare let her gift expand more than ten.

Focusing her gift saved her from blinding headaches and pain, but it didn't give her the knowledge she was used to. Archers could strike and she'd never know the arrow was coming. Even a child with a strong arm and a throwing blade could be a threat she never sensed. She tried to compensate with her other senses, but it required constant vigilance. No matter how attentive she was, though, she always felt exposed and vulnerable without the ability to expand her sense.

Her training last winter with Daisuke helped. He made a heightened state of awareness almost second nature to her, but she still tired easily being inside a city with so many people packed so closely together. She ended every night exhausted, even if all she had done was walk around.

Mari's days were as filled as Asa had ever seen. She held meetings in secret, sent letters and notes, and collected more information with every passing moment. Asa felt as though she was watching a master put all her pieces in place before striking. Despite Asa's anger at even being here, she couldn't help but be impressed. She could see why Koji felt so strongly about the lady, and why he had wrung an oath out of Asa to protect Mari.

Thoughts of that last argument still stung. Asa disapproved of the way in which Koji tied himself to Mari's fate. Part of her feeling was tradition. Blades weren't supposed to align with any one ruler. But that ideal had been destroyed over the past few moons, and Asa was still uncomfortable with their new role. Aligning with rulers made them partial, and with the strength of the blades, even reduced, that loyalty would cause greater problems in the future. The Kingdom relied on the blades to be as impartial as possible.

She recognized that they had been caught in a web of their own making, a web she'd had no small part in creating when she'd killed Kiyoshi. What truly angered her was that she had no desire to be attached to any political causes. If she believed in anything, it was helping the blades survive this crisis. In her mind, there were far better ways to accomplish that than guarding Mari all day.

Koji had insisted, though, as stubborn as any mule. Eventually Asa had let herself be convinced, even though the cause was not her own. Koji's conviction overrode her ambivalence.

So every morning and afternoon was spent following Mari around as she tried to gather support. They had been in the city now for five days, and Asa worried that if Mari didn't make her move soon, it would be too late. It didn't take long to solidify power. Mari must have felt the same, because she worked even longer days than Asa could handle.

Keeping Mari safe was proving to be no small task. No attack had materialized yet, but Asa's worries grew by the day. Stonekeep was a city of sharp corners, narrow passageways, and tall buildings. She understood from a military standpoint it was almost invincible, but the same qualities that made it so easily defensible made it perfect for ambushes.

The inn was another source of strife. The guests in the common room seemed to be permanent fixtures there. Optimistically, Asa figured that perhaps they were in the same situation Mari's guards were: trapped in the city for an extended stay with no better place to sleep. But Asa couldn't help but see spies everywhere, and there was no shortage of people interested in their little party. To make matters worse, Mari had shown her face, however briefly, in the common room when they first arrived.

They were returning from yet another meeting. Mari had decided to return to their rooms early, as she was expecting a collection of new intelligence today. Asa followed her, all her senses working constantly to keep them safe.

They arrived at the inn without incident, but even so, when they stepped inside the common room Asa immediately checked the surroundings. A number of the usuals were there. A big man with two deep cups of beer in his hands laughed heartily. A woman with a small scar down her cheek sat reading in the corner. One particularly nasty man, wearing no fewer than three swords, was staring at them as they entered. He always stared at new arrivals.

Asa forced her hands to remain still. It would be so easy to draw any of the weapons hidden on her, but she couldn't attract attention, not now. She could only defend, never attack.

The nightblade walked with Mari to her room, then relaxed a little. There were two honor guards inside. They couldn't stand outside, or they'd draw attention. But Mari was safe until she left the room again. Asa could afford to get some rest.

Knowing it would be difficult to calm her mind, she went downstairs to the common room and ordered beer. She took the overflowing cup to where a few of Mari's honor guard were drinking and playing a dice game. She sat down next to Takahiro and politely declined to join in the game. Gambling had never interested her.

Takahiro glanced away from the game. "You look like you could use some sleep."

Asa held up her cup for his inspection. "I'm working on it."

"What's bothering you?"

She looked around, then spoke softly enough that only he could hear. "I don't know how you stand being a guard. There are too many avenues for attack here. Trying to track them all is exhausting. Isn't there any place we could be that is more secure?"

"Not unless she comes out in the open. Until then, this is the best we can do."

"Aren't you suspicious? The people here seem quite interested in us."

"Of course, but until there's something solid to defend against, there's nothing we can do."

"Can't you buy out the whole inn?"

Takahiro's response was dry. "That would also attract attention."

Asa cursed. Life would be a lot easier if Mari would just make her move. In an uncharacteristic moment, she gulped down the remaining half of her beer in one swig. Perhaps that would be enough. Bidding the guards farewell, Asa turned to go to her room, desperate for sleep.

ASA FOLLOWED Mari through the winding streets of Stonekeep. Even though they had been in the city for days, Asa still only had the barest of ideas where they were at any given time. Mari navigated the streets like the local she was, taking narrow alleys and tight corners with confidence. Because Mari shifted directions so quickly, and because the high walls often blocked out the sun, Asa fought for her bearings at every turn, only to have them pulled away moments later.

Today was no different. Another day of meetings and letters had passed, and Asa's unease had only grown. Mari needed to act. Her time was slipping away. The sun was setting, and from what Asa could observe, Mari seemed no closer to taking action.

The lady took another corner into a long alley, dark in the falling light of the early evening. Here in the mountains the sun set earlier than Asa was used to, and although the sky above was still light, Stonekeep fell to darkness early. Mari walked confidently, Asa muttering under her breath as she followed.

A few moments later, a woman came into the alley from the direction they were heading. She was unremarkable, of medium build and height. Asa noticed that she moved well, her steps always in balance, but paid the other woman no more mind. As they passed, Asa noticed that the woman had a small scar on one of her cheeks.

The hair on Asa's arms suddenly stood straight up, and she knew she was missing something. Then it struck her like a thunderclap.

The woman was a regular in the common room of the inn.

Asa reacted before she could even process a thought, knowing the coincidence to be too unlikely. She spun, her arms coming up to draw the blades hidden on her back. The woman with the scar was already turning, though, and Asa now sensed her intent. A knife glittered in the darkness, but Asa wasn't the target.

Asa snapped her right arm down, slapping the attack away less than a heartbeat from the moment it hit. Asa wasn't fast enough to stop the blade, but she sent it spinning, causing the hilt of the throwing knife to strike Mari in the back, warning the lady that something was wrong.

Asa had deflected the attack, but it distracted her from drawing her swords. Her left arm, still close to the hidden hilt of one blade, reached back, but she suddenly felt the cold bite of a chain as it wrapped around her left wrist.

She cursed. How was she not sensing the attacks?

The chain pulled hard on her wrist, and she received part of her answer. The attacker was on the roofs above, high enough to avoid the detection of her sense.

Asa sensed the scarred woman's next attack, a slash aimed at her neck from a large knife. Asa managed to twirl around her outstretched arm, just managing to avoid the cut. The woman positioned herself for the next attack and Asa realized just how poor of a situation she was in. They were in close quarters, the alley so narrow even Asa's short swords were potentially too long. Her left arm was trapped overhead, greatly limiting her movement and abilities.

The situation became worse when Asa saw another man step into the alley. Twin knives glittered in his hands. Their attackers had certainly come prepared for close-quarters combat.

Asa needed to get her arm free, but wasn't sure how to go about that. She suspected whoever was above was larger than her. No matter how hard she pulled, her arm didn't budge.

Her sense warned her that she was out of time. The woman sliced again, and this time there was no escape. Asa tried to spin again, but couldn't get away completely. The cut aimed at her neck ended up cutting through her upper-left torso. Pain seared through her body as blood poured from the wound.

Asa couldn't play their game. Grimacing against the pain, she grabbed the chain with her left hand, bracing against it as she ran her feet up the wall. Upside down, held in the air only by the chain, she twisted and tried to kick at the woman. She ended up flopping over more than launching a well-executed attack, but it was enough to make the woman back off a few paces. It gave Asa the heartbeat she needed.

Drawing her sword was pointless. Strung up as she was, in such a confined space, she wouldn't have a chance even with her sense. But her right hand did find its way to a set of three throwing blades hidden at her waist. Asa pulled one in a smooth motion and sent it sailing into the woman. Asa had aimed for the heart, but the attacker's reflexes were too quick. The woman shifted her weight and the blade sank into her left shoulder. It would hurt, but if the woman was as good as she seemed, it wouldn't do much more than slow her down a bit.

Asa was reaching down for a second throwing blade when her left arm was heaved up violently. She heard and felt her shoulder dislocate, and she screamed. Whoever was above watching the fight didn't like what he saw. Asa's feet left the ground and she started spinning around the chain, kicking helplessly. The moment only lasted for a heartbeat, but it ruined her positioning. Distracted, Asa didn't find her feet as the chain dropped her back down. She collapsed, apparently catching the man above by surprise.

In that single moment, he must not have expected all her weight. She pulled him off-balance and saw his silhouette as he fell from the roof. His head hit the opposite wall as he fell, the crack audible even below. Asa just managed to roll away as the man crunched into the stones beside her.

Asa didn't have time to congratulate herself as she was attacked by the woman again. Asa rolled farther, hitting a retreating Mari and almost causing the lady to fall over. There wasn't enough space to fight, and Asa needed to stand up.

The woman went after Mari's exposed back, but Asa shifted her weight and kicked out at the assassin, knocking her back a few paces. Asa took the moment to stand up.

The situation could be worse, she supposed. The chain around her wrist was still attached to the man who had fallen, but she had more freedom. Unfortunately, they were surrounded by two people armed for exactly this type of fight.

She took the brief moment of freedom to draw her sword and ensure Mari was still unharmed. So far the lady was fine, but the assassins were approaching from both ends of the alley, and Mari wouldn't last a moment against either of them. Asa couldn't let them both close the distance. She needed to isolate and kill, and quickly.

The chain around her wrist complicated matters. She didn't have time to unwrap it, and it limited her mobility. Besides that, her left arm was as good as useless. But perhaps it could still be a benefit. The other woman didn't know Asa was still connected to the dead man from above. She might consider the chain a free weapon. Gritting her teeth against the pain, Asa stepped toward the woman with the scar, flinging her left arm as she got close.

The woman reacted, immediately bringing her knives up to block the strike from the chain. When Asa's arm suddenly jerked to a halt, the chain reaching the end of its limit, the assassin's eyes went wide.

Asa's own eyes teared up at the pain, but she didn't waste the moment. Her right arm snapped around, a single cut that sliced through her opponent's unguarded neck less than a heartbeat later. The woman's eyes turned glassy as she collapsed to the ground.

Asa couldn't celebrate her victory, though. The last man still stood, and Asa assumed he was just as dangerous as the other two. In her condition, he might be good enough to beat her.

The man had seen his partner fall and darted in to kill Mari. The lady was between Asa and the man, blocking her own rescue. Asa turned and ran toward Mari from the other side, leaping off one of the alley walls to pass just over Mari and place herself between the killer and his target.

That was her plan, at least. The chain jerked at her arm, sending her off balance as she was about to land. It twisted her body in midair, sending her spinning uncontrollably.

Asa felt a knife cut into her leg, but the different

sensations of pain blurred together as she crashed into the man and the stone walkway. She tasted blood in her mouth, and the entire left side of her body burned. The world spun woozily around her, and she blinked away the disorientation. Beside her, the man groaned. Her crash had taken them both out. That was some small comfort, at least.

Asa pushed herself up with her one good arm. Her short sword lay several paces away, out of reach. Beside her, the man also began to push himself to his feet. She realized just how much danger she was in. Once he stood up, the fight was as good as over.

Asa swept her legs, bringing him back down before he could find his balance. She sensed a knife coming at her but deflected his wrist with her right arm. They rolled for a moment and she found herself on top of him. She kneed him in the chin, snapping his head back.

With an angry roar, he threw her off. Desperate, she rolled and launched herself back at him. His knife hand responded, slicing an angry gash in her already-useless left arm. She threw her right elbow into his face, and the man's nose gushed blood. She sensed the knife again and was forced to roll over him to avoid it.

Heartbeats passed and Asa lost all sense of control. The match was a flurry of arms and legs, each fighter desperate to survive. Their grunts of effort echoed in the alley and Asa could feel her pulse pounding in her head. Her world was darkness and sharpened steel, her scant attention focused on his blade hand. She stayed alive only because she could sense his attacks moments before he made them. Her defenses weren't measured, but they kept her alive as the two enemies battered one another.

The struggle was brutal, bloody, and impulsive, Asa always managing to slip away just before the man landed a blow she wouldn't live through. But the fight was slowing, and she was losing. He was physically stronger, only had to fight one opponent, and all four of his limbs still worked. Asa's sense wasn't enough against those advantages. She wasn't sure she could win.

She sensed the strike coming but didn't believe it. She moved out of the way just in time to make sure she wasn't cut, and a knife blade drove deep into the upper part of the man's right arm.

Mari had joined the fight. She had grabbed one of the knives lying around the alley and waited for opportunity to strike. Asa avoided the wild cut, but the man didn't. He roared in pain, and for just a moment, Asa found herself left alone without a relentless series of attacks to deal with. It was only a moment, but a moment was all she needed.

The first weapon at hand was the chain, still wrapped around her useless arm. She grabbed it with her right arm, then looped it around the man's neck and twisted her entire body, bringing the man down to the ground. In terms of sheer strength she was far outmatched, but there were ways around that.

Asa got a full twist in the chain before the man responded, grasping at it with his own hands. Fortunately it was already tight enough he couldn't get his hands between the chain and his neck. Using the powerful muscles in her legs, Asa pushed herself away from the man as she wrapped the chain around her right hand, too. The agony in her left arm almost caused her to lose consciousness, but she fought against the blackness.

For all the combat she'd seen, Asa had never fought like this. Her head was pounding and she swore she could feel every move the man made through her feet and hands. He was rolling around, flailing uncontrollably. Mari threw herself on top of him, just to help hold him down. Asa wished she would get away, but was grateful for the help. On her own, she wasn't sure she'd have held on, especially as she lost her own strength.

Life drained out of the man slowly. Even after he stopped moving, Asa held on, afraid he was faking his own death. She didn't stop pulling until Mari got off the man and came over to her, gently.

"It's over," the lady said.

Her heart still threatening to escape from her chest, Asa gingerly unwrapped the chain from her hand and from around her left wrist. Her wrist and hand looked horrible, bruises and cuts already discoloring the bluish skin. Asa didn't look forward to the healing she would have to undergo if they made it back to the inn.

It felt like it took all night for Mari to get Asa back to her feet. Eventually Asa gathered her weapons, but still, no one had responded from the city watch. Asa didn't have the ability to even wonder about it. She couldn't walk without Mari's support. Instead of guarding Mari, she was now a liability. There was only one reason she didn't send Mari to the inn on her own.

Asa wasn't sure if this was the only attack, or only the first of the night.

5

At the very least, thought Koji, tracking an army was an easy task, especially when that army seemed dedicated to leaving nothing but destruction in its wake. In his training, Koji had heard of such practices, used occasionally throughout history, but he never thought the day would come when he'd see such dishonorable conduct in person. Katashi, the lord of House Amari and the commander of the army they pursued, was a man without a shred of honor. This most recent transgression was just one more to add to the list.

Katashi had killed Mari's brother under a flag of truce, then stuffed Mari into a chest and carried her away, attempting to wrest her house lands away from her through deception. He was also the one who told Mari what Koji had done, poisoning their relationship.

The young lord had given Koji plenty of reasons to detest him. This was another.

Half a league away, Mari's army marched after Katashi's. After the siege of Starfall, Katashi's forces retreated. The combined force of Mari's soldiers and the nightblades was too much. Mari's commanders had hoped and speculated that Katashi would retreat all the way back to his house lands. Whether or not that would be the case remained to be seen. So far, Katashi's forces were headed in the right direction, but Koji didn't trust the lord to make a full retreat. He was too devious.

Koji wouldn't even call Katashi's movement a retreat. This was brutal, purposeful, and calculated. Fields and villages burned, the ground soaked by the blood of Mari's people. The stores, meager as they were after the relentless winter, were further depleted by Katashi's men, leaving next to nothing behind. Women were taken and only sometimes returned. The places Katashi's army visited became living ghost towns.

The place where Koji stood was one.

Smoke had been spotted at first light the day before. Unfortunately, such sights were not infrequent. A field would burn completely in the time it took for Mari's forces to catch up to Katashi's. Even after days of hard marching, they were still days behind at best. Towns, villages, and houses burned the longest, embers continuing to transform into flame long after the real damage had already been done.

Fumio had slightly changed the course of his army upon seeing the smoke. The first time, they had followed the path of devastation, thinking there would be something the army could do. The first village put that idea to shame. All the young men had been murdered, leaving behind only the old, the women, and some children. The storerooms were looted and burned. Katashi left the greatest number of mouths to feed with the least possible supply.

There had been no help to offer. Fumio left some food, but it was a token only. He couldn't spare what little he had if he wanted his men to fight. The dayblades healed some wounds, but the deepest scars weren't physical, and many of those who had been gravely wounded had died before the force could arrive. For all their strength, the combined forces were hopeless against Katashi's ruthlessness. The best they could do was send the people toward Stonekeep, promising aid there. The promise felt thin, even to Koji.

The army had left the village, every soldier forced to witness the despair brought upon their people. For the rest of the day Koji had worried that the army would begin to desert come nightfall to better protect their own homes. Fortunately, Fumio had the same concern. That night, he spoke to all the troops, reminding them that if divided, the whole house would suffer the same fate. Somehow, Fumio had turned despair into anger, and the army marched with a vigor that bordered on madness.

The main force didn't approach villages any more. Everyone knew what the smoke represented, but Fumio believed it better if not everyone was forced to see. All the same, the mood of the troops was somber. At every village, Koji volunteered to lead a party to search for survivors and provide what help they could.

Unfortunately, even Koji could do little. He didn't have food to spare. He hunted as he could, but most of the game had either perished in the fires or been driven off. Even with his skills there was little to do. He offered what he could and directed them towards Stonekeep. The journey would kill some, but it was the safest place he could think of.

This village was no different. Koji wasn't even sure it was large enough to be named. The remains of five small houses stood before him, but there were no survivors. Tracking individuals was nearly impossible after the army had been through, so Koji wasn't sure if everyone had been killed or if some had already left their home for safer places.

He fought down his emotions as he looked at the devastation around him. Doubtless, the houses here had stood for generations, housing family after family as they made their living from the surrounding land. In the course of a single day, all of that history had been destroyed. Lives hadn't just been taken, they'd been shattered.

Koji saw six corpses from where he stood, and didn't even want to think about how many more were scattered around. Their flesh was charred, and in one case, the fire had burned so hot only the bones remained. Koji wasn't even sure what to do with the remains. The fire had been so consuming he wasn't sure they'd have time to collect firewood for a proper pyre. They'd have to journey too far.

In the end, he decided to leave them as they were. To act would take valuable time, and his responsibility had to be toward the living. Koji hoped they fared better on their next trip through the Great Cycle. By midday a few nightblades had returned from scouting the surrounding area, reporting that they'd found no survivors. There was nothing to do but catch up to the army and avenge the wrongs when they got the chance.

He had killed lords before. He had killed his own master and a king. Each of those lives haunted him, waking him at night and consuming his thoughts during the day. But hopefully, killing Katashi would silence the ghosts of his past.

KOJI WAS EATING a small meal of rice and vegetables with a handful of other blades when he got the summons from Fumio. The food wasn't much, but it was more than many received these days. The arrival of the messenger caused him to frown in confusion. According to Mari's commands, Koji commanded the contingent of blades that had elected to fight Katashi directly, but there'd been little interaction between the two of them. For now, Koji followed Fumio. He used the blades as volunteers for some tasks, like checking on the villages, but otherwise marched them with the army. So far, in this young campaign, he didn't know what else to do. Fumio seemed content with the arrangement as well, and the two hadn't had much need to speak to each other.

There was respect between the two, though. Mari trusted Fumio, so Koji did as well. Likewise, Fumio had made it clear enough that Koji was always welcome in the command tent, but to this point, Koji had seen little need. He didn't deceive himself with the belief that he was a general. Their lack of interaction made the summons curious, though.

He didn't let any worry show on his face as he bid the other blades to finish the meal without him. Although the days had been trying, both mentally and physically, spending the evenings with the blades almost made the suffering worth it. Koji eagerly awaited the time each day when the sun set and the camp was made. There was something special about being among those who understood what it meant to be sense-gifted.

Koji left the warmth of their small fire as he followed the messenger to the center of the camp. Fumio was in conference with the other army commanders. Compared to the fire Koji had just left, surrounded by friends, this one felt cold and empty. There were no smiles, and every statement was whispered with harsh authority.

Koji was announced briefly by the messenger. He tried to keep his back straight and his bow formal, but it required his attention. Such formality wasn't observed in his daily life, but better to make friends than enemies in this circle.

"Koji, I'm glad you were able to come so quickly." Even his thanks sounded like a command, but Koji had learned that was the nature of Fumio's personality. He'd been a great commander for almost as long as Koji had been alive.

"How can I be of service, general?"

Fumio drove straight to the point. "I'm not sure if you've had word yet, but we're within two days' march of Katashi and his force. We just received notice that they've turned to the south."

Fumio had predicted as much. Like Koji, he didn't expect Katashi to give up the land he'd conquered so easily. "Do we know his purpose?"

Fumio gave a single shake of his head, even that everyday action decisive and quick. "No, and that is only one of my concerns. Our best guess is that Katashi and his generals believe that the terrain to the south will give them potential advantages. They might be right, too."

Koji studied the map the generals stood around. He saw the position of their army, Katashi's force, and the surrounding geography. He frowned. He wasn't an expert in warfare at this scale, but he saw an immediate problem with Katashi's maneuver. He pointed at the map. "Doesn't moving to the south mean that their supply line is exposed?" Both armies were nearing the wide river that separated House Kita from House Amari, but the bridge Katashi had used—and the focal point of his supply line—was more to the north. Turning to the south exposed it to attack.

Fumio nodded. "Yes, but attacking the supply line brings us right up to the river. It wouldn't be unreasonable to expect Katashi has forces stationed there." The general shuffled some pieces around. "He could wheel around behind us and attack our own supply lines, catching us between his two forces without supply."

Koji bit his lower lip. He hadn't thought of that, but as he looked at the map he realized how obvious of a ploy it was. Again, he was grateful he didn't command armies. Then he frowned again, another thought occurring to him. "I assume Katashi knows as much of our movements as we do of his?"

"A fair guess," Fumio replied.

"This might be an opportunity for the blades to separate from the rest of your forces. You could move to intercept Katashi's expeditionary force, acting as though you are ignoring the supply lines. Then you won't risk being flanked. At the same time, I could lead a group of blades... here." Koji found a likely place on the map. "If your information is accurate, their supply line passes through this stretch of woods. It will reduce the threat of their archers to my warriors. We can break, or at least harass, their supply lines, giving you a chance to attack the main force."

The commanders looked skeptically at one another. Fumio spoke for them. "Katashi's no fool. Those supply carts are well guarded. You'll be heavily outnumbered, and if there's one place they'll be expecting an ambush, it's in those woods. Without numbers, your chances seem slim."

Koji trusted himself with this, though. Large maneuvers of armies were beyond his training, but ambushes he knew. More than that, he knew the heart and skill of the blades with him.

"Perhaps. But these are the men who burned our city. They will fall to our swords."

Fumio took in the mood of his commanders with a glance. There was another fact at play that everyone was too polite to say out loud. Who here would care if there were fewer nightblades? Koji didn't ask for a detachment of well-trained soldiers. Even if the blades lost, they would damage Katashi's lines, distract him, and force the enemy to commit more resources to defending their supplies. Koji suspected that Fumio had no particular love for the blades. So he would happily use them as tools.

His suspicion was confirmed moments later. "Very well. We'll try it. Report back here by first light for more planning."

Koji tried again to do a formal military bow, then left without another word.

The time had finally come for them to fight back.

KOJI SAT IN A TREE, focusing on his breath and on his surroundings. He was a ways off the ground, sitting above a road the supply train was traveling down. The scouts had already reported, and now it was only a matter of time. He started to run through the plan again, but stopped himself. The plan was far from perfect, but it was as good as any, and it was too late to change now.

In the woods, his sense was alive. He could feel the energy of the trees up high and connected below the ground. Birds flitted from branch to branch in the warm spring air and the floor of the forest was alive with new energy. If he wasn't preparing for battle, he would have been content to sit here for days on end and enjoy the gradual unfolding of life. He felt sorrow for those not as gifted as he was. So many people went through their days, unable to understand the beauty of the vast web of life that surrounded them. They were blind and didn't even realize it.

The same could be said for the supply train heading

their way. Although they were still too far away for him to pick out individuals, he could tell that the supply carts were guarded by dozens of soldiers. Fumio hadn't been wrong. Katashi was no fool, and had learned hard lessons from the warfare that had already occurred. Weak supply lines threatened an army.

Koji waited, as patient as necessary. He kept his sense alive and open, always directed towards the oncoming supply train. They didn't slow or hesitate. Instead, as they entered the woods, Koji sensed them pick up their pace. They knew the forest was a prime place for an ambush. But even so, they had little chance of spotting the blades. They were limited by their normal senses, and in the thick woods Koji's gift, and the gifts of the others, traveled much farther than sight or sound.

From his perch, he could only make out small parts of the road below. Several layers of limbs sheltered him from the sight of the road, protecting him from detection. But he could sense the first Amari scouts carefully testing the way below.

Fooling the scouts was the first challenge. Koji was the front line of the ambush, with almost a dozen blades hidden in the woods behind him. He would lead the attack, waiting until the carts had passed. Once he dropped, the others would swarm.

Koji kept his breath steady and observed the scouts as they passed underneath. He could sense their wariness in the way they moved, one slow step after another. Though they moved cautiously, they moved forward steadily, and soon they were well behind him. He breathed a slow sigh of relief and steeled himself for the battle to come.

There were more carts than he had expected. He

counted twenty before he sensed the rear guard, still a ways away.

Koji considered the task before dropping. His blades weren't just outnumbered, they were significantly outnumbered. The supply train was larger than expected and had the protection to match. The wise decision wasn't to attack, but to wait for a better opportunity.

But in his mind's eye, he saw the burned bodies of the families in the villages they had passed. His grip tightened on his sword. He wouldn't live in a world where such crimes went unpunished. If the risk was greater, he simply needed to fight harder. He took a deep breath and dropped from his perch.

Time slowed down for him as he fell. He dropped from branch to branch, only putting his weight on each large limb long enough to slow his descent a little. Less than a heartbeat later, he was dropping from the lowest branch onto the nearest guard.

The guard was looking up, alerted by the heavy rustling of the leaves. His mouth hung open, disbelief painted on his wide eyes as Koji dropped from above, drawing and cutting in one smooth motion. The cut was perfect, slicing through the guard's neck, his head sliding off his shoulders, the look of surprise the last expression he'd ever wear.

To Koji's senses, the guards around him seemed to be moving underwater, their movements slowed by the very weight of the air. He dashed among them, none requiring more than two moves to kill. One archer tried to loose an arrow in his direction, but Koji sensed the release of the string and slid to the side, and the arrow passed harmlessly by.

He sprinted toward one of the carts as the archer drew again, climbing up the wheel in one smooth move and vaulting over it as another hastily-aimed arrow cut the air behind him. On the other side of the cart he engaged with a handful of guards that had come together, seeking to overwhelm him with numbers.

The idea was sound, but the four of them weren't enough. Koji let his momentum carry him into their midst, keeping his guard close and his cuts small. The metallic ring of steel clashing against steel echoed in his ears, but even with four they weren't fast enough to break his guard. Koji crouched low as another series of cuts reached out for him, the four guards suddenly aware they were as much a danger to each other as they were to him. Swords clanged above him as he made his cuts low, his steel slashing through tendons and blood vessels in the legs.

He didn't kill them all, but they all fell to his sword, losing their balance and their strength. He left them behind. They were no immediate danger, and they could be killed later when the blades cleaned up the site.

The archer who had harried him on the other side of the carts had crossed over in front of a pair of horses and Koji caught a glimpse of his steely-eyed determination. He sensed the release of the string and knew this was no hastily aimed shot, but an arrow shot directly toward the center of his body. Koji twisted, bringing his sword around and trying to present as narrow a target as possible.

The flat of his sword slapped against the rear of the arrow, a chance move he wasn't sure he'd ever be able to duplicate. The arrow twisted, striking him sideways across his shoulder. The impact stung, but nothing worse.

The archer was fast, another arrow already nocked in the bow, his arm coming back. But Koji was only a few paces away, too close now. The archer had enough time to release the arrow, but not aim. The arrow went wide as Koji covered the last two paces between them. His sword finished the job as he passed the archer, drawing a thick red line across his neck.

Koji attacked another set of soldiers, then another when the first set had fallen too quickly. Time lost meaning as Koji lost himself in the battle. He only came back to himself when there was a break in the fighting.

Looking for new opponents, Koji realized there weren't many enemies left to fight. He cut down another two guards with easy moves, but no others remained close by. Only blades were left standing.

Koji met their eyes, and he imagined he saw hints of the same anger he possessed burning in their own eyes. A number of the guards were still alive, injured and crawling along the ground, either to get to safety or to fulfill whatever orders they had.

As the blades looked around, Koji knew he wouldn't need to give the order. They all felt the same. They clutched their weapons and finished their mission.

THE NEXT DAY, the blades received new orders from Fumio. He requested that the blades break off their attacks of the supply line and return to the main army. Koji held the short note in his hand and frowned. One attack, successful as it was, wouldn't change the course of the war. He had intended to stay and lay further ambushes. But Fumio's tone was urgent, and Koji wondered what the general knew that he did not.

He did consider the possibility of disobeying the summons. Although pledged to Mari and House Kita, taking orders from one who was not a blade rankled. Worse, Fumio didn't explain the reasons for his orders. As a general, he probably wasn't used to doing so. But Koji needed to know retreating from the supply lines was the right move.

Ultimately, he had to trust. He'd chosen to become part of this war, and his obedience was a responsibility he'd have to shoulder.

They'd lost two nightblades in the skirmish. The deaths pained him, but given the odds they had been against, it was better than he had any right to expect. A few other blades had been seriously wounded, but the two dayblades had kept them alive. Koji hated knowing the deaths were his responsibility, but they were, and he had to make their sacrifice worth something.

He gave the orders, and after two days of travel, they came upon the army. Koji had spent most of the trip in silence. The other blades gave him space, and although he hadn't asked for it, he appreciated it.

They arrived to cheers from the rest of the army. Supplies were quickly becoming the vital ingredient to winning these wars, and Koji's blades had just brought an impressive amount.

That night, though, the blades sat alone, as they usually did, around their campfire. That made Fumio's appearance even more surprising. Koji would have guessed that if the general wanted an audience, he would have summoned the blade. Instead, he approached slowly and bowed slightly to Koji. "Would you walk with me?"

Koji considered inviting the general to the campfire, but he had the look of a man who had taken a leap he was now regretting. Koji didn't press the issue. He could feel the muscles of his back tighten as they walked away from the warm fire, Fumio clearly looking for a place to speak in relative privacy. Koji had no wish for more intrigue and secrets. He'd had enough to last him a lifetime. Koji believed anything said to him could be said in front of those he fought with. Unfortunately, those he served still held onto their precious secrets.

Finally, Fumio spoke. "I'm sorry to request your return. I would have liked to keep you there, harassing the lines, but events have happened faster than expected."

Koji kept his face neutral, but he was surprised. He hadn't expected Fumio to begin with an apology.

"Word of your deeds has already reached me," the general continued.

Koji frowned. "What deeds?"

Fumio stopped and looked up at the younger blade, a sudden understanding there. "You haven't heard what they're saying about you?"

Koji shook his head. He hadn't heard any talk about him, but then again, he hadn't spoken with many people the last few days. Was that why the blades had given him space?

Fumio continued. "The other blades have spoken of little but your prowess in the ambush. They say that even they had trouble tracking your movements. They say you killed over a dozen enemies on your own."

Koji was shocked. That couldn't be right, could it? Like all battles, the fight had become a strange combination of hazy memories and crystal-clear moments. He found it hard to believe that he had killed so many, but the truth was, he couldn't say for sure either way. He shook his head, trying to get his thoughts in order. "Thank you for letting me know, general, but I assume there is more."

Fumio stopped again, and Koji noted that they were now far away from prying ears. "I wanted to speak to you in private because I want to learn of your intentions."

The question unbalanced Koji. He'd never made any

secret of his intentions. "I plan to help Mari win peace in her lands, and, if the opportunity presents itself, I will kill Katashi for the crimes he's committed."

"A few moons ago that would have been treason."

"A lot has changed," Koji acknowledged.

Fumio stared off into the distance. "I don't think you'll get your chance soon. Katashi's forces have changed direction again. They are making for the bridge south of here, the last one that could lead them to the safety of their own lands. I think your raid hurt them more than we predicted. They pushed too far, too fast, and now they're scared of going back through that forest. If I had to guess, they'll plant themselves on our side of the bridge, then route supplies to their army through Katashi's lands."

"So what are we going to do?" Koji demanded.

Fumio shrugged. "Wait. Their position is solid, but there's more. Lord Isamu has invaded from the south."

Questions swirled in his head. "The other houses have allied against Kita?"

"It looks that way. Perhaps it is because we've allied with the blades. Perhaps they just think we're the weakest, or perhaps they've been thinking about this for a while. Regardless, now we're fighting a war on two fronts, against two armies, each of which is larger than our own."

"Does everybody know about this?"

Fumio shook his head. "I wanted to speak to you first. The other officers will learn tonight. But there's a limit to what I can do. And there's a third problem." Fumio handed over a note with the seal broken. Koji glanced at the man and he shrugged. "I apologize. An overzealous clerk took it upon himself. He's been punished."

The explanation wasn't nearly enough. Fumio openly spied on letters being passed between the blades. They were allies, but they still didn't fully trust each other. Koji took the letter and read it by the light of a nearby torch. The order made no sense. It came from Hajimi, calling all blades to the valley below Stonekeep.

"Why would he do that?" Koji wondered aloud.

Fumio looked decidedly uncomfortable, and Koji now understood his earlier concern. He wasn't sure if the blades would remain with his army. "I wish I knew. I was hoping you might have some insight. My own decisions with this army are affected by your presence. If the blades are parting ways, it limits our options. We don't have the strength to destroy Katashi's forces unaided, especially with Isamu tying up our other units in the south."

Koji felt as though he was being torn apart, just like the Kingdom was. He couldn't serve both the blades and Mari, not if Hajimi was recalling the blades in the middle of a campaign. Who did he serve?

"I'll go," he told Fumio. "I don't know what this is about, but the loss of one warrior is better than the loss of many. I will find out what Hajimi desires, and you shall know. Until then, the blades will be yours. I'll make the arrangements and leave at dawn's light."

Fumio nodded, and Koji could see the man had wanted something more, something solid he could believe in. Unfortunately, Koji didn't have anything to give. His loyalties were as split as everyone's in the Kingdom.

6

The assassination attempt in the alley galvanized Mari. In retrospect, while every preparation she'd taken had been necessary, she realized she had been avoiding the inevitable confrontation. Her move was still far from a sure bet. She'd secured support, but wouldn't know if it would be enough until the deed was done. Too many nobles refused to take any stand, content to wait until she was in power before supporting her. As much as she wished for it, one could never fully predict politics. Nothing was ever certain. Victory required action, not endless planning.

Mari thought her decision would please Asa. The blade struck Mari as someone who hungered for action, someone who detested the reactivity necessary in being a bodyguard. But Asa sat listless in the corner, waiting for others to prepare. Every loyal blade and warrior was in the inn, strapping on their weapons and preparing for battle.

She hoped tonight wouldn't come to violence, but Mari recognized that the chances of Tatsuo simply stepping down were slim. The assassination attempt meant that at least one person knew Mari was in Stonekeep, and that someone was willing to kill the last surviving member of House Kita. Though they had no damning evidence, the signs all pointed to Tatsuo. For Mari, the attempt had pushed her over the edge. Tatsuo needed to be dealt with, now. If that meant violence, that was a sacrifice she was willing to make.

Mari watched as Asa stood up and quickly ran her hands over her body. The movement was quick, and almost looked natural. But Mari was fascinated by Asa, and had studied her enough to know that the nightblade was ensuring all her weapons were present. Mari had grown up around military men, but still had never met someone who carried as much sharpened steel as Asa. Some days, Mari was surprised Asa didn't accidentally stab herself just sitting down.

Mari wasn't about to go into the night unarmed, either. Today a short blade rested on her hip. Partly it was a symbol, letting her followers know that she was more than just a noble, that she was willing to fight as well. She also halfway planned on using it before the night was through.

The assembled group slowly quieted as the warriors finished their preparations. Mari stood up and advanced to the door. Glancing around the room, she saw the determined set of everyone's faces, Asa's being the one exception. There was little to say. No one in this room needed further encouragement, and their plans had already been well laid. "Are we ready?"

Her question was greeted with the stony silence of the assembled warriors.

"Then let's remove this traitor from my throne."

They slipped out of the inn, stealth no longer a concern. The time was early, and the sun hadn't yet risen. Mari and Takahiro suspected the guards would be least wary at this time. If all went well, by the time the sun struck the streets of the mountain city, Mari's reign would be solidified.

They walked through the narrow streets toward the courtyard in the city center. Tatsuo hadn't yet worked up the courage to move into Mari's family's palace, and so remained in what was considered merely a large estate by Stonekeep standards, only a few streets over from the city center.

One or two early rising citizens saw the group marching, and they immediately made way. Mari, for the first time since her arrival, walked the streets of Stonekeep without her hood up, without fear of being noticed. Even that simple difference lent a spring to her step. She walked tall, proud of her position in her own city. From the bows she received, she could tell she was recognized by the few passersby they encountered.

Soon they came to the last corner before Tatsuo's residences. Asa, who had acted as a rear guard during the march, wormed her way through the crowd of soldiers to stand by Mari. The lady looked at her. "Are you ready?"

Their eyes met, and Mari knew that Asa understood she wasn't referring to physical preparedness. Asa's face was blank as she nodded.

Mari couldn't help but feel uncertain. She trusted Asa deeply, but Asa did little to maintain the trust she had earned. And now Mari had little choice but to rely on her skills.

Together, the two of them walked past the corner and approached the main gate of Tatsuo's residence alone. The gate was open but guarded by two very alert sentries. Mari had hoped they'd be drowsy, but Tatsuo would be the type of man who only hired the best, guards who didn't slack in their duties.

The women approached casually. Asa wore her traveling clothes, washed after their previous journey. To a casual observer, they were just two women walking in the early morning. The sentries stopped them once they drew within five paces of the gate.

The two guards looked almost identical in their uniforms. Both stood a full head taller than the two women. One was slightly broader across the shoulders, but besides that, they could almost be twins.

The slightly thinner man, clearly the superior, addressed them.

"Lady Mari, it is a pleasure to see you."

Mari gave a short bow. So he knew her, then. How would he react?

The man gave a quick nod to the other, who turned around. Mari assumed they were going to escort her into Tatsuo's residence.

In her peripheral vision, Mari saw Asa blur forward, her hand swinging out faster than Mari's untrained eye could follow. The bigger man, who had turned around, sprouted blood from the side of his neck. The thinner man's eyes opened wide and his mouth opened just in time for Asa's hand to punch him in the throat. When her hand came away, it left behind a short dagger.

"Asa! What have you done?" Mari had hoped to avoid violence. She'd told Asa! She'd trusted the blade.

The nightblade uttered an almost silent curse and pointed to the wall behind the first man she had killed. There was a horn there Mari hadn't noticed. "He was about to sound the alarm. I sensed it."

Mari had no way to evaluate the truth of that statement, and it didn't matter now. Asa had decided their course.

Behind them, Takahiro and the other soldiers jogged up. No doubt they had seen.

Mari kept her orders concise. "Don't kill unless necessary. Go."

The soldiers streamed out in front of her. In moments, the entire house would be in an uproar. Asa remained behind, standing next to Mari as the warriors cleared the passageways in front of them.

"You don't believe me," she said matter-of-factly.

Mari glanced over. She wouldn't even try lying to the blade. "It is much to ask on faith."

Asa accepted that. Mari was grateful for that aspect of the difficult blade. The woman respected naked truth more than half-lies. If only more were like her, perhaps the world would be an easier place to navigate. Maybe more frustrating at times, but straightforward, at least.

Not long after, the first sounds of swords clashing came to their ears. Mari made a decision. "Let's go. Your strength may be valuable." Asa didn't argue.

They entered the house and Mari was glad to see that in several rooms her soldiers were keeping the occupants at bay without resorting to murder. In one room, a woman and children huddled together under a guard's watchful eye. In another, a man with a bloody nose lay sprawled on the floor, attended to by his family. They were all servants and had no part in what was occurring.

The two of them walked deeper into the house. Suddenly, Asa stepped in front of Mari. "Hold here."

For a moment, nothing happened. But then, from a small closet, a young man flung himself at them, a kitchen knife in his hand. Mari, even with Asa's warning, jumped. He must have been missed by the initial sweep, but even in the short glance she had, Mari saw he hadn't seen more than fifteen cycles. She opened her mouth, afraid Asa would kill him, but couldn't form the words quickly enough.

Asa's open palm crashed into the boy's face, her other arm easily deflecting the wide swing of the knife. The boy crashed to the ground, unconscious.

The two women locked eyes and Mari gave Asa a slight bow. "Thank you."

Asa gave the barest of nods as she led the way deeper into the house. Mari saw that the violence became more pronounced the deeper they went. Guards had started to react here, and more than a few bodies littered the hallways. Mari fought the bile rising in her throat. The cost was necessary, but these were her citizens.

Asa led her to what appeared to be a receiving room near the center of the house. Tatsuo sat there, in his evening clothes but otherwise looking completely at peace. He fixed Mari with an unwavering stare as she entered. "You are too late, Lady Mari, and this mistake will cost you everything."

She couldn't believe his confidence. He was surrounded by her men, yet believed he was in control of the situation. She would have to disabuse him of that. "Surrender your traitorous claim, and possibly I will let you live."

He gave her a look as though she was a child who hadn't gotten her way. "No, Lady Mari. Your house has become mine. Call back your soldiers and I will allow you to live in exile."

Mari took a single, deep breath. For all the groundwork she had laid, the future was still unwritten. Tatsuo clearly believed he had the support of most of the nobles. He might be right. Mari knew their support was divided fairly evenly. A shadow of doubt fell over her.

Then she remembered the farmer, turned away from justice only a few days ago. She remembered that this was a man who easily resorted to assassination. No, Tatsuo couldn't have her house. Only one path was clear, as much as she detested it.

She stepped toward Tatsuo and drew her short blade. Tatsuo's all-knowing grin never wavered. He still thought she was bluffing, that she didn't have the will. "You should put that away before you cut yourself," he said.

He never expected her to slash at him, the sharp steel cutting a deep, uneven line across his neck. His eyes went wide, and for the last few heartbeats of his life, he realized just how wrong he'd been.

THE SUN ROSE on Mari's first day of rule. After the attack, they had returned to the inn, where Mari changed into her finest robes. While Mari changed, soldiers loyal to her flooded through the streets. Down at the gate, some of her soldiers were coming up the pass to reinforce her position. She hated that Stonekeep would have such a strong military presence, but it was needed to ensure the smooth continuation of her rule.

She glanced at herself in a mirror before leaving the inn. The emblem of House Kita sat prominently on the robe, a reminder to all who would challenge her. According to her information, Tatsuo had planned on holding a small council meeting today, no doubt to consolidate his own power. The open council was for the people, but the small council was where the direction of their house was decided.

Mari made her way toward the council chambers, the path familiar to her from the days of her childhood. Although she hadn't had the same upbringing as Juro, or even Hiromi, their father still expected her to be present at small council meetings. He believed each of his children should possess at least a basic understanding of how the house lands operated.

Mari and her entourage were the first to arrive. Takahiro took a torch and lit the lamps in the small, stone room with thick doors. As a child, Mari had always considered the room warm and comfortable. Her father and his advisers had argued in this room for half the day sometimes, but it had always felt safe. Under her father, this had been a space where people could disagree with one another and not fear for their lives. Today, despite the growing heat of the summer, the room seemed chilly.

Eventually the other nobles arrived. Mari recognized them all, and they recognized her in return. Some nobles she'd already made contact with. From them, she received small nods, the only acknowledgment she'd receive that they'd cooperated. Others looked surprised, some even taken aback, at her presence in the room. She assumed by now most had learned of her presence in the city, but no small number of them might have been involved in the plots to assassinate her.

Arata was an old noble Mari remembered well. She hadn't seen him for over a cycle, but he looked unchanged, like a weathered rock immune to the storms of time. His white beard was long and well maintained, and he moved with a grace that belied his advanced years. He had been a military commander long before even her father had taken control of the house. Unfortunately, he was one of the nobles whose loyalty to their house was uncertain. As such, she hadn't approached him yet. His reaction seemed genuine.

He knelt down the moment he recognized her. "Lady Mari! I had heard you were dead, killed with your brother near Starfall. I am glad to see you alive."

Mari gave the old noble a small bow. Though circumstantial, the fact he'd mentioned that particular rumor indicated he probably hadn't been involved in the plots against her. He had always seemed too honest for such scheming, but one could never be sure. She relaxed toward him, but not completely. "It is good to see you once again. It has been far too long, Arata."

As old as he was, and Mari guessed he had seen over eighty cycles, Arata's eyes were clear and sharp. He saw that Mari was sitting at the head of the table, but he made no mention of the fact. He took his seat, waiting for developments to unfold.

Two other nobles who had walked in behind Arata were well known to Mari. She had visited them both in the past several days and earned their support. Their names were Naoki and Isau, both who had seen about forty cycles and had been close friends of her father. She bowed slightly towards them, and her gesture was returned by a pair of deeper bows. They were solidly on her side, then.

The other nobles trickled in one and two at a time. Some didn't seem surprised to see her, while others were shocked. Mari made note of each reaction. More than a few faces didn't seem pleased that she sat at the head of the table.

The final noble to arrive was the one Mari knew she would have the most problems with. Yoshinori stepped into the room, laughing at some comment his bodyguard had made when his eyes met Mari's. His gaze immediately hardened, and he took in the room and the rest of the nobles with a quick glance. Mari didn't need to be a mind reader to know he was doing the same math she was. Who supported whom? That question would determine the fate of the lands. In many ways, this meeting held even more importance than her actions the night before.

Mari wished she felt as confident as she looked. She had been very careful when meeting with the nobles over the past several days. One wrong move would have given away the element of surprise, and she'd been more cautious than necessary. Now she wished she'd been bolder and sought out more support before she acted.

Yoshinori sat down. He had been Tatsuo's closest ally, according to everything she had heard. He began the meeting without formalities. "Where is Tatsuo?"

Mari decided not to lie. "Dead."

Loud murmurs immediately erupted around the table. Even the nobles who had already pledged their support to her looked surprised. Yoshinori looked as though he was about to stand and shout, but reconsidered. "You killed him?"

Mari nodded. "I gave him an opportunity to rescind his claim peacefully. He refused."

Silence settled over the room as the various nobles considered the implications. Yoshinori, of course, sought to take advantage of the confusion. "We must choose a new leader for the house."

Mari stopped him before he could continue. She'd predicted the move, and couldn't let Yoshinori frame the argument. "I agree. None of you are fools. I'm sitting here today because I intend to protect these lands and my people. I am the last surviving member of my family, and I *will* rule. But it will only be by the consent of the majority of the nobles here."

Yoshinori stood up now, his face turning red. "How dare you presume to rule? You are a woman!"

Mari met the noble's fire with an icy gaze. Yoshinori

sputtered as the other nobles judged him for his outburst. Mari knew of his temper and hoped to use it to prove how unfit a leader he was. "I am well aware my position goes against tradition, which is why I'm asking for your support. Without you, the people will not follow. With you, they will."

Yoshinori muttered loudly about the disgrace of the situation.

Arata spoke, his voice firm. "What you ask is very unusual, Lady Mari. I have long supported your family, but if what you say is true, and you do seek to protect the people, why should I support you and not another?"

Mari gave the older noble a small bow. "A good question. Since I was young, my father insisted that we be part of his rule. I did not receive the depth of training Juro did, but I am also no stranger to the ways of the lordship. Perhaps more important, I have the allegiance of General Fumio, who is now in command of the army on our western border. I also have the allegiance of the blades."

Yoshinori spat. "The assassins who killed our lord and the king? You've made your bed with snakes, Lady Mari."

Mari felt her heart race at that. She thought of Koji, reflecting on how strange a world it was where she counted the man who killed her brother as one of her most loyal supporters. The nobles here could never know how close the two of them were, another reason she had sent him away from her instead of making him the head of her guard.

"They are also the only force strong enough to protect us in our time of need," she replied. "We are under attack from the other two houses. Without the blades, this house will fall."

Yoshinori's retort was immediate. "You don't even trust our military? Your lack of faith is unbecoming of a ruler."

Although anger rose in her throat, she couldn't allow herself to show it. The nobles needed to see she would handle a crisis with calm, rational decision-making. "I trust our military, but I'm also a realist. Hiromi's actions decimated our forces, and although our men are well-trained, we are substantially outnumbered. Our only hope is the blades, as unpleasant as that truth might be."

Arata verbally stepped between the two of them. Mari didn't remember him ever being quite so vocal during meetings. "Your words are reasonable, Lady Mari, even if I find them difficult to accept. There is one other question, though. Do you plan to marry?"

Mari leaned back in her chair. The question wasn't unexpected, but it was the one she was the least enthusiastic about answering. But the long arm of tradition could never be fully escaped.

"At some point, yes. I believe there are more important matters at stake now, but I desire to see my family line continue. I refuse to make it a priority at this time, however."

Arata wasn't pleased with the answer, and looked like he was about to push the issue.

Mari spoke before Arata could reply. "I do plan to marry, and I recognize how important giving birth to an heir will be. But we must first look to the safety of the land. Our people must come first. I am happy to entertain potential suitors, as time allows. If I receive support from you all, it would allow me more time to consider such issues."

She knew she walked a fine line, but she saw little choice. The nobles around the table were silent as they considered her statements. Yoshinori, in particular, seemed thoughtful. Mari hinted at the possibility of greater roles within the ruling of the lands. She expected that he underestimated her, that he saw opportunities both for marriage into the family and to assume greater responsibility behind the scenes.

Yoshinori had called the blades snakes, but he was one if she'd ever met one in human form. If he saw a way to slither his way into power, perhaps he would publicly back her for the moment. Otherwise, he needed to try for the throne today, and he knew as well as she did that any vote taken at the moment was razor-thin. If he supported her now, he would be a continuing threat, but she was willing to push the problem into the future if she could at least solidify her rule today.

She ended with her strongest move. "You've asked, reasonably, why you should support me." She paused, waiting for all eyes to focus on her.

"It is true that I have the support of the military and the blades. That gives me strength. But a good ruler does not rule by strength alone. As we speak, I'm distributing papers throughout Stonekeep and the land, proclaiming the truth that I was the Lady in White so many have spoken about. The legend has grown in the telling, but the people will know what I did for them this past winter. If you support me, the people will know that the nobles support them. In this time of crisis, we all need what stability we can find. I am the best hope for that stability."

She left plenty unspoken, but the nobles understood well enough. The legend of the Lady in White had grown, and Mari would muster the support of the people. By itself, such support wasn't a deciding factor. But combined with the support of the armies and the blades, the nobles knew they'd have chaos on their hands if they didn't vote for Mari. And the vote would be public. Mari had done all she could to trap them in a corner, giving them only one reasonable way out.

Yoshinori seemed to be the first to arrive at that conclusion. He watched her for a moment, and Mari thought she saw a combination of respect and hatred in his eyes. "My peers," he began, "I, for one, believe in Lady Mari, and she shall have my support. I will call for the vote now."

She fought the temptation to smile. It was a smart move, and left him several avenues towards power. He would forever be known as the one who had called for Mari's vote. He would indeed be trouble in the future, but for now, he served her purposes.

By the time the sun hit its zenith, the vote had been tallied, and Mari was the undisputed ruler of House Kita.

MARI RUBBED AT HER TEMPLES, wishing she knew of a way to get the ache behind her eyes to go away. Too many problems required attention she didn't have to give. With the throne secured, she'd spent the rest of the day handling what seemed like an endless series of crises. She didn't know how the land had held together as long as it had. And now, at the end of the day, another crisis loomed. She read the note one more time, then threw it on her writing desk.

Takahiro was the only other person in the room. He too had read the note, but refrained from commenting until she asked him. Right now, she wanted to think about anything else.

She held her head in her hands. "So, how did I do?"

"There were some missteps near the end of the day. For example, I think you'll need to lend more credence to Arata's concerns about the distribution of food reserves. But overall, you did well. As well as any lord I've ever seen."

Mari appreciated the honest assessment, and his comments stirred a long-distant memory. Takahiro had seen several more cycles than her, but he had been with her family as a bodyguard for so long she sometimes forgot he had existed before he became a bodyguard. "You're from a noble house yourself, aren't you?"

"A disgraced house, but yes. Our lands are tiny, and when I elected to become a guard for House Kita, my younger brother assumed the responsibility of heading our house. I have renounced my claim. It was the only way your father would allow me to serve."

"Do you ever regret your decision?"

Takahiro chuckled, a sound Mari found particularly pleasing after the events of the day. "Do I miss councils, complaints, and arguments over how one's lands should be run? Never once. I was not made for rule, my lady."

Mari smiled at the comment. She understood the draw of power, but the responsibility of rule was a burden, and always should be. The thought made her groan, knowing there was more to do. She desired sleep, but not quite yet. She picked up the note. "Come. There's one last task to complete before the day is over."

Takahiro gave a short bow and followed her without question. She assumed he could guess where she led him.

The streets were dark but the sky was still light when they got to the inn. Mari had missed that about Stonekeep and the tall mountains. She loved how the sun would set behind the sheer granite faces, casting the city into darkness while the sky shone dark blue overhead.

Mari found her target sitting in the corner of the common room with a cup of beer. Mari took a seat and ordered a beer of her own. She'd never been much for drinking, but tonight she'd gladly partake. One didn't become the first lady to rule one's lands and not celebrate, after all.

Asa looked up, her expression something between curiosity and annoyance. She didn't speak, waiting for Mari to take the lead. Once the beer arrived and she'd taken a nice, long pull, she did.

"That's good. Just what one needs after a day like today." She glanced at Asa, wondering if she would receive any response.

There was none.

Mari passed the note over to Asa, who read it without speaking. The nightblade's face didn't so much as twitch.

One could say many great things about Asa, Mari thought, but her manners and conversation would not be among the qualities listed. The blade continued to sit there in silence, waiting for Mari to get to her point.

Mari capitulated. "What do you think he wants?"

The letter was from Hajimi, demanding that all blades meet in the valley below Stonekeep to plan their future. A copy had found its way into Mari's hands.

Asa shrugged. "He's up to something."

Mari fought the urge to slap the girl. Anyone could understand that. She'd hoped Asa would have some insight. If the nightblade knew more, she would have said more.

At least, she hoped as much. She trusted Asa, but recognized the blade was torn between different loyalties.

"Will you go?" Mari asked.

Asa nodded. "I will ensure there are others to lead your guard while I am gone, but whatever Hajimi plans, I must be present."

Mari held back a sigh, though she'd expected as much. The meeting wasn't for several days yet, as Hajimi no doubt wanted most of the blades present. But much of Mari's strength relied on the blades. If Hajimi renounced his support, the ramifications could destroy her. She felt as though she had a knife to her throat.

Actually, she felt like she had several knives to her throat. The other nobles were sharpening theirs as well. Which made her think of the other reason she'd come here tonight.

"Asa, I'd like you to start a new group of guards, a core group within the honor guard."

Asa frowned. "Why?"

"Because I want them to be women."

Asa set down her mug slowly, and Mari got the impression she only did so to prevent spilling beer by slamming it down. Beside her, Mari could feel Takahiro's tension. She hadn't given him any warning about this idea.

"Why?" Asa repeated.

"Because I am going to need protection everywhere I go, including during my baths and when I dress. I don't care to be ogled, or to have a guard distracted when he should be protecting my life. I need women who can and will fight to protect me."

She didn't say that it served a political purpose as well. Even a small number of women, present and visible as guards, would begin changing perceptions, which would be necessary if Mari was going to continue to rule. They would need to keep her alive, of course, but that was why she needed Asa to find and train them.

"That will be a challenging task. Where shall I find women who can fight?"

"I had hoped you would start with blades. In time, perhaps, others will come who can pass your training."

She could tell Takahiro wanted to argue. She turned on him. "What?"

"You risk yourself unnecessarily," he said. Asa might not guess at her hidden motives, but he could see them.

"I disagree. Could you fight your best, without distraction, if I stood naked beside you?"

She'd never seen the shade of red on Takahiro's face, and she felt a small measure of satisfaction at the reaction. He didn't argue her point, though.

Mari turned back to Asa. "Will you do it?"

Asa didn't look enthusiastic, and Mari wondered what was going through her mind. Truthfully, she didn't know if the blade would accept or not.

"Fine. I will. But I cannot guarantee my length of service."

Mari knew she couldn't ask for more, not from one whose loyalties were so torn. But when Asa gave her word, it was good. She released a sigh of relief. "You can discuss specifics with Takahiro. I imagine it will take some time to make the changes."

Mari took another giant pull from her beer, amazed at how good it tasted. She began to understand now why her father drank as much as he had. She could already feel her muscles unknotting after a full day of hard decisions. She felt good, though, as she'd accomplished much today.

Asa, on the other hand, looked like someone had tied a noose around her neck.

7

In two days, the blades would meet. That meeting, Asa was increasingly certain, would set the path for the blades moving forward. She hadn't heard so much as a whisper, but she had gained something of an understanding of Hajimi in the past few cycles. He would be looking beyond the war to what came next, but he wouldn't move without the blessing of the remaining blades. That gathering, so close yet so far away, would be very interesting.

Compared to her days now, the gathering would be a welcome relief from her daily boredom.

Asa stood behind Mari, who was seated on the small dais in the courtyard. She had volunteered for guard duty today. Young women had flocked to her over the past few days, trying to prove they had the martial skill to become a guard. Asa didn't understand why. Were they desperate for gold, or did they see honor in guarding their lady? Asa had to turn aside at least nineteen of every twenty, and the ones she did admit for training were almost always a far cry from a warrior.

Today Asa took a break from the madness, but she

wasn't convinced guarding Mari was any less a waste of her time. Although the day was young, there had already been several encounters where she worried she would have to draw her sword. Today was open council, flooded with complaints of the people, and Mari's decisions often left few happy.

Asa found she detested the workings of a noble house. Compared to Mari's complex challenges, the life of a warrior was a slow stroll down a straight path. She hated the never-ending complaints of the people. Too often, people came to Mari with problems Asa believed they could easily solve on their own. One couple had even come with a marital dispute!

But worse than the meaningless complaints were the ones that had some merit, or the ones that involved political maneuvers beyond Asa's understanding. Already this morning, Mari had listened to a farmer who demanded military protection for his farm. The lady sent him away, his request unfulfilled. A particularly daring young noble came next, barely bowed in front of her, and asked publicly for her hand in marriage. Those gathered to watch had leaned forward eagerly to see how Mari would react. The young man spoke for some time about his suitability, and no small number of onlookers seemed to agree. Asa believed the man talked far too much, and every word he uttered made him less appealing. Mari ejected him from the courtyard before he had even finished listing his desirable attributes. That decision, at least, Asa agreed with.

Another farmer came next, asking for seed for his farm. It was late in the season to be planting, but his fields had been destroyed by Katashi's retreating armies. Mari granted him a bag of seed over the objection of some onlookers who believed it was a waste this late in the year.

She rebuked them sharply. "Our seed does no good in the storerooms, and we have precious little food as it is. I'd rather risk some on a chance than the certainty of starvation this winter."

After the farmer, Mari's treasurer stepped forward. Asa glanced warily around the room. The treasurer was the only person to approach the dais whose presence had been arranged by Mari. Normally such business would be conducted in private, but Mari, influenced by the strange teachings of Takashi, believed that as many dealings as reasonable should be handled in public.

"My lady," the treasurer, Naoki, began. "I have worked the figures and submit them to you now, with copies, as you requested."

Mari nodded, and the onlookers were given small sheets of paper with numbers written across them. Naoki offered Asa a sheet, but she declined. She didn't feel any need to complicate her life any further than it already was. From the expressions of the onlookers, Asa had a decent idea of how the assembled nobles felt about the proposal. A wave of angry muttering passed over the crowd.

Mari gave everyone a few moments to study the sheet before speaking to Naoki. "You believe this constitutes a fair price for the food our armies need?"

"Yes. The prices are based on current market values."

Yoshinori stood up from the crowd. In the time since Mari had taken her throne, he had become the leader of the opposing faction. His complaints always sounded like support, but his intentions were clear. Asa believed that Mari would be better off if Yoshinori found a sword through his stomach one day. But Mari detested such tactics.

The noble spoke loudly. "Lady Mari, I admire your attempts to better the lives of your people. But don't you think it sets a dangerous precedent to pay for what has always been given?"

Mari didn't waver. "I think you mean to say 'taken.' The food has only been provided because of the forces the nobles wield. This proposal allows those who provide our food to feed their own families."

Yoshinori spoke as though he addressed a child in the basics of how the world worked. His voice was kind but condescending. "Lady Mari, all farmers are allowed a certain amount of what they grow. That is how they feed themselves, and it has been enshrined in our laws for countless cycles. This idea of yours threatens to upend a system that has sustained us through good seasons and bad. Why change what doesn't need repair?"

Mari's gaze could have frozen steam. "And if I were to send auditors to your lands, would they find that all farmers have received their fair share? A noble who doesn't provide the fifth to those on his land faces severe consequences."

Yoshinori's face didn't show any reaction, but Asa could tell from the way his balance shifted he hadn't considered that Mari would push the issue this far. They still underestimated her.

In front of the nobles was a proposal that was radical, at least within this house, as far as Asa understood. For generations, the allotted share of the farmers who worked the land for the nobles had been one-fifth. The nobles, in turn, provided one-fifth of their total to the house to feed the armies.

In many cases, the system worked well. Mari told Asa that most nobles usually cared for their farmers, giving from their own stores when the seasons were difficult. But lately, that had changed. With the great uncertainty from the bitter winter and the political upheaval, many noble families were taking more than their fair share and hoarding the food. Other lords might have chosen a single noble family to make an example of, but Mari didn't think that way. She hated the idea of strong-arming people into doing what she wanted.

Instead, she offered a new choice. Farmers could, if they chose, sell a tenth of their labor directly to the house. Mari would guarantee a certain price. Mari's solution meant the nobles might lose some of the food they had been hoarding, but Mari loved the idea of giving the farmers more choices.

Asa struggled to care. Force seemed an easier route to her, but Mari had strange ideas about governing.

At the moment, though, the question was how Yoshinori would react to Mari's implied threat. Mari knew Yoshinori was one of the guilty parties, a noble who had taken more food than was allowed by law and not sent enough onward to the house. She could have his lands taken from him by force. Asa much preferred that idea.

Would Yoshinori accept her compromise and lose one tenth of his food, or would he push the matter?

He proved to be the coward Asa believed him to be. He sat down without another word.

Mari looked over the crowd. "Are there others who wish to speak?"

Asa's hand twitched towards her sword. Many of the nobles looked as though they had plenty to say, but they all remained silent. That worried her more than angry outbursts. That silence meant they would speak later, when Mari's back was turned. No doubt, Yoshinori would be in the center of most of those conversations.

Mari had won the seat of her house, but her position, and her life, were far from secure.

· · ·

ASA FINGERED the note in the folds of her robe as she neared the temporary encampment of the blades. The camp sat in the valley below Stonekeep. Not only was the location convenient to the seat of the house lands, the mountains rising around it acted as a natural defense. Asa's robes allowed her entrance into the camp, but the note, sealed with Hajimi's own seal, would get her into the inner circles of the impromptu city.

The note had found her the day before, requesting a semi-private audience before the gathering. The note gave no other reason, but Asa would seize any excuse to leave her current responsibilities behind. The gathering was to start about noon, and the sun had just risen in the sky.

Asa hadn't visited the blades' tent city before. By the time they'd all migrated from Starfall, she'd already been inside Stonekeep, embroiled in the intrigues within. The camp was clean and orderly, but Asa still felt the stab to her pride to see her people living in tents.

The mood around the camp seemed to agree with her. People completed their daily tasks: cooking food, carrying water from the nearest well, washing their robes, training, and more. But Asa heard no laughter, no lighthearted conversation. Every blade she observed looked as though they carried a great burden. And, in a way, they did. Asa didn't think on it often, but the blades here were the majority of everyone that was left. In the entire Kingdom, there were maybe only a thousand of them left. Would they wither away and die, like a tree overshadowed by its larger neighbors?

She couldn't let that happen. She'd found something in Starfall worth fighting for: her people. Growing up, she'd never put enough importance on the fact that she was a blade. Now she did. She would fight for them, and maybe even die for them, if that was required.

Soon she made it to the center of the camp and was admitted into Hajimi's tent. Even though the shelter was larger than most, it still felt small. Hajimi's living space closed in on her, the same way the Kingdom seemed to be suffocating the blades.

Asa stopped when she saw Koji in the tent. Until that moment, she had thought he still fought in the west. She'd heard rumors of him only a few days ago. The man could barely make a cut without creating a new legend somewhere.

He gave her a bow that almost seemed apologetic. Had her life contained more light in it, she might have thought of being angry at him for not informing her of his movements. But between her responsibilities above and the questions of their survival below, she found that it was just good to see him again. If nothing else, he was a rock in trying times.

Hajimi didn't waste time in polite conversation. A servant poured tea for them, and Hajimi promptly ignored it as he motioned for them all to sit. "The council has decided to form groups of volunteers to lead expeditions for a new home. The rest of the blades will learn of this when the gathering begins."

Asa didn't catch the nuance as quickly as Koji did. The legendary nightblade was a methodical thinker, but his intuition sometimes made leaps ahead of others. "I find it hard to believe we'd find any other land to settle in besides this," Koji said.

Asa felt as though there were a question in the statement, but she still didn't understand. Then insight struck. "You're planning on leaving the Kingdom."

The lack of expression on Koji's face told Asa he'd

already figured it out. Hajimi just gave a small nod. He looked older to Asa, time slipping past the head of the blades faster than it did for others. Not for the first time, Asa felt grateful not to be in his position. "Not planning, exactly. Preparing, perhaps. There is still some hope that a peaceful resolution can be found among the houses and the blades, but it seems less likely by the day."

"You're giving up," Koji said.

Asa couldn't detect a hint of emotion in Koji's voice; it sounded as though all hope had been drained from him. Asa could imagine his feelings. Koji wanted the blades fully behind Mari, but Hajimi wasn't foolish enough to gamble their entire future on one person. Everything Koji had worked toward over the past moon was slipping away from him.

"Quite the opposite," replied Hajimi. "My responsibility is to the future of the blades. One of those possible futures is here in the lands of House Kita. I wish that to be the case, but I must prepare for all eventualities. Mari's victory in this conflict is far from certain, and there will be no home in the other house lands. I'm not giving up, but giving us a hope for new life."

Asa saw Koji's eyes flicker upward, cold fury behind them. Something in him had changed, Asa realized. A few moons ago, this conversation would have had him up and pacing. But now that willpower that made him so dangerous on the field of battle contained his energy. He had matured, and that made him more dangerous. Even Hajimi wilted a bit under that gaze.

"Why did you ask us here?" Koji asked. "You wouldn't if you didn't have an ulterior motive."

Hajimi regained some of his composure. "I wished to discuss the council's decision with you before the gathering.

Many of the blades look up to you, and it is due to your argument at our last gathering that we are here now." He paused, then looked at Asa. "And you are closest to Lady Mari. We must walk a fine line between protecting our interests and aiding her."

"You want our support," Koji said.

"I do."

For a tense moment, the silence in the tent pressed against her. She hadn't expected any of this.

"I will speak out against your decision," Koji decided.

Hajimi looked pained. "Surely you understand the position we find ourselves in."

"Yes. But you risk splitting the blades at a time when we need a unity of purpose."

Hajimi pushed back. "The world is not as black and white as that, Koji, and the blades are not children, obsessed with whatever goal I put in their sights. We can handle the complexity of this new world."

Koji looked ready to argue the point, but Hajimi stopped him with a motion, as though an idea had just occurred to him. "Perhaps we can borrow a method from Mari herself."

Invoking Mari's name was enough to get Koji to truly pause. "What do you mean?"

"Let the people decide which path they want to take."

"Another vote?" Asa finally found her voice.

"No. Koji is right to be focused on protecting Mari's interests, but the expeditions *will* happen. But the council can give you time to speak, Koji, to ask for volunteers. You fight for Mari, and you can make the case for what you do. Those who choose not to fight can volunteer to be sent on expeditions."

Koji nodded thoughtfully as he thought about the idea. Asa, having been involved with Mari's dealings for the past moon or so, felt a tickle in the back of her mind. Something about this didn't sit quite right with her.

"That seems fair," Koji finally decided. Asa saw the briefest flicker of a smile across Hajimi's face, and then she understood. From beginning to end, this whole scene had been scripted. Hajimi caught her gaze, and she saw that he knew that she knew what just happened.

The ploy was brilliant, now that she thought about it. Many, if not most, of the blades would follow Koji. Given the nightblade's growing legend and conviction, he'd form a force of blades larger than any seen in dozens of cycles. And Koji was the right person to lead them. Hajimi might have been manipulative, but that didn't make him wrong. Koji would guarantee that the other houses' armies didn't get close enough to Stonekeep to threaten the blades, giving them time to find another home, or potentially even bring an end to the war and make the whole issue moot.

It also gave the rest of the blades another goal. Koji was right about the blades needing purpose. Hajimi simply realized they couldn't all serve one master.

Asa couldn't imagine what the Kingdom would look like without the blades, but for the first time in recorded history, that possibility seemed all too real. She knew, too, why Hajimi had invited her. She needed to convince Mari to continue to extend her protection to the blades, even as the blades made plans to leave. She finished her tea and stood up. "Thank you, Hajimi, for your service to the blades. Knowing the plans for the meeting frees me to return to my duties immediately. I shall take my leave."

A look passed between her and Hajimi. She gave him a small nod, to let him know she was aware what must be done.

"Give my best to Lady Mari, please." Hajimi bowed.

As Asa left the tent, she felt elation pass over her. Next to Koji, she couldn't have expressed her feelings, but the idea of leaving this broken Kingdom behind them sounded like a dream come true.

ASA BARELY MADE it a dozen steps before she sensed Koji coming up behind her. Even in the crowded camp, his energy stood out to her, like a bright torch lit in the middle of the night. His strength made even the other blades look like children in comparison. She wondered if he knew how strong he felt to others.

"Asa, wait!"

She stopped, knowing already the argument the two of them would have. She didn't want to fight. With all the struggle in her life, she wanted this to be easy. But Koji rarely took the easy path.

Koji sensed her displeasure, but guessed wrongly. "I'm sorry that I wasn't able to warn you about my coming. I only just made it here myself, running several horses to the ground to get here in time."

Asa wrapped her arms around him and he stiffened, the display unexpected. She held him close for a moment as he awkwardly returned the embrace. She liked the feeling of how stable he was. Even now, caught off-guard, she wasn't sure she could push him over: his stance was solid, his feet rooted to the ground. As frustrating as he could be, she appreciated his simple consistency.

That consistency had meant the world to her back when she'd been lost in doubt. Perhaps more than any other reason, that was why she had always cared for him. No matter how mad the world seemed to become, Koji would always be there, as unmoving as a mountain. In the world of shifting loyalties that defined her time back in Stonekeep, Koji was a breath of fresh air.

After a few moments she stepped back. "You will lead the blades against Mari's enemies, then?"

He gave a small frown, as though she had just asked a question so obvious it didn't need an answer.

Asa almost laughed at his expression. It never even occurred to him that others would feel differently, his belief was so strong. "Don't you think it would be nice to go on one of those expeditions, exploring unknown lands, trying to find a new home?"

He shook his head, as Asa knew he would. "Not when there is so much to do here."

She realized it would be hard to have this conversation. Their starting points were so different from one another. The temptation to skip it was powerful, but she couldn't. Koji needed to know how she felt. She'd made her decision almost immediately after she left Hajimi's tent.

"I would like to go on one of the expeditions," she said.

Koji looked as though he'd been slapped across the face. A moment of doubt passed over his face, as though he thought she was joking with him. Then he realized how serious she was. "You would abandon Mari?"

Asa swept out her hands, indicating the temporary city surrounding them. "I would abandon the whole Kingdom for the blades."

"There are no blades without the Kingdom."

"Maybe not in the past, but there's nothing that says we need to remain here. We are strong, and perhaps even stronger on our own. What keeps you here?"

She knew part of the answer already, even if he couldn't articulate it himself. He felt tremendous guilt over his past, and he saw the defense of Lady Mari as his redemption.

"Asa, people are suffering out there. I've seen villages burned, women taken by soldiers, and fields destroyed. I have the strength to do something, so I must."

She reached out to him, feeling the pain in his voice. "I know how you feel. But you can't save everyone. Why not focus on saving the blades? We are your people."

Koji pulled away from her touch. "It's wrong, Asa. If we focus only on ourselves, we'll lose everything." He paused for a moment. "Does this mean that you'll not guard Mari?"

Asa didn't answer, the implications of her intentions obvious.

"Asa, you can't. If Mari isn't protected, everything we do, all the blades we've already lost, will be for nothing."

His conviction moved her, but she couldn't be swayed.

He pushed forward. "Don't you see? Even if you're right, and the blades need to leave the Kingdom, Mari needs to be protected. She's the only noble willing to give us shelter. If she dies, the rest of the lords would band together against us, and we couldn't defend ourselves. If we're going to find a new home, we need time. Mari needs a strong warrior protecting her. I've heard of the assassination attempts, so you know it's true. Others can go on the expeditions. To protect the blades, you need to stay with Mari."

Against her desires, she had to admit he had a point. A hundred rebuttals ran through her mind, but they all sounded like the whining of a petulant child. Koji was right.

"Will you go with me, when the time comes?" she asked.

He looked at her curiously. "You mean leave the Kingdom?"

"Leave everything. Leave the lives of the blades behind. We can start a life somewhere new, together. A life where we can avoid violence instead of running toward it."

Koji looked out into the distance, staring at something Asa couldn't see.

"Yes. I would," he said, stepping closer to her and wrapping her in his own embrace. "I would leave it all behind with you."

8

K oji stepped out of his tent, surprised at how hot the morning already was. Summer was near its peak, and while the long days made for plenty of time for training, they also brought more than enough heat.

Despite the heat, Koji looked around him with a deep sense of satisfaction. He was surrounded by blades, over a hundred total. Together, they marched toward Fumio's army, prepared to join the battle for Mari's lands.

Although the gathering had happened just the way Hajimi predicted, Koji still found himself surprised every morning to discover he still led a band of dedicated blades. He had over ninety nightblades at his command and over a dozen dayblades. They were the largest single force of blades the world had seen in generations. His heart beat faster when he looked at them, knowing that he could change the course of the war with a force this size.

He would need to, too. Thanks to Lord Isamu's actions to the south, Fumio had been forced to tear off units of his cavalry to reinforce Mari's weaker forces near the southern border. The lack of men was already telling, and Fumio absolutely needed the blades before the battle was joined.

A smaller force of blades had also left from the valley below Stonekeep to reinforce Mari's southern armies, commanded by General Masaaki. Koji had never met the general personally, but he heard the man was a solid commander.

Koji's days had been full as of late. He had two pressing responsibilities. The first was to reach Fumio to provide support for his battles. The second was to prepare the blades for those battles. Rarely in the history of the Kingdom had so many blades been summoned to one task. Nightblades were used to fighting alone or in small groups. They had no training in formations or large-scale battle tactics. Koji needed to prepare them before it was too late.

So half their days were spent traveling, the other half spent training. Koji experimented with dozens of different strategies, welcoming suggestions from all those with him. Every night, around the fires, the entire unit discussed what had worked and where they had struggled. The blades were all excellent warriors and learned quickly, but Koji wasn't convinced they were learning fast enough.

Time had become one of their many enemies. Katashi's forces seemed willing to sit for now, but Isamu was moving up from the south. It didn't take a master to see that both lords would attack at roughly the same time. Koji and his forces needed to reach Fumio by the time that happened. Ideally, they were three days away, but they were now in position to ride hard for one long day if needed. That, at least, was one pressure off Koji's mind.

They received a bird that afternoon, right after they set up camp to train for the rest of the day. Fumio's handwriting was terse and filled with information. Katashi's army had begun to move. Fumio responded by moving his own troops. Mari's general expected that within the next two days, the subtle maneuvers for control of the battle location would be over and the true fight would begin.

Koji elected to ride hard for Fumio. He would have preferred another few days of training, but better to be at the battle rested than to be rushing in at the last moment. They packed up their tents and rode well into the night to reach Mari's forces.

The next morning, he allowed the blades to sleep in late. The Great Cycle favored them, and Koji received a message that the battle would not happen until tomorrow. Koji ordered the blades to engage in some light training, but then to rest. Tomorrow would be hard enough without being exhausted.

The heat on the day of battle felt oppressive, as though the weather itself judged their actions. A messenger came to Koji before sunrise with his orders, orders he didn't find surprising in the least. He summoned the blades together.

"As expected, Fumio has placed us just off the center of the battlefield, where some of the fiercest fighting is expected. We've been given uniforms of House Kita, so as not to make an obvious target of ourselves. Our mission is straightforward. We're to break their lines and threaten their headquarters. Our spies tell us that Katashi will be present on the battlefield, and if we can kill him, we have the opportunity to end this war before any more lives are lost."

Pride twisted Koji's stomach into knots as he looked around the circle of warriors. He tried to memorize the faces of each of the people under his command. He wasn't naive enough to think they were all going to survive. They had trained with new tactics that would hopefully protect them, but the Great Cycle would call some of them home today. It was certain.

"Remember why we fight. If we can give our lives to protect others, our sacrifice is not in vain. I will be front and center with you, and we will break Katashi's lines. We will end this war today."

He was surrounded by faces filled with silent determination. Today he would show the world the true strength of the blades. A final thought occurred to him.

"Remember that this is the same army that burned Starfall to the ground. Let us remind them how much of a mistake that was."

Koji and his blades were at the lines when the sun rose over the battlefield. The day promised excruciating heat, but Koji could still feel a hint of cool morning breeze. It seemed a shame, he thought, that they would fight on a day that promised to be so beautiful. The morning sky was painted in shades of purple and dark blue, with barely a cloud to be seen. It just didn't seem right to die under such a beautiful canopy.

He wondered how many warriors on both sides of the battle would agree with him. Never in his life had he been part of a fight of this scale. Thousands of warriors lined up behind him, but Katashi's forces across the plains and shallow valleys seemed as numerous as the grass. From his vantage point, Koji could barely make out the end of the enemy lines. It was one thing to know your forces were outnumbered, but to see that difference in front of you, knowing that a sea of steel and flesh stood between you and your target, was something else entirely.

Koji's heart raced and his hand sweated against the hilt

of his sword. He knew from long experience that once the battle began his nerves would disappear, but the waiting that came before battle was always the worst. He couldn't allow himself the luxury of showing the fear he felt. The blades watched him with an unwavering focus, taking heart from the confidence he displayed.

He didn't fear for his own life. It wasn't arrogance or even confidence. If he died today, he died for a worthy cause. The numbers in front of him didn't matter. Once he drew his sword, if there was a single enemy or a thousand, he would fight without holding back.

He sweated because of the burden of leadership. His own life was his to spend how he wished, but these blades had chosen to follow him. They looked to him because they trusted him, and he feared that every death would be a betrayal of that trust. He knew there was only so much one could do, and he resolved that he would sacrifice his own life if it would save one of the blades behind him.

In the stories, this was the moment when the leader gave a speech that stirred the hearts of soldiers. But Koji had never been strong with words. His tools were steel. He turned around, gave a bow, then turned back to the front and waited.

The blades were a few ranks away from the very front of the lines, protected by the lives of some of General Fumio's standard infantry. Koji hated the general's logic, but couldn't deny the wisdom of the positioning. As many blades as possible needed to survive the charge so they could turn the tide of the battle. Had they stood at the very front, they would have fallen early. Fumio had pinned most of his strategy on them. Outnumbered and almost outmaneuvered, Koji's small group held Fumio's best chance at victory.

There was no opportunity to speak as the drums sounded the advance. The shouts of commanders went up across the line, and as one large mass, Fumio's army started forward.

Koji's blades marched side by side with the common infantry, hiding in plain sight. With every step they took, Koji's hands dried and his heart settled into a steady rhythm. The waiting was done, now only the work was left.

What did other soldiers think on the eve of battle? Did they think of homes left behind, better times that existed only in the comfort of memory? Despite his politics and his actual reasons for being there, when the battle started, all Koji thought about was the brothers and sisters at his side.

From the opposing lines, arrows numbering in the thousands shot into the air, darkening the sky with the deadly beauty of their flight. Koji allowed himself to watch for a full heartbeat, observing a few arrows colliding in midair and knocking several others off course. Then he drew his shield and held it overhead.

Like all nightblades, Koji despised the use of the shield. It was a cowardly device, but after the siege of Starfall, and knowing that not all large-scale battles were as honorable as a one-on-one duel, Koji had insisted that all his warriors use shields. A nightblade with an arrow through the chest was no more useful than any other wounded soldier.

Koji felt several impacts to his shield, jarring his arm, but his group kept their shields tight together, forming an almost impenetrable roof above their heads. They kept the shields up as they continued marching forward, and again and again Koji felt the blows against his arm that would've brought death or injury under other circumstance.

The beat of the drums changed behind them, and the infantry that made up the front lines switched from an orderly march to an all-out sprint. The lines had closed. Three lines in front of him, the warriors ran, yelling as loud as they could. Then the next line sprinted, then the one in front of him. Finally, Koji took a deep breath and ran forward himself.

He screamed, unleashing all the fear that combat evoked. He embraced his sense, feeling the power of the army around him, the spirit of men and women willing to give their lives so that others may live in peace. He screamed for Asa and for Mari, and for those who stood solidly behind him.

The sprint, such as it was, lasted only for a few dozen paces. Just as soon as the charge had begun, it halted viciously as the song of steel on steel rang in the air. The front lines had clashed. Koji threw his shield off to the side, sensing the warriors behind him doing the same. They pushed their way to the front of the lines, waiting for the blue uniforms of House Kita to give way to the red uniforms of their enemies.

Koji thought the battle began slowly. First, one red uniformed officer seemed to stumble through a sea of blue, causing Koji's sword to flash once. A few moments later another came through, and Koji's sword sang again, ending the man's life with a single cut. Then two more came through, then more than Koji could handle on his own. They began to surround him and move beyond him. Koji and his fellow blades, in their nondescript uniforms, didn't attract any special attention from the enemy infantry.

Any order that had existed prior to the lines meeting was gone. Soldiers hacked at one another with abandon, many of them forgetting even their basic training. The infantry that had protected the blades on the advance were either dead or had fallen away, overwhelmed by the number of enemies they faced. Koji and his warriors were surrounded by a sea of red uniforms, but Koji didn't mind. He pushed even harder, wanting to surround himself entirely with the enemy. Only then did he feel as though he was fighting as hard as he could. He lost himself in his sense and relied on his training, gliding between cuts as easily as avoiding trees in the forest. No enemy came close as his sword sliced down over and over.

He felt strangely energized, his cuts strong and precise even as the battle went on. Enemies filled his vision and his sense, but he felt more alive than ever.

Koji lost all sense of time. With the press of people, he couldn't extend his sense for more than a few paces in any direction, but within that small kingdom, he was king. His world filled with bloody steel, sweaty and grunting soldiers, and the dust of thousands of feet with nowhere to go.

One danger was in straying from the other blades. He fought at the point of the mass of blades, and sometimes, as the chaos flowed around him, he found himself alone, cut off from the others. Twice he stood his ground and waited for the blades to reach him, but once he needed to retreat and take shelter.

He felt odd, being a part of the fight but still separated from the larger scene. He didn't know how the battle went or even if they were winning or losing. When he spared a glance at the sky, he was surprised to find the sun straight overhead. He'd had no idea so much time had passed. Suddenly, a wave of exhaustion rolled over him, and he allowed himself to be swallowed by the other blades, falling back into a small space of relative safety.

The short break from the fighting allowed him to obtain a better idea of his surroundings and the battle at large. Their forces had advanced farther than he'd thought. With luck, they'd pull through this. Far more inspiring, though, was the work of his warriors.

The blades fought in pairs, never allowing one to get too far in front of another. Each pair took turns fighting near the edge of the group and then fading back into the center, giving themselves time to rest and to breathe. They couldn't relax completely, of course, but few red uniforms made it through the wall of fighting blades. Also within the center were a handful of dayblades, ready to heal at a moment's notice.

Koji searched the entire battlefield again. Despite the progress they'd made, there were still far more red uniforms on the field than blue. They needed to attack Katashi. After a few moments of searching, he found the flag, off in the distance on top of a small rise. The lord was viewing the fight from the rear.

The lord's actions only confirmed Koji's belief that the man was a coward. He needed to direct the blades toward Katashi. Taking a deep breath, he left the relative safety of the center of the group and took point once again, heading straight for Katashi's flag. The other blades followed suit, making slow progress against the sea of bodies pressed against them.

The resistance against them increased. For every soldier Koji felled, two seemed to spring up to take his place. Koji didn't know if his group was attracting more attention, or if they'd just made enough progress to leave the rest of Fumio's line. The why didn't matter, though. All that mattered was killing Katashi and ending this battle.

Driven by his need for justice, Koji slipped again into a near-trancelike state. Swords cut all around him, and the fighting was thick and fast enough that more than once he needed to choose between taking a cut or certain death. His life trickled from half a dozen little gashes, but Koji only noticed the pain in the rare moments he wasn't being attacked. His world became nothing more than a long series of dodges, parries, blocks, and strikes.

Somehow, a single voice penetrated his consciousness. It was one of his fellow blades, yelling his name. He turned around and glanced at her, seeing her covered in blood that wasn't her own. "Koji! Get back here!"

At first, the order didn't even register. Why did he need to return? Then he shook his head and decided to listen to those who fought by his side. Making sure that his guard never fell, he retreated until he was within the circle once again. As soon as he dropped out of his trancelike state, a wave of exhaustion, unlike anything he'd ever felt before, crashed against him. He didn't know a body could be so tired. His knees buckled, and two of the nightblades standing near him stood him up. He tried again to stand, but his body seemed unable and unwilling to respond.

One of their dayblades came to him, summoned by the small group that surrounded him. The dayblade took one glance at him, laid his hand on Koji, and closed his eyes. A moment later, Koji felt a cool wave of energy trickle through his body. It felt like taking a sip of water after walking for leagues with an empty water skin.

As suddenly as the sensation began, it ended. Koji felt like a dying man as he lay on the ground. The dayblade stared daggers into him. "I have done what I can, but you need rest. There is no other healing for the damage you are doing to your body." With that the dayblade left, leaving Koji with more questions than comfort.

Due to Koji's inability to move, the circle of blades had stopped advancing. Without their forward movement, many of Katashi's men seemed willing to let them simply stand there. No doubt Katashi's soldiers thought them some sort of elite unit. No regular infantry squad approached them unless necessary. The pressure against them lessened, while the battle raged around them.

Slowly and carefully, Koji got to his feet. The nightblades on either side of him looked uncertain, their hands hovering near his arms in case his legs collapsed once again. Fortunately, his strength held. His legs wobbled and shook, but they held his weight. Koji looked around the battlefield to plan their next steps.

As he had wondered, his warriors had advanced far beyond the reach of the rest of Fumio's forces. They were surrounded by a mass of red, and although they were largely being left alone, it was only a matter of time before attention returned to them and disaster struck. He spun around, looking for Katashi's flag. When he saw it, he could barely contain his surprise. The flag was there, but it was retreating, growing smaller in the distance.

Koji cursed to himself. The young lord had realized the danger of his situation and moved to another location. Then he heard the beat of the drums in front of him, and the entire battle shifted in a moment.

It was one of the nightblades standing next to him who first realized what was happening. "They're sounding the retreat," she said.

Koji's eyes narrowed as he watched the battlefield. She was right. All around them the red uniforms retreated, and he thought that the sounds of battle behind them were fading in intensity.

The warriors looked around, eventually focusing their attention on Koji. What should they do next? Did they fight, or did they make their way back to their own lines?

Koji was torn by indecision. If the other force was

retreating, that meant that Katashi would live to fight another day, and the war would go on. But a victory was a victory, and Koji wasn't sure they had the strength to launch into pursuit. His desire, strong as it was, wouldn't be enough. The decision was painful, but necessary.

"Hold your position. Only engage if attacked. We are done here today."

As their enemy retreated, the blades were left almost entirely alone, as few had the desire to become a casualty after the battle was done. Soldiers in red passed by on either side of their small circle, eyes blank and wide with shock. Koji's warriors no doubt shared the same look.

A strange silence descended over the battlefield, quiet only in comparison to the battle that had so recently raged all around them. Koji could still hear the groans of the wounded, the cries for help as each side reformed their lines, but the sounds were strangely muted, as though his ears were still ringing from the clash of swords.

Koji fought the urge to sink to his knees and close his eyes. He couldn't, not in front of his warriors. But for the day, it was over. They had won the battle.

9

M ari released the string on her bow, watching the arrow fly straight into the target, its flight ending with a satisfying *thunk* against the wooden man. Though she kept her face neutral, she felt the warm glow of pride within her. She hadn't shot in far too long, but her skills hadn't faded much. Beside her, Takahiro released his arrow, the shaft barely sticking in the edge of the target.

They stood in a long hallway in her family's home, a hallway that occasionally became an impromptu archery range. Mari had occasionally shot her bow in this hallway as a child. Back then, Juro had shot with her. Today, Takahiro unwillingly joined. She'd practically had to order him.

She didn't like shooting indoors, but the hallway was easy to guard, and concerns over her safety had only grown over the past days. Though they had no specific evidence, both Takahiro and Asa were certain that rebellious factions were targeting her. At least shooting indoors was better than not shooting at all.

Though Takahiro didn't speak, Mari could hear his

objections all the same. He thought they should be working on the problems facing their house lands. Though he'd never voice the opinion, he worried that she wasn't taking the challenges as seriously as needed.

Nothing could be further from the truth, however. Mari had thought of almost nothing else for days. But her tired mind needed a break, and she hoped the archery would shake loose the blocks forming in her thoughts.

They'd received word from the western battlefield that morning, and were expecting word from the south at any time. Fumio's news had given Mari a mixed reaction. The victory made her grateful, but the reports of the losses had been almost too much for her to take. They'd won the battle, but at the cost of thousands of lives. Fumio had lost almost a quarter of his army, and Katashi had made an orderly retreat before his lines truly shattered. The cost of victory had been too high. Katashi still had an overwhelming advantage of numbers.

Mari didn't let those thoughts into her mind yet again. She focused on the motion of the bow, pulling the cord back to her cheek as she focused her spirit on the target. Taking a slow, deep breath, she released again, and again the arrow ended up quivering near the center of the target. Takahiro questioned her desire for archery, but he didn't understand it was one of the only times she felt like she could focus.

Her world was crumbling around her. Though she was the head of her house, the nobles who should be supporting her conspired against her. The blades, who she'd risked her own soldiers to save, considered leaving the Kingdom. The other two lords worked together to destroy her land. She felt besieged on all sides, with no place to run to.

Mari heard the shuffling of feet behind her and she put

down her bow. A messenger entered, delivered a message to Takahiro, then retreated. Takahiro read the letter quickly, then handed it to Mari. "General Masaaki ordered a retreat before his forces could get routed. He plans to move north for a few days, then settle into another defensive position."

Mari cursed silently as she read over the letter. Masaaki wrote with flowery script, using more words than necessary. Mari didn't much like the man, but he was a competent general and loyal to the house.

Masaaki hadn't expected to win, but the news was nevertheless disappointing. His forces were vastly outnumbered by Isamu's, and Mari had given him clear instructions that retreat was far preferable to a heroic last stand. No doubt the traditional general had balked at those orders.

Even though she'd expected the loss, the words still hit her with the force of a backhanded slap. How could she possibly make this work? They were outnumbered, and her enemies surrounded her on every side. The list of allies she was certain she could depend on seemed to dwindle by the day.

She tried drawing her bow again, but couldn't find the focus necessary. She put the bow down without releasing. For the first time, she considered just giving in.

Mari had little doubt what kind of ruler Katashi would be. The man was manipulative, with a strong focus on himself. Perhaps he'd pledge to treat Mari's people as his own, but she couldn't imagine a world in which that was the truth. The people her family had protected for generations would be under the thumb of one who would abuse them to no end.

Isamu might be marginally better, but Mari also couldn't see a world in which Isamu was made king.

Katashi was too devious, and seemed to have the upper hand.

But the whole Kingdom desperately needed peace. The early and harsh winter had frozen crops, meaning all the houses had to dig into their reserves. Mari knew hers were desperately low, and if they didn't have a successful harvest this cycle, famine would take more lives than war. Whenever Mari looked at a map, she thought about how each movement of the army essentially destroyed a field that wouldn't produce that cycle.

In the histories she'd studied, wars often lasted for cycles. But this one would be over within a season. It had to be, or they were all doomed.

Takahiro looked up from reading the letter a second time to see that his lady suffered. "Mari, what's wrong?"

She fought to keep the distress from her voice. "Do you think I should surrender?"

Takahiro looked taken aback. "You can't surrender because you've lost one battle!"

"No." If anyone else saw the larger truth, it was Takahiro. "It's not about losing in the south. It's about all the challenges we face. If I am a responsible ruler, I need to ask the question: are my house lands better off if I surrender?"

A lesser adviser would have spouted empty platitudes, but not Takahiro. He stood there, letter in hand, asking himself the same question Mari didn't trust herself to answer.

"No," he finally said. "If you step down, Yoshinori would almost certainly take power. You know the way he'd treat your people, especially if Katashi demanded concessions from him. Anyone who isn't a noble would suffer. You are the land's best hope."

Mari took comfort in the words, but hated the burden

Takahiro laid on her. There would be no rest from her duty so long as he remained her adviser. She appreciated that in him.

She didn't even realize she was crying until a few heartbeats after it began. Takahiro stepped forward and wiped the tears from her face, then stopped. The two of them rarely touched, but at that moment, Mari welcomed the gesture.

An awkward silence began, but Mari cut it off before it could settle between them. "Thank you."

She took a few moments to gather herself. "So, if surrender isn't an option, and victory is necessary, what actions are left to us?"

Other advisers might have considered the question rhetorical, but not Takahiro. He looked thoughtful. "Perhaps there are other ways of winning this war."

She watched him as the gleam formed in his eye. As he explained his idea to her, she quickly found herself nodding along. The ideas were unconventional, and she wouldn't have expected them from a man as honorable as Takahiro. Slowly, hope began to live again in her, like a young plant just breaking through the hard soil.

TIME. Being back in Stonekeep, being back in the house she'd grown up in, was making Mari reflect on her past. As a child, she'd always wished the days would go faster so that she could become an adult and do as she pleased. Now, time was a merciless enemy, marching relentlessly against her.

Takahiro's ideas could work, but they would need time, and time was a precious and fleeting resource. She hated having to reach out for support, but she saw no other way around it.

Part of her wished Takahiro could be here for this meeting. His presence would have reassured her. But he was needed elsewhere, drafting the orders that would go to the generals. The birds needed to fly today, and everything had to be in place.

A servant knocked and announced that her guest had arrived. He was earlier than expected, a sign he took the request to meet with appropriate significance. Mari looked around the room one last time at the minute details set in place, either for her guest to notice, or to create an atmosphere that would encourage the conversation she sought. She nodded at the servant and went back to working at her desk.

Arata entered a few moments later. Mari saw him take in the scene, saw the hint of satisfaction in the lines of his face. Arata radiated nobility. Mari figured the effect was some combination of his age and calm demeanor, but his presence alone made her want to be a better ruler. The noble offered a deep bow. "My lady."

Mari returned the bow. "Thank you for coming on such short notice. How are you?"

Arata gave a grim chuckle as he approached her desk, covered with maps. "You may skip the formalities. When you get to be my age, and your return to the Great Cycle seems more imminent with every passing moment, you learn that, sometimes, brevity is wisdom."

"I agree. Tea?"

He waved the offer away as he studied the maps. His eyes and mind, despite his age, were sharp. After only a moment he looked up. "We're losing, then."

Mari almost argued against the assessment, but decided to save her breath. "That is why I asked you here."

He gave her a curious look.

Mari cleared off some of her papers, so the map and the units on it could be seen more clearly. "We're heavily outnumbered, and while General Fumio managed to drive Lord Katashi back, the victory cost us dearly. In the south, General Masaaki was forced to retreat rather than be routed."

She assumed Arata had gathered as much from his glance at the map, but she wanted to ensure he knew what she knew. When he didn't respond, she continued. "I am going to order our forces to retreat to the foothills of the mountains. Fighting a war on two fronts, out in the plains of our territory, will destroy us."

Arata frowned. "Many nobles won't like such a plan. Many of your strongest supporters have lands in the plains."

"Which is why I need you. The other nobles look up to you, and know that you won't support me without cause. If we don't retreat, we're doomed. But without your voice supporting me, I'm not sure I can keep us together long enough to win this fight."

Arata looked thoughtful. "And how do you plan on winning this fight?"

Mari pointed at a few points on the map. "In the west, we're going to modify the strategy that I used as the Lady in White. Groups of nightblades will attack supply convoys and possibly return them to us. We'll starve Lord Katashi's armies." There was more, another part of the plan, but one she wouldn't share here.

"And in the south?"

"I still need to speak with Hajimi, but I am sure that he will bolster our forces there, holding Lord Isamu at bay. Once Lord Isamu's men approach the mountains, they'll be nearly useless against our troops. We only need to hold them long enough for Lord Katashi to break. I'm certain Lord Isamu will follow close behind."

Arata studied the maps again. "It could work, and I don't see many other options at the moment. I do fear we rely too much on the blades, though."

Mari had expected this complaint. She'd heard it often enough in her short rule. "Their purpose is to maintain the peace of the Kingdom. They protect us on our home land against the invading houses. They are fulfilling their duties. And," she lowered her voice, "I'd much rather lose blades than soldiers of House Kita."

Arata's eyes came up to meet hers. Mari didn't say any more. She had to deal with enough rumors of her affection for the blades. Let Arata think he understood a different truth.

Arata stood up straight, and Mari knew she'd won him over. "Lady Mari, perhaps it is forward of me to say, but I am honored to support you. Did you know at one time, I considered trying to take the house from your father?"

Mari stiffened, wondering where Arata was going. In her mind, Arata had always been faithful to their house. "No, I didn't."

"It was during a rough year, with many crops failing, and your father had hard choices to make. I was younger then and couldn't see the entire problem. I thought only of my own lands and their well-being." He paused, lost in the past. "Your father discovered my plans and invited me to tea. I thought I walked to my death that day. But then we talked about the problem facing the whole land, and how he had to make these decisions. In many ways, our meeting today reminds me of that day. I left then knowing I served an honorable man, and I leave today knowing I serve an honorable lady. You will have my vocal support on the closed council."

The comment both warmed Mari's heart and stabbed her at the same time. She served her house on behalf of the people, but the ghosts of her ancestors, all well-respected rulers, stood ever over her shoulders. She hoped Arata never had to learn the lengths she would have to go to protect and lead her people.

THAT NIGHT, Mari made her way to where Asa trained the new recruits. Mari didn't pay as much attention to her guards as she should. She knew that much. Her own father had known each of his guards by name, as well as what was important to each. Mari had plenty of memories of her father laughing alongside his guards, or supporting them in their times of need.

Mari always meant to strike up conversations with those who risked their lives to protect hers. As her father had made abundantly clear, a guard who views you favorably will protect you that much more fervently. But a dozen other tasks always demanded her time, and she'd never made the effort.

Despite that, though, she did know that Asa's training seemed to be working. There were more women in her guard now, protecting her as she changed, or when she took a bath. Occasionally, they were rotated in for other duties as well.

When she stepped into the training hall, she realized that she hadn't actually been here since she'd returned to Stonekeep. As a girl, she hadn't been allowed into the training hall, and it simply hadn't been something she'd thought about since her return. As a child, she'd wanted nothing more than to be here, and now that she had the option, she chose not to take it. Perhaps it was time to reform that practice.

Mari saw that Asa noticed her immediately as she entered, but the nightblade didn't give her any particular recognition. She had work to do, and she went about it without interruption.

Not for the first time, Mari thought that in different circumstances, she and Asa could have been friends. Mari respected the way the nightblade went about her duties, and even though it was clear Asa had little patience for politics, the woman always kept her word. Mari felt safe so long as the blade was near.

Though she had more important tasks, she decided to wait and watch the training for a few moments. Asa had the women working partner drills. The blade walked up and down the line of trainees, fixing mistakes that she saw and sending them through endless repetitions. Mari felt as though she'd stepped back in time, and her father was training some of his personal guard. Her father had been an impressive swordsman as well.

One woman stood out from the group. Even Mari's untrained eye could see she was a cut above the rest. Her sword was always a step ahead, and in the short time Mari observed, she easily won each of her matches.

Eventually, Asa called for the group to halt and take a break. When they did, Mari got a better look at the woman dominating her peers. She was less a woman and more a girl. Mari guessed the young warrior hadn't seen more than seventeen cycles.

Asa came over to Mari as the potential guards stretched and drank water. The warrior that stood out from the group didn't join the rest, continuing to practice her forms.

She used the sword like she'd been born with it in her hands.

Asa gave a barely perceptible bow. "My lady."

Mari gestured toward the lone woman. "Who is she?"

"Her name is Suzo. You noticed her skill?"

"Yes. Who is she?" Mari wondered if she was the daughter of some noble house, having received training somewhere else before.

"No one of note. Her mother died a few cycles ago in childbirth. Her father is a farmer, but wasn't able to feed her. He was considering selling her to one of the brothels, but then she heard of the training here. She displays unusual aptitude for the sword. If I didn't know better myself, I'd think that she had the gift, but she does not. She's simply talented."

Mari's heart went out to the girl. But her story confirmed Mari's own plans. Under her rule, everyone would have opportunities. She would make sure of it.

Mari turned her attention from Suzo to Asa. "I came to ask you a question."

"I assumed as much."

"It's about Koji."

Mari saw a flash of emotion cross Asa's face, but it was gone so quickly as to almost be unnoticed. Mari knew the two had fought, but wasn't interested in their personal problems. The needs of her lands were greater. "I am considering giving him an order that he might find detestable. If I do, will he follow it?"

Asa's answer was immediate and bitter. "I imagine he'd do almost anything for you."

Mari had suspected that was the case, but the confirmation reassured her. She gave Asa a short bow and then turned to leave.

Asa wouldn't let her leave so easily. "He's one of the most honorable men I've ever met. You'd take that from him?"

Mari didn't have any response to that. She continued out the door without answering, heading toward her chambers, where she would write the orders that would hopefully bring an end to the war plaguing the Kingdom.

10

Asa had never much liked beer before. She'd imbibed on several occasions, but she couldn't drink much without feeling the effects, and she preferred to have her head clear.

These days, though, it tasted better than ever. In addition, being in the common room of the inn allowed her to be surrounded by people. She could watch and forget the responsibilities that weighed on her for a time.

She understood more about herself now than she had before. Asa didn't like the world as it was. She detested the political maneuvering that defined so much of Mari's life. She hated that the three lords of the Kingdom fought over the right to rule. But most of all, she hated that she wasn't out on one of the expeditions, trying to find a new place for the blades to live. Koji's arguments still held true, of course. By ensuring Mari's safety, she gave the blades time to decide their next steps. But it didn't feel like she was doing much. Guarding Mari, watching as she wrote letter after letter, made her feel useless.

So she drank in the evenings and watched. Depending

on her mood, she found the behavior of the other patrons either fascinating or despicable. Tonight she found the drunken antics to be more the latter than the former.

A man, completely unremarkable, came and stood next to her. Every once in a while, one would try to engage her in conversation. Usually, a stare was enough to get them to leave, but this one looked as though he'd be persistent. He had a hint of a smile on his face, as though he knew a joke about life that no one else knew. "May I join you?"

"No." Asa had found that being rude hastened the exchanges.

The smile never left his face. "Rough day?"

"Sure."

For a moment, Asa worried the man was going to keep trying, but she didn't have to fear. He gave her a short bow, that half-smile still present. "Well, perhaps I'll see you again soon, then. Under better conditions."

The man melted into the background, and Asa wondered if she'd maybe had too much to drink. She lost sight of him almost instantly, as though he'd never been there. She considered quitting, but the night was young, and her head was still too full of thoughts. Raising her hand, Asa ordered another round. Thankfully, being the head of Mari's guard paid well.

After Asa had nursed her next beer for a time, another shadow passed over her. Asa was about to growl at the stranger, but when she saw who it was, she stopped. Suzo stood there, looking out of place and awkward. "May I sit?"

Asa worried about one of her guards drinking with her, but then stopped herself. Why should she care? She hadn't wanted the position anyway. And she liked Suzo, for as little as she knew about the trainee. She motioned for the girl to sit.

The girl sat down and ordered a drink, looking uncomfortable all the while. She looked like someone who'd never been to an inn in her life. Perhaps, Asa thought, she hadn't. The girl said she had only left her farming community a handful of times before coming to train.

Asa didn't mean to make the girl more uncomfortable, but she had no desire for conversation at the moment. She sat there, waiting for Suzo to speak her mind.

"So, do you come here often?"

"Often enough that you knew to find me here."

The girl looked down, as though ashamed that Asa had realized this meeting wasn't coincidence. "I'm sorry. I just didn't know when else I could speak to you alone. During training, there are always other people around." The girl's voice was tense, more anxiety in it than Asa could remember hearing before.

Asa kept silent, waiting to hear the reason Suzo had come.

"I don't want to speak out against the other trainees, but I'm worried about them."

"Why?"

Suzo fumbled around. "Well, as you know, people have some different feelings about what we're doing."

Asa had heard as much. Some people thought the female guards were wonderful, or fascinating. Though they didn't speak to her directly about it, Asa heard enough to know several men were interested in the new guards. Women who fought were... exotic, Asa supposed, to the average man here. Others derided the women as foolish, attempting to do something that was the right and responsibility of men.

"Some of the women have men who are interested in them, but I'm nervous."

Asa got tired of Suzo dancing around the questions. "Say what you mean."

"I think some of the men might be interested in the women only to learn what the guard rotations are like."

That was news. Asa felt herself responding slowly, but she did respond. "What makes you say that?"

"Well, the other women listen to instructions, and they don't say anything directly, I don't think. But they plan out their meetings with the men days in advance, and most of the women have suitors right now. It just occurred to me that if someone was planning something, they could piece together the rotation if they wanted to."

Asa leaned back. All the women in the selection process were single. It had been required, as Asa had wanted women who could commit fully to the process of learning the sword. And if almost all the women had found interested men in such a short time.... Her thoughts trailed off. She'd never thought of it, but something certainly seemed worth investigating.

"Thank you, Suzo. I will look into it."

The girl looked relieved, but didn't leave. Asa's eyes narrowed.

"I'm sorry, but there's one other question I wanted to ask."

Asa gave her a look that clearly stated she should ask it and leave.

"Am I a nightblade?"

Asa stopped sipping her beer mid-sip. She hadn't been expecting that question. "No."

Suzo's face fell, as though her closest family member had died. "Oh."

"Did you want to be one?"

Suzo glanced up. "Yes. Well, no. I'm not sure. But it feels

right to hold a sword, and I know I'm good. I thought that maybe I was one, and no one had noticed when I was young. I don't remember ever being tested."

Asa felt a stirring of compassion for the young woman. "You're very good, Suzo. But you aren't a blade. I haven't sensed anything from you. I'm sorry."

Suzo looked down at the table again, at her untouched drink. "It's fine." She paused, then looked back up, a sudden fire in her eyes. "I just want my life to matter. And this is the first time it feels like it has. Thank you."

With that, Suzo stood up and left, not even taking the time to say goodbye. Asa watched the girl go, finding herself suddenly missing the company.

SUZO'S CONCERNS left Asa with a predicament. The enemy you knew was far safer than the enemy in the shadows. She'd rather uncover this particular plot than scare them into hiding, only to try again later. She didn't feel comfortable asking the other women to share what they knew. A single wrong word might be enough to alert the conspirators.

So she put herself in their shoes. Asa believed in the women she recruited. She didn't believe, after the intensive interrogation each woman subjected herself to, that anyone was actively trying to harm Mari. If the plotters were interested in the guard schedule, it probably didn't actively involve the guards.

Asa recognized the assumptions she was making, but had to stick by them. That meant the traitors most likely were looking for times when no nightblade was present. They probably felt more sure of their chances when only the ungifted were guarding Mari. Although only a guess,

Asa felt the logic to be true. Her move, then, was obvious. Until now, guard shifts always included a nightblade. Most of the trainees hadn't been ready to face threats on their own.

The day after Asa heard Suzo's concerns, she announced to all the trainees that they had graduated to full guards. They would still train daily, but they were now allowed to guard Mari without the presence of nightblades. When Asa and Takahiro made the schedules, Asa deliberately chose three nights to not have a nightblade present. The only people who knew of the plan were Asa, Takahiro, and Mari.

During those open windows of time, Asa made sure to hide nearby, alert for any possible attacks. The first and the second night passed without incident, and by the middle of third night, Asa began to wonder if she'd made a mistake.

She sat quietly in a corner of a room, hidden by a changing screen. In the center of the room, Mari took a bath, attended by two of her personal attendants. Two of Asa's guards stood by the door, their shift almost over.

Asa had just begun to believe she'd been entirely wrong when she sensed an unusual presence below her. The room they were in sat on the top floor of Mari's estate, and a window looked out over parts of Stonekeep. The presences Asa felt were outside, climbing up.

Asa nodded to herself. Although only two guards were in the room, the castle swarmed with them, and she'd wondered how the traitors would try to enter. Climbing had been one of her best guesses. The walls of Mari's estate weren't easy to climb, but for those who had grown up in the mountains, it shouldn't prove too much of a problem. Asa sensed four men climbing up, their pace indicating they were having an easy time of it.

She fought the temptation to warn everybody of what

was coming. She wanted to capture at least one of the attackers and see if she could determine who was behind these plans. Mari suspected Yoshinori, but Asa wasn't as sure. Yoshinori felt too political. He would make his moves in the closed council and in teahouses. The only way to know for sure, though, was to question one of the would-be assassins. She needed them to come in, and the only way to do that was to make sure they saw nothing but what they expected.

Asa drew her swords slowly, making sure not to make a sound. Then she waited, focusing on her breath to pass the interminable moments until the battle began.

The men, whoever they were, were careful. The window, for obvious reasons, had a changing screen sitting between it and the bath. Between the screen and the darkness of night outside, the men cast no shadows as they slid one at a time through the small opening.

Asa gave them a hint of credit. After such a climb, she wasn't sure she'd be able to move in such a smooth and controlled manner.

As soon as they moved the screen aside, the room fell into immediate chaos.

The women watching the door, unsurprisingly, were caught completely off-guard. Neither of them had experienced an attack before, and it took them several precious heartbeats to draw their weapons. Asa noted their reactions, though, and believed them both to be in genuine shock. Neither of them had expected this attack. Had Asa not been there, they wouldn't have had a chance against the invaders.

Asa came around her own screen with her swords ready, further confusing the guards. The guards hadn't swept the room as they should have before letting Mari in, and they'd had no idea she hid there. Of the four men, three turned to meet the new threat, their stances relaxed. They expected an easy fight.

The fourth man raised his sword to cut at Mari. He became Asa's first target. She leaped at him, ignoring the wild attacks his partners used to try to stop her. The assassin looked up from his killing blow, unable to react in time. Asa smashed into him, knocking him to the floor and cutting across his torso as she rolled to her feet. She wasn't sure it was a killing blow. She'd leave another alive, just in case.

The other three moved in, attacking at the same time. But the room was dim, and Asa wore her loose, dark robes. The men couldn't see her moves well, and she could sense each of theirs before they even attacked. Asa sliced her way through two of the men in only a moment, then kicked the fourth back into the corner she'd hid in, sending him crashing into the privacy screen.

The chaos immediately subsided. Knowing the fourth man was alive, Asa turned quickly and killed the assassin she'd tackled first.

The last man alive finally found his feet. Blood trickled from a cut in his forehead, making him wipe it away from his eye. The two guards in the room advanced on him, too. He was outnumbered, and now that he had time to see Asa's robes, knew that he fought a nightblade as well.

"Who sent you?" Asa asked.

The man stood up straighter, apparently reaching a decision. For a single heartbeat, Asa worried the man would try charging through them all in a crazed attempt to kill Mari. Instead, he yelled, "I will not let this land fall into madness. This house begs for a true ruler!"

Asa knew what the man was about to do, but was too far away to stop it. He slammed his sword into his own stomach, eyes bulging with pain as the reality of his action caught up with him. The man bled slowly, a painful way to go. No one had ever told him stomach wounds didn't kill quickly.

Asa bent down in front of him. "Who sent you? I can ease your pain."

The man tried to spit at her and failed. Shaking her head, Asa stood up and walked away, letting death do its slow work.

11

Koji avoided the battlefield after the battle ended. Under the orders of the dayblades in his group, he'd been forced to rest and recuperate. Though he'd never say as much out loud, the time was necessary. His body didn't act the way it had in the past. He knew himself capable of tremendous feats of endurance. The recent battle had been evidence enough; he'd fought longer than any other blade. But the cost to his body went beyond mere physical exhaustion. When the battle finished he'd felt entirely drained, as though his spirit itself was diminished.

Rest healed the exhaustion, though he slept like the dead. Days passed without much activity. Fumio had his men strip the battlefield and burn what bodies they could. Even though he slept through most of the days, Koji heard enough to know that Katashi had retreated all the way to the river, pressed up against the bridge that led back to his lands. With the difference in their numbers, Fumio would be foolish to attack.

Both sides rested, healing their wounds and making

their plans. Several days after the battle ended, a messenger came for Koji. Fumio requested his presence.

Walking to the general's tent required a fair amount of his stamina, and Koji took note. Whatever was happening to him gave him strength and speed, but if he pushed too hard, the cost might be more than he could pay. As he walked, Koji heard the murmur of voices around him. Several warriors bowed in his direction as he passed. He barely noticed, focused as he was on putting one foot in front of the other.

When he entered the command tent, everyone within stood and bowed deeply toward him. Koji frowned. "What's the meaning of this?"

Fumio answered, "Stories of your deeds have spread throughout the camp. Your force was vital in breaking Lord Katashi's line, and tales of your own effort in the battle are now legendary."

Koji was too tired to take that in. At the moment, he was simply grateful he'd made it to the tent while still standing.

Fumio gestured to a chair and ushered the others out. Soon the two of them were alone.

"How are you?" the general inquired.

"Exhausted, but good. You?"

"Well. We've won our first engagement, and that will matter. I mean what I said. If not for you and the blades, I think that battle would have been hopeless. You ground their center down and allowed us to carry the day. Thank you."

"You're welcome."

Fumio looked him over for a moment before handing over a sealed note. Koji looked at Mari's seal, then up at Fumio. His question must have been obvious. "There were two copies of this order sent. I already know what it says."

Koji tore open the letter and read, his eyes opening wide. Then he read the letter again, to make sure he'd read it correctly. He set the letter down and stared blankly at the canvas walls of the tent.

"Will you do it?" Fumio's question sounded like genuine curiosity, as though the decision could go either way.

Koji knew he would do it, but saying so out loud was more than he could bear. Finally, he nodded.

"You don't have to."

"Can you think of another way?"

"Not without a great deal of luck, no."

"Neither can I."

The two of them sat in silence, each lost in their own thoughts. Fumio broke the quiet first. "It's a horrible task she's given you."

Koji nodded. "Were there another way, I would leap for it, but I do not know what it might be."

Fumio stood up and gave Koji another bow. "You bear much of our safety, and our shame. You have my gratitude and my respect, come what may."

Koji returned the bow, a wave of feeling washing over him. "I will leave most of the blades with you. Their new commander will report by the end of the day. I will not order anyone to follow me, but some will, I am certain."

Koji left the tent, his mind surprisingly calm. He'd been given orders, and no matter how he felt about them, he would complete them. The lives of countless people depended on him.

He walked toward the camp where the blades resided. He'd have to take volunteers, because he'd never order anyone to follow the instructions Mari had given him.

. . .

ENTERING Katashi's lands proved to be more straightforward than Koji expected. After considering a few different options, Koji decided his group was small enough that they didn't need to fight over one of the contested bridge crossings. He only had a dozen blades with him, and there was no point in risking lives needlessly. Instead, he hired three small boats to ferry them across the river at an unguarded location in the middle of the night.

The crossing wasn't without challenges. One of the boats ended up getting lost in the current, depositing the nightblades who rode in it almost a league downstream from the others. Fortunately, they had planned for such a circumstance, and the group united before daybreak at a prearranged location.

The blades dressed in traveling clothes, but Koji led them away from well-traveled roads and towns. The fewer people who saw them, the better off they would be.

Koji didn't like his orders, but his approval wasn't necessary. His logic was straightforward and simple: he believed in Mari and would go to any lengths to see her dream of a peaceful land realized. If that required someone to engage in horrible acts, he would shoulder the burden.

Their trek through Katashi's lands made him reflective, though. He was born here, and while he no longer had any particular attachment to the area, he found his mind wandering frequently. After two days of travel, his primary realization was how little difference there was between this land and Mari's.

The grass and crops here were in no better condition than the land they had left. Drought had struck here just as much as it had leagues away. The people here suffered from hunger and starvation as well. In truth, the situation might even be worse.

Koji supposed there was a lesson here. It was easy to assume your enemies led an entirely different life than yours, that there was some fundamental difference that couldn't be overcome. However, as Koji and his fellow blades traveled, he realized just how mistaken that idea was. Farmers here fought against the land and the drought just as they did in Mari's lands. Knowing the suffering he was about to inflict on them made his head spin. But for Mari's peace, his actions were necessary.

After a few days of traveling, Koji decided that he would risk approaching a village to gather more information. One of the blades, a young woman named Sakura, volunteered to join him. The other blades set up camp far away from prying eyes.

The village they entered could barely be called that. The entire place consisted of no more than ten homes, all grouped together with a small clearing in the center for gatherings. Koji and Sakura approached as travelers, their swords well-concealed. Sakura, in particular, hated the idea of hiding her weapons. Her pride as a nightblade directed many of her actions, and if she'd had her way, she'd have walked straight into the village with her sword on her hip, proclaiming who she was as loudly as the black robes they usually wore.

As they neared, Koji's eyes took in new details. Every house looked as though it had seen far better days. Where there was paint, it peeled away from the wood, old and faded. Windows were cracked but not replaced, and at least one roof had a hole. None of the wear made the houses uninhabitable, but in Koji's experience, people tended to take better care of their homes if they could.

The people didn't look to be in much better condition.

One older woman in particular looked like a skeleton draped with loose flesh.

Koji noticed the lack of fighting-age men. One elderly gentleman looked as though he'd seen over sixty cycles. Other than that, the oldest male Koji saw was a child who couldn't have seen more than eight cycles. Even the boy moved lethargically, as though each step carried a heavy weight.

Koji didn't consider himself naive. He knew war affected civilians as well. When the army went to war, so did everyone else. But he'd never seen suffering like this in a place that had seen no battle. This village lacked the people and supplies necessary to survive. He'd heard that Katashi's land lacked resources, but to see the lack with his own eyes almost made Koji doubt his purpose.

The elderly man approached Koji, his voice wary. "Greetings, traveler. What brings you here?"

Koji noted the hint of suspicion. He was a terrible liar, but fortunately they'd come up with a story on the way. Koji bowed. "Greetings, elder. I work for a noble from the south, and I'm traveling the land to assess the needs of the people, and to see what can be offered in trade."

The old man glanced suspiciously at Sakura, and Koji stepped in before he could ask his question. "My wife. She wished to travel, and there was no denying her."

The elder still gave them suspicious glances, but he didn't question them. His doubt receded further when Koji presented a small selection of their supplies. "By this point, most of our goods are gone, but we offer these to your village to ease your burdens."

Looking around, Koji realized that the small bag of rice they had brought would do very little good. All the same, the elder lit up and bowed deeply to the pair. "You have my gratitude."

They sat down on logs in the center of the village, and Koji inquired about recent events.

The elder spoke more freely, the rice effectively buying his trust. "As you can see, the past few moons have been difficult. Our food stores are low. But our faith in Lord Katashi is absolute, and we know that our victory is assured by the end of the season. Do you deal personally with our lord?"

Koji, unsure of what to say, nodded.

A fanatical gleam lit in the older man's eye. "Will you tell him that he has our full support? Every one of us here is willing to do anything necessary to ensure our lord is successful. Will you tell him that, the next time you see him?"

Koji nodded. He became distinctly uncomfortable under the old man's gaze. The depth of his belief rattled Koji. From everything the blade could see, Katashi had done nothing but take from this village, and yet their belief in him was absolute, defying the reality of the situation.

The old man looked down at his hands. "I only wish that these hands were stronger, so that I could continue to serve my lord and cut down his enemies."

Koji didn't know how to respond, but continued nodding in agreement. Fortunately, the man was beside himself with fervor, and didn't notice Koji much at all anymore.

In time, Koji felt it prudent to leave. The man knew little of any troop movements, or any information of value. Koji had seen firsthand how Katashi treated his people, and that was enough for the moment. They bid farewell and left, making sure to travel in a false direction until they were beyond sight of the village. But even though they'd left the village behind, Koji couldn't help but feel queasy at the unquestioning devotion he'd just seen.

AS NIGHT FELL the next day, the small group of blades came to their first target. Working with Fumio and the information he'd had from spies, Koji had a list of potential places to strike. Damaging any of them would hurt Katashi's war effort, and the more they struck, the better.

Their destination was a small estate, the home of the noble who owned this part of Katashi's lands. It stood on the plains, defying the winds and storms of the open prairie.

As far as estates went, this one wasn't much. A short wall surrounded the house and the grain storage, but Koji and his warriors would almost be able to jump over it. The wall served more as a demarcation of the property than a defensive fortification. At the distance they stood, Koji couldn't sense the individual lives inside. Instead, he could feel the combined energies. Though it was little better than a guess, he didn't think the grounds held too many people. The other blades with him agreed.

The group waited for the cover of night. Koji would have preferred to slip into their traditional robes, the black fabric that blended in so well with the darkness of the evening. But they didn't want to bring blame back on the blades. They remained in their everyday traveling clothes, and the blades spent the evening enjoying a light meal before their mission truly began.

The mood around the campfire was subdued. Every blade was a volunteer, but that didn't make the task in front of them easier. They knew the consequences of their actions. They chose willingly, and each bore the burden of that responsibility.

Once the sun had been down for some time they moved forward. Koji advanced, tall grasses swishing around his knees as he walked. The lives of the estate in front of him resolved in his sense as he neared. His initial assumptions had been correct. He only sensed two people on the walls, and they didn't feel particularly strong.

He motioned to the group and released them. Everyone with him knew what to do.

Koji had expected more resistance. Somehow, the fact that it was easy only made it worse for him. If he'd had to fight, if he'd had to fear for his life, then perhaps he could have justified their actions. But the men on the wall were killed without problem, not even knowing their death was coming.

His warriors crawled over the wall and into the estates. Koji led a group of four into the house while others set about freeing the horses and burning the storehouse of grain. Koji glanced out a window as the fire quickly caught. Originally, they'd hoped to send the grain back to the lands of House Kita. But at the moment that would have required traveling with dozens, if not hundreds, of people, and sending them far to the north to an uncontested bridge across the river. They didn't have the time or the people to spare, and Koji had wanted to travel with a much smaller group.

It pained him to burn the food. There was so little. But the nobles held all the reserves, and all the supply carts originated on estates like this one. Instead of attacking the supply lines, Koji and his people were attacking the stores themselves.

The attack was devastating, though. Food was already scarce, and some of this food went to local villages. Koji didn't know how this particular noble was dividing the food between his villages and the army, but burning this food was as good as killing hundreds. They all knew it.

So, apparently, did the noble who owned the lands. He came rushing out of his bedchamber, his eyes wide with shock and fear. Too late he realized strangers had invaded his house. The alarm hadn't even been raised. Koji and the blades had been too effective against too few.

Koji drew his sword to kill the noble. Their mission was simple: destroy the food and kill the nobles. Send Katashi's land into chaos.

Koji didn't know anything about this particular noble. Perhaps he ruled the land well, making difficult decisions about where to send the food, trying to protect those who lived on his lands. Or maybe he was a tyrant, starving others while he profited and thrived. Maybe he was somewhere between those extremes. Regardless, he owned the lands that Katashi used to drive his army forward. Koji wouldn't ask anyone else to carry this burden for him.

He didn't have to. Before the noble had even understood what was happening to his home, Sakura had drawn her blade and cut his head off.

Koji stopped, shocked at the quick action. He'd told the others he would kill the noble, but Sakura showed no more emotion over the murder than if she'd just killed an annoying insect. She wiped her blade clean on the noble's bedclothes and sheathed her sword again. She didn't even look back at Koji.

For a moment, Koji was grateful to her. He'd never killed an unarmed man before, and although he was sure he could bring himself to do it, he was glad he had some time yet.

They moved quickly through the rest of the house. Their invasion had been so successful, most of the house was still asleep. No guard had awoken the others, and no one on the property was alive and awake to alert the rest of the house about the fire on the property.

A storm had just passed through, so Koji wasn't too worried about the fire spreading to the rest of the estates. As far as he was concerned, his work here was done. He was about to turn around and order them to leave when Sakura hissed at him. He approached as she looked into a small bedroom. A young man slept there in fine clothes. The boy clearly was the noble's son, and had seen eight or nine cycles.

Sakura gave Koji a meaningful glance, and Koji realized she was asking if she should kill the boy.

Koji considered it.

Suddenly, realizing what he was contemplating, he shook his head. The family was probably as good as dead anyway. There wouldn't be enough food, and the boy was too young to rule. Koji didn't know what the family would go through in the next moon or two, but he was certain it wouldn't be pleasant. They didn't need to add to the family's pain.

Sakura looked displeased, and for a moment, Koji worried she wouldn't obey his order.

Then, with a low growl, she left the doorway of the room, heading outside.

Koji looked at the sleeping boy, his heart unable to go out to the young man. All he felt was emptiness inside him.

He turned around and left the house. In the morning, the family would awaken to tragedy, but by then, the nightblades would be long gone.

12

E ven though the sun shone brightly overhead, Mari shivered. The air felt cold against her skin, even as the sun warmed her. Perhaps it was only her imagination. She never had quite gotten used to the sight of dead bodies.

She'd been in battle before, and she'd even killed. Violence was no stranger to her, and yet somehow, this was different. She couldn't put her finger on why. Perhaps it was the lack of steel anywhere near the body, or the meaninglessness of it. Why had she insisted on coming here in the first place? She should be in bed, recovering from last night's assassination attempt. Mari's faith in Asa had been rewarded handsomely.

Unfortunately, the previous night had not been a complete victory. Her enemies, it seemed, were every bit as determined to overthrow her as she was to rule.

Mari looked again at the body of Isau. He had been a minor noble, but one of her most fervent supporters. For him to die now, like this, was a blow. Not only did her position among the council weaken, but it felt as though someone was sending a message directly to her. If she remained in power, those who supported her would suffer the consequences.

Asa came out of the house, the sounds of wailing servants following her as she slid the door open and then shut it again. She looked up at the balcony two stories above them, then down at the body sprawled on the ground with a look of shock on his face. Asa looked deep in thought.

After a while, Mari tired of the silence. "What are you thinking?"

Asa looked around, as though checking to see if anyone was listening. But Mari's guards had cordoned off the area, and they were alone. "You say that Isau was one of your supporters?"

Mari nodded. "One of my strongest. His family has long ties to mine. I remember him as a young boy when he came over on their annual visits to Stonekeep. He will be sorely missed on the closed council. Why?"

Asa shook her head. "I'm certain Isau was pushed off the balcony."

Mari's stomach tightened into knots. She'd been fairly sure as soon as she'd heard the news. Isau dying on the same night of Mari's own assassination attempt was too coincidental. But still, hearing Asa confirm it felt like a physical blow. She knew she wasn't directly responsible, but that didn't stop the feelings of guilt from nearly overwhelming her.

Asa looked back up at the balcony. "Isau was considered a strong climber. He wasn't a warrior, but if he was a frequent mountaineer, as his family suggests, his balance and coordination should have been fine. According to his guards, he wasn't drinking yesterday, so he shouldn't have suffered from any impairments."

"Accidents do happen." The defense felt hollow, even to Mari's ears.

"Yes, but the rug on the balcony is also disturbed, as though there was a scuffle. And I refuse to believe one of your key supporters died randomly on the same night you were attacked."

Although Mari detested the line of reasoning, she agreed with Asa. She felt the dishonor of the act as a personal affront, offended that someone would even dare do something so base in her lands.

Asa brought her out of her reverie. "Who benefits most from this?"

Mari didn't need long to answer that question. "Yoshinori."

If she had died last night, Yoshinori would have effortlessly ascended to the rule of the house. Even though he'd failed at assassinating Mari, it looked like he had plans within plans.

Asa frowned, not liking the answer. "Do you believe him capable of something like this?"

Mari considered. "A moon ago, I would have said no. Now, I'm not so sure. The case against him keeps building. I can't think of anyone else who would benefit as much as he would. If I were to fall, I have little doubt that he would become the new lord of the lands. But still, I've always thought of him as a purely political enemy. I wouldn't expect such violence from him."

"How much will the loss of Isau affect your support in closed council?"

Mari shrugged. "Most still support me, although Isau was vocal and persuasive. I'll survive, but he'll be sorely missed."

"Tell your other supporters to double their guard and

never be alone. If someone is coming at you through them, they might also be in danger. At the very least, ask them to be cautious, and maybe not to stand on any balconies in the near future."

Mari agreed to that much at least. She couldn't afford to lose much more support.

MARI SAT in her small office, the true seat of power in her house lands. The throne room was large, ornate, and impersonal. For making a statement of power, there was no place better. To achieve anything of worth, there was no place worse. Whenever she needed to think or do any work that was beyond that of a figurehead, this small office was where she retreated, just like her father had, and Juro after him.

There were mementos of both of them in the room. On one hall hung a long scroll, decorated with a rural scene an artist had created many cycles ago. Mari now suspected that her father had always wished for a simpler life. To live the life in that painting, fishing in a stream without a concern, had always been his deepest desire. It was a shame he hadn't had enough time after his rule to make his dream a reality. By the time he'd passed the house onto Juro, he was already at death's door.

Juro's largest contribution to the room was a small dagger, ornately jeweled, that sat on the desk. He'd received it as a gift from a noble house on his ascension to the lordship. He'd hated the blade, hated that good steel could be ruined by such decoration. Her brother had been a deeply pragmatic man, and he ended up using the blade to open letters and break seals. He found no end of delight in making the useless gift useful.

Mari still hadn't brought anything of her own into the room. Somehow, it didn't feel quite right. As comfortable as she felt here, the idea of making the room her own still felt like a trespass.

She felt a connection to her family here, deeper than in other parts of the small castle. She felt a bond, a string connecting past, present, and future. Her family made hard decisions here, decisions that changed the course of their lands. But their house had always survived. She felt like she owed it to her ancestors to succeed, to make the most out of the sacrifices they'd made.

Because of that, her profound sense of failure was even more pronounced at the moment, digging deeply into her, darkening her heart. So many before her had worked diligently to keep their people safe and their land secure. Though she believed in the work she did, she wondered if she had fooled herself. Maybe she wasn't as fit to lead as she believed. After untold generations of lords, would the history books record her as the final ruler of House Kita?

The thought shook her, circling in her mind again and again, no matter how hard she tried to focus on anything else. She could not fail. She refused.

But the challenges continued to pile up against her. Did she even have a chance? Everywhere she looked her lands collapsed. Even her own nobles, whose support could have changed so much, were not united behind her. They might even be trying to kill her. She was being attacked by multiple enemies while her supposed allies held her hands behind her back. And now this.

A single tear broke through her frustration as she pounded the desk and stood up. She paced from one end of the room to the other in five quick steps, turning on her heel and marching back to her desk as though it was a battlefield.

In a sense, it was. Her war would not be won with steel and strength alone. Hers was fought with wits, guile, and courage. Her quill and her voice were her weapons, and despite the setbacks, she believed them every bit as strong and necessary as the soldiers under her command.

There was a knock at her door, and from the intensity of it she knew that it was Takahiro, coming to visit her once again.

What would she do without him? Not only was his support instrumental in keeping some of the nobles in line, but he always gave her the truth, and his advice, as near she could tell, had never been tinged with self-interest. With a hundred of him, she could've taken over all three of the house lands and restored the Kingdom to the glory it once possessed.

"Come in," she said.

As predicted, it was Takahiro, somehow looking as though he had just gotten a full night of sleep and had taken most of the morning to clean and prepare his uniform. She had no idea how he continued to pay such attention to the details of his dress, considering the amount of work she gave him every day. She'd asked once, but he'd given a mysterious grin and refused to answer.

She was jealous of him. A quick glance at a small mirror sitting on the desk was more than enough to reveal the bags under her eyes and strands of hair falling everywhere. No matter how many times she put her hair up in the course of one day, it always seemed to come out moments later.

Takahiro took in her state at a glance, able to read more in a single look than most understood after talking with her for an entire morning. "I take it you've read the latest dispatches?"

She gave a small nod toward her desk. "I keep looking for news that I can hang any hope on. But no matter how much I look, everything seems to be crumbling. You've confirmed the information?"

"Yes. It's been verified by several units. Isamu and his forces are pushing harder than ever, grabbing as much territory as they can as quickly as they can."

"Is there anything we can do to stop them?"

Takahiro sighed. "Hajimi sent the blades we requested, but it won't be in time to stem the worst of the problem. By the time the blades arrive, at the rate we're retreating, we're going to be back in the mountains anyway. But it should stop there, at least for a time. Isamu's units aren't trained or prepared to fight us in the mountains."

Mari looked at the maps on a separate table. Almost a third of her lands would be lost by the end of the moon, and another third was hers only because no one had decided to attack it yet. If Katashi decided to cut the northern third of her land off, there wouldn't be anything she could do about it. She didn't know enough curses sufficient for the rage she felt.

Mari paced to a small cushion and sat down, forcing herself to stillness. "Is there no good news?"

Takahiro looked uncertain. "I do not know if it is good news, and I haven't passed it on because I haven't verified it, but it seems the numbers that Katashi is advancing with are far fewer than expected."

Mari frowned. It *could* be good news, but with Katashi being as devious as he was, it could also mean he was hiding troop movements from them somehow. "Why?"

"I'm uncertain. My first guess would be that Koji's

actions behind the lines are starting to have an effect. Perhaps Katashi needed to divert some of his troops back home. It would explain a great deal. We don't have scouts in position to monitor retreats. But Katashi hasn't moved the forces anywhere else in our lands, so I don't think he's up to anything. But I can't be sure."

Mari leaned back on her cushion and rubbed her temples as she considered the implications before her. Her generals were looking for more guidance, a simple direction that she wasn't willing to commit to. On one hand, she could order them forward, to fight and defend every acre of land to the best of their abilities. Otherwise, she could order them to continue to retreat, to save their strength for when it was most needed.

She leaned towards the idea of retreat. It would bring most of their units up into the mountains, where they were much better equipped and prepared than the other armies. Mari wasn't sure how much of an advantage the terrain would be, but perhaps it was just what they needed to turn the tide of this devastating campaign.

But she needed to consider the ramifications of her decision. In the council, either choice would be unpopular. If she decided to send the troops forward, her opponents would call her impulsive and complain that she risked the lives of their troops for little gain. If she retreated, they would claim that she had no concern for the land that was lost, that she was willing to give up precious land because she lacked the courage to fight.

Few of the council members seemed to care about serving or saving the people. They cared only about preserving their own power. How could they not realize that if they continued down this path, there would be nothing left for them to govern, that the house would dissolve, and all that power they fought so hard to maintain would cease to exist in any form?

At least she could trust Takahiro's guidance. "What are your thoughts?"

"My instinct is to retreat into the mountains. Fumio will balk, but it's a good order. Fighting in any other conditions will only guarantee that you'll lose more troops. I hate to lose the land, but the troops are more important." His voice was firm, but Mari heard the pain. He didn't want to give up that land any more than she did. His own family lands, small as they were, would probably be sacrificed.

"And what about the people left behind?"

He gave a small shake of his head. "You can send out messengers to tell the people your plans. There may be some who are not willing or able to leave their house lands, but with warning and reason, you can give them a chance to escape."

"It's not enough," she said.

"Nothing is." In a surprising move, Takahiro sat down next to Mari and met her gaze. "We need to win this fight, but I do not know how."

Instinctively, she leaned in toward him, and he wrapped his arm around her. Sitting there with him, she didn't have any answers, but she felt his strength, his solid nature. Takahiro was like a mountain, unmoved by the chaos around them. She took a deep breath and realized that he'd even had time to take a bath recently. He smelled clean.

A wave of exhaustion passed over her. There was a council meeting soon, but she was just so tired.

Before she knew it, she was asleep, Takahiro's arm comforting her.

· · ·

MARI AWOKE to a gentle shifting beside her. Her eyes snapped open, and she realized with a start that she'd fallen asleep on Takahiro. Apparently, her head had slid down until it was resting on his lap. She blinked away the sleep and sat up. She felt ashamed. To sleep against Takahiro, of all people.

"I'm sorry. How long did I sleep?"

His grin was soft. "Almost the whole morning. I decided you should probably have some time to get ready before the council meeting."

She couldn't believe she'd slept most of the morning. She'd been tired, of course. "Why did you let me sleep so long?"

"You needed it."

She hated to admit it, but he was right. She felt better after the nap than she'd felt in days. "Thank you. I'm sorry for falling asleep against you."

"I didn't mind."

Mari heard something else in those words, something she hadn't expected to hear from Takahiro. But she shook her head. She needed to focus on the council meeting. "I'll meet you in the chambers."

Takahiro nodded and stood to leave. Before he stepped out, Mari spoke softly. "Thank you, again."

Her adviser bowed, then stepped out the door. Mari saw the guards outside and wondered what they thought.

She couldn't worry about such problems right now. She needed to worry about the council. They needed news of Isau's death and her decision to retreat. She didn't expect that it would be a pleasant meeting.

By the time she'd bathed quickly and changed, the meeting was almost about to start. She made her way through the hallways until she reached the council room, then took a moment to compose herself before stepping in.

As usual, the council room was a hive of activity. Given that the meeting was about to start, she was among the last to arrive. Normally, that would have bothered her, but today she was grateful for the rest she'd gotten. The nobles clumped in small groups, and Mari could see that the divisions among her council were as strong as ever.

She classified the nobles into three groups. One group supported her. Their head was Arata, and their support was the backbone of her rule. Yoshinori headed those who were against her. But there was a third group, more undecided than the rest. Their support could swing either way, and that made Mari nervous. For now, they backed her, as no one openly opposed her. But their continued support was far from certain.

A few other nobles arrived and the meeting began. They began with official, regular reports. Nothing was reported that wasn't already known, but the nobles had the opportunity to ask questions and get more details. Most of the information had to do with food distribution and tax collection. Important, but far from exciting.

Next came the issue of Isau. Mari stared longingly at the place where he had knelt at the table. She missed his vocal support already. "Ceremonies for Isau will be held in two nights' time. Notices have been posted throughout Stonekeep. We will celebrate his life."

She took a respectful pause. "Isau had a son, but he's young. Still, I would like to bring him onto the closed council. Isau had good advisers, and I have no doubt that his son will learn even more from sitting in on these meetings."

She'd sent messengers the moment she'd had the time to after finding out about Isau's death. Isau had left a wife and children at his family estates. Mari harbored a hope that Arata would take the child under his wing.

Yoshinori spoke. "Your decision is wise, Lady Mari. As soon as I heard what happened, I sent an escort from my own house guard to complement Isau's. I expect them here within a fortnight."

There were murmurs of approval from around the table, and Mari fought back a curse. The child would be poisoned against her by Yoshinori's 'escort' before they even reached Stonekeep. The action was suspicious. Mari had sent messengers immediately, but if Yoshinori was so confident his people would arrive first, it indicated prior knowledge. Perhaps the evidence was circumstantial, but it was no less damning in Mari's eyes. Unfortunately, there was nothing to be done. It sounded as though Yoshinori had potentially gained one more seat of support at the closed council.

"Thank you," Mari forced herself to say. "Next, I must inform you all that I've ordered our generals to retreat even farther, into the mountains. We will make our stand there."

The announcement sent the room into an uproar. Mari wondered if her father had ever had to deal with such disrespect, or if the fact she was a woman worked against her here too. Regardless, it took some time for the room to quiet.

"Might I ask your reasoning, Lady Mari?" asked Yoshinori.

"Always," she replied. "Our troops are heavily outnumbered on both fronts, and both Lord Katashi and Lord Isamu are pushing hard into our territory. As much as I hate giving up land to the invaders, these are battles we cannot win. By retreating into the mountains we save the lives of our troops until a point where we might have a chance at winning."

Several objections were raised. As she'd expected, several claimed she lacked the courage to fight. Yoshinori didn't make those claims, though. He was sitting thoughtfully. His gaze traveled slowly over to her, and she saw the calculations happening behind those eyes. He cleared his throat and the room quieted. Mari cursed his control over the environment. They wouldn't have silenced themselves so easily for her.

"Lady Mari, might I ask why you haven't sued for peace?"

Because such an idea was doomed to failure, she thought. But she didn't say as much. "We're in no position to bargain with the other lords."

"Perhaps. But if we continue to sacrifice land, the same will still be true. Although it doesn't seem like it these days, we are all still part of the Kingdom. The other lords could see reason."

Mari didn't believe that for a heartbeat. This invasion had been coordinated, planned. Katashi, in particular, wouldn't be satisfied until he could call Mari's house lands his own.

As she looked around the room, though, she realized that she wouldn't find much support for her belief from these nobles. Peace made sense. At the least, striving for peace was necessary. They were fighting what appeared to be an unwinnable war. Of course they'd want to see it come to an end. They didn't agree that such a treat would be as harmful to their house lands as Mari believed.

Yoshinori continued. "If you wish, I would be willing to head a peace envoy to one or both of the other lords. If you gave me terms, I'd be happy to deliver them."

Mari thought quickly. Yoshinori had just confirmed he'd been in contact with the other lords, though he hadn't said as much. She'd suspected, of course, but this was as much proof as she needed. She couldn't allow him to become an envoy. He would make her a puppet in no time at all. But she also couldn't leave Stonekeep. She had no doubt the gates would be barred to her if she tried. Her hold was too tenuous. Then inspiration struck.

"You are right. We do need to sue for peace. Of the two, I believe Lord Isamu would be most amenable to a treaty. Do others agree?"

There were sharp nods around the table. The enmity between Katashi and House Kita wouldn't be erased anytime soon. "Then I propose we invite Lord Isamu here. He can see the strength of Stonekeep again, and we can offer terms."

If Yoshinori was disappointed, he didn't show it. "A wise decision, Lady Mari." His voice sounded cold, though.

The decision didn't require much debate, and Mari left the council with her mind spinning. A peace treaty could be a disaster, but it could also be an opportunity. An opportunity she wouldn't waste. Perhaps this could work to her advantage after all.

13

Asa swallowed her beer in a few long gulps. Immediately, she felt the warmth of the drink spread within her. She'd been looking forward to this moment all day long. She raised her hand for another, and the attentive barkeep had another frothy mug in front of her in an instant. Asa considered drinking this one quickly too but decided against it. She still had too much work to do tomorrow.

Isamu's acceptance of Mari's offer to meet was all that anyone in Stonekeep could talk about. No doubt, Mari viewed the meeting with more trepidation than Asa did, but Asa didn't think anyone in the city had to work as hard for the lord's arrival as she did. The guards required more training, schedules needed to be planned, and routes and meeting spaces had to be inspected and guarded in preparation for the visiting lord. And, if either Mari or Isamu decided to change any part of the plan, Asa needed to have contingencies in place. She'd been working from sunrise to sundown the last few days without taking so much as a break.

The additional duties made Asa question her place more than she already had. She kept thinking about the expeditions and the opportunity to explore unknown lands. Asa had spent most of her younger cycles on the road, and although time masked the suffering of those days, she longed for the open road again. She wanted nothing more than the freedom to determine how to spend her days.

But she'd given Koji her word, and she couldn't bring herself to break it. Protecting Mari was the best use of her skills, whether she liked it or not.

She looked down into her mug, realizing over half the beer was gone again. She'd been so lost in thought she'd barely noticed.

Asa had come back to the inn's common room again. She hadn't slept in the building for over a moon, but she found the familiar atmosphere calming. Also, for the most part, no one paid her much mind.

She looked around the room, the soft murmurs of pleasant conversation filling the air. She liked that the room rarely became rowdy. Some taverns always seemed to be the source of fights, but the patrons of this inn tended to be quieter. Asa imagined the higher costs of the drink had something to do with that.

A small group of performers sat in one corner of the room, their heads together, planning something Asa couldn't even guess. A nondescript man who looked vaguely familiar sat in another corner. Two young men were having a friendly argument down at the other end of the bar.

Asa didn't have her sense extended very far, but she felt the woman enter the room behind her, pause for a moment, then walk straight toward her when she was recognized.

Suzo sat down next to Asa. "Do you mind?"

Asa shook her head, surprised that she really didn't. She

imagined that being the head of the guards meant she shouldn't be drinking with the younger woman, but she didn't much care. So long as they could fulfill their duties tomorrow, they had little to worry about.

With a gesture, Asa ordered a beer for each of them. She hadn't planned on having another, but Suzo's company seemed reason enough for her. Suzo nodded her thanks and they both drank deeply from their mugs.

"How can I help you?" Asa didn't believe that Suzo was there by coincidence.

The other woman looked uncertain for a moment, an expression Asa was not used to seeing on the face of one of her most promising guards. After a moment's hesitation, Suzo replied, "Honestly, I only wanted to spend some more time with you. You are the only one I know who doesn't judge me for my skill. Compared to yours, I suppose mine isn't that great anyway."

Asa almost thought to argue, but Suzo's words rang true. Suzo didn't seem to have many friends. Her skill and her dedication to improvement made her an outcast even among the women who were forging a new path.

Asa took another long sip of her beer, enjoying the companionable silence. She had always liked Suzo and her desire to accomplish more than anyone else. Perhaps she saw a little of herself in the woman.

Eventually Suzo got around to asking a question, and Asa got the distinct impression that it had been one of Suzo's primary motivators for visiting. "If you don't mind me asking, why do you lead the guards? It doesn't seem to be a task you are particularly interested in."

Asa contained her surprise, realizing there was no way Suzo could have known she was thinking about that very subject. Her first impulse was to lie and talk about duty or honor or any of the other vague and nebulous concepts so many used to justify their actions. But one glance at Suzo prevented that. The woman deserved better than empty words. "I'm not really sure," Asa admitted. "I began because I couldn't think of anything better to do, and I continue because of a promise I made to a friend. But it is not a task I would've set for myself."

Asa worried that Suzo would panic, but she received no such reaction. Suzo just nodded, as though she'd expected as much. "Do you ever worry that your lack of dedication will be a danger to Lady Mari?"

The words weren't uttered in judgment, but Asa felt their sting all the same. "Sometimes. But even though I struggle, I would be devastated if anything happened to her. I want to see her succeed."

Suzo let the silence stretch for a few moments, even though Asa could see there was more she wanted to ask. "Do you mind if I ask you a more personal question?"

Asa considered saying no. She didn't tend to be the type of person who liked deeply personal conversations. But the beer had loosened her defenses, and she nodded.

"What do you want from life?"

Asa suddenly felt as though she was in front of Kiyoshi once again, the old man's eyes digging into her as he quizzed her about her desires and plans. Then she blinked, and she was back in the present. Looking at Suzo, she answered honestly again. "I want to leave this land and explore beyond the boundaries of the Kingdom. I want to find new lands and face new challenges."

This time, Suzo did look taken aback. But it was a move of surprise more than of judgment. "You'd want to leave? But you're a nightblade."

"That's exactly why I want to leave."

"I don't understand. Just by wearing your robes, everyone around knows you're one of the best and strongest swords in the Kingdom. *Everyone* knows how powerful the blades are."

Asa understood what concerned Suzo. "Strength and power are hardly what they're made out to be. By themselves, they are worthless."

"I think I would give almost anything to have that respect, though."

Asa shook her head. "It is more fear than respect."

"Still."

Asa wasn't sure how to respond to someone so certain in her beliefs. She felt tossed about like a ship caught in a storm at sea, but Suzo seemed focused, cutting through choppy waves with certainty. Asa decided to turn the conversation more toward the young guard. "What about you? What do you want?"

Suzo's answer was direct, as though she'd been waiting for just that question. "I want your position."

As soon as she said it, she seemed to realize just how forward she'd been. "When you're not in it, of course."

Asa laughed and held her mug up in a silent toast toward Suzo. "When you're ready, you are more than welcome to it."

Suzo smiled and tipped back the rest of her beer.

THE NEXT DAY, Asa regretted having as many drinks as she had. Suzo had turned out to be excellent company, and the two of them had remained later than was wise. In many ways, the two women were mirrors of each other. Asa had the power and respect that Suzo craved, and Suzo had the dedication to her work Asa wished she felt.

Asa made her way through the halls of Stonekeep castle, surprised when she ran into an old and familiar face. Hajimi was just leaving the castle. He hadn't been expected, as far as Asa knew. She bowed to the leader of the blades. "I didn't think I'd ever see you here," she said.

Hajimi didn't look particularly pleased about being present either. "It would not have been my first choice, but I felt it was necessary. Can you walk with me for a while?"

Asa realized that bumping into him might not have been quite as random as she'd first believed.

She nodded and joined him as they left the interior of the castle. They paused at the front gate. The castle stood on one of the highest points of Stonekeep, and from the front gate one could look out over the city and the valley below. Far below, the camp of the blades was visible, looking pitifully small from this height.

"We believe we have found a place," Hajimi said, his voice soft.

"So soon?" Mari couldn't hide the disappointment in her voice. She realized a part of her had been hoping that the strife in the Kingdom would end soon enough for her to join a new expedition.

"We were extremely fortunate," Hajimi said. "The location is nearly ideal."

Asa started, understanding the full implications of what Hajimi said. Suddenly, her dream of leaving the Kingdom became that much more real. "Is that why you're here?"

"No. I didn't tell Lady Mari, and for the moment, I'd appreciate it if you wouldn't either. I've sent another small expedition, looking for some more information. But it looks promising. It's an island in the Northern Sea. I believe soon we're going to have a large decision in front of us."

Asa agreed. What would the blades decide? Would they

even have a choice, once the chaos settled? If the blades left now, the slim chance Mari had of surviving this war disappeared. Hajimi seemed to be reading her thoughts.

"There's time. Mari still has our support, which was the real reason I made this journey. I'd heard about Isamu's visit."

Asa began to understand. "You want to have a seat at the table."

Hajimi nodded. "Once, such an idea would have been nearly unthinkable. But now I worry what decisions might be reached about the blades if we aren't present. I won't have us sacrificed for political ends."

Asa understood Hajimi's concerns well. Though she hated to admit it, she could see Mari using the blades as a bargaining chip in the negotiations.

They walked down the narrow streets of Stonekeep. As challenging as ascending to the castle could be at times, the walk down made the price worth it. Views of the valley below kept opening before them, and even though Asa now made this walk daily, she still felt the urge to stop and stare. She understood now the connection Mari felt with the mountains.

"I don't know if it matters to you, but perhaps I should warn you: Isamu isn't preparing for peace."

Asa started. "What do you mean? Is he going to make an attempt against Mari's life?"

Hajimi shook his head. "I doubt it. Weak as he is, Isamu is generally honorable. No, he is breaking up his armies to strike against Mari's flanks. If I had to guess, he plans on either using threats or moving against Mari immediately if his demands aren't met. We still need time, and Mari can't fall yet."

"How do you know this and Mari doesn't?"

Hajimi sighed. "General Masaaki, while a plenty capable commander, is too cautious. He's brought even his scouts in as they approach the mountains. He doesn't know the full extent of Isamu's moves against him. I used the information to extract a promise from Lady Mari to give us a place at the table."

As they neared the gate that led from Stonekeep, Hajimi turned to her. "Do you ever miss Kiyoshi?"

The question made Asa stop in her tracks. Despite the time that had passed since she'd taken the old man's life, she still thought about him often. Cycles had passed and she still wasn't sure she could sort out her feelings about the man who had killed her father. She nodded in response to Hajimi's question.

Hajimi looked out at the valley below, his eyes passing over the blades under his care. "I do too, sometimes. If anyone could have pulled us out of this fire safely, it was him. There are days when I wish I hadn't sent you on that task."

With that, Hajimi turned and left Stonekeep, leaving Asa alone with her churning thoughts.

Asa decided that when she was reincarnated, she was going to do everything in her power not to become a guard again. The preparations for Isamu's visit continued to grow in complexity with every passing day. Thankfully, Takahiro had been able to guide Asa through large parts of the task, but Asa was exhausted. As she stumbled into the inn for a drink, she felt as though she could barely keep her eyes open.

She noticed the change in attitude immediately as she stepped into the room. Even though the volume wasn't much louder than usual, there was a different energy in the room. Expectation ran rampant. Everyone knew the war needed to end soon. If it went on much longer, the consequences would begin compounding. Though the summer was just over halfway through, people spoke about the lack of food for the upcoming winter. Stores were already depleted, and the war took or destroyed much of what little remained.

Isamu's visit tomorrow represented a chance for a better future. If Isamu and Mari could sign an agreement, then perhaps Katashi would join behind them. They could put the war behind them and focus on survival. Everyone had seized on that hope, holding on tightly to it like a child holding a favorite toy at night.

Asa couldn't bring herself to be so optimistic. There were too many factors at play. Isamu was making secret troop movements in the south. She still believed Isau had been murdered. And Yoshinori and his schemes couldn't be controlled by Mari. Too much could go wrong for her to find hope.

But listening to the snippets of conversation around the common room, she could almost believe. Isamu's honor guard could now be seen from the gate. Tomorrow they would make the journey up the narrow road to Stonekeep. Until then, Asa had decided to enjoy the calm before the storm. Her preparations were all in place, and she'd invited Suzo to come drink with her again tonight. The girl's shift wasn't due to end for a bit yet, but Asa figured she might as well get a head start. The girl couldn't quite hold her drink yet.

The innkeeper brought her a mug of beer, and Asa sipped eagerly, forcing herself to go slowly. If she wasn't careful, she'd be drunk by the time Suzo arrived. The brew refreshed her as soon as it touched her tongue.

She looked around. The inn was more crowded than usual. Word of the peace meetings had spread and merchants had flocked to the city, hoping to take advantage of the influx of people. Some of the regulars were present, but many of the faces were new. Asa was grateful the merchants brought their coin, but she hated that they made her work harder. More people and more strangers brought additional challenges to protecting Mari.

Despite her efforts at restraining herself, she still found herself at the bottom of her mug in short order. It would probably be a little bit before Suzo arrived, but Asa figured another one wouldn't hurt. She ordered, and soon enough a full mug sat in front of her, eager for her attention.

Just then, a group of four large men came into the room. While most of the inn's patrons were merchants, these men obviously were not. They were laborers of some sort, and loud at that. Asa didn't recognize any of them. Almost as soon as they came in, the loudest of them, the one Asa identified as the leader, laid eyes on her. He took in her dark robes and the swords at her hips and he stumbled forward.

Asa cursed. The last problem she wanted to deal with today was a drunk interested in a nightblade. Usually, men saw the robes and walked the other way as quickly as possible. Or at least they left her alone. But once in a while, a man got it in his mind that bedding a nightblade was a unique challenge. This man, inebriated as he obviously was, seemed to be one of the latter. He stopped just a few paces behind her.

"You're a nightblade, aren't you?" His words were slurred.

Asa tried ignoring him, but it didn't work. He stepped

forward, until he was close behind her. He practically towered over her, and she noticed that he had stepped around the sheath of one of her swords, standing over it, leaving her sheath in a particularly dangerous position. His breath reeked of drink when he leaned over her, putting his hands on her shoulders.

Asa grabbed the hilt of her sword and pushed down as hard as she could. The other end of the sheath levered up quickly, striking the man square between the legs. She wasn't looking at him, which was a shame, because she would have loved to see the expression on his face. But he dropped to the ground, holding himself in a voiceless scream.

Before his friends could come to his rescue, her sword was out of its sheath and she was standing, her back to the bar. "He got off easy. Don't come near me again."

For a few moments, Asa worried they might push their luck. Men always underestimated her, even if she was wearing the robes of a nightblade. The group gave her short bows of surrender, grabbing their unfortunate friend and pulling him out of the room, back into the street.

Asa looked around the room one last time. Something seemed off, but after a few moments of wondering about it, she decided she was just being paranoid. She turned back to the bar and took her seat. Her beer had never looked more inviting. She drank it down quickly and frowned. This mug was particularly bitter, but it was still refreshing. Suzo should be along shortly, but Asa didn't see why she shouldn't have a third. She'd have to cut herself off soon after, though. She raised her hand to order.

Her third drink tasted normal, but she noticed that she was feeling pretty drunk already. Had she remembered to eat supper? She'd been so busy. She couldn't recall.

Asa decided to slow down. She could finish this one when Suzo came, then go get some good sleep to prepare for the big arrival tomorrow.

But even as she stopped, she felt sluggish, and the world started to wobble in front of her eyes. She put her head down, suddenly feeling even more tired than before. She needed to get home.

A strong arm put itself around her. Asa looked up, expecting Koji. But he wasn't there. The face was familiar, but she couldn't quite place him. It was a young man, his lips turned up in what seemed to be a perpetual smile. She'd seen him before. She was certain of it. But she couldn't get her mind to work. Every time she tried to hold onto a thought it slipped away from her, like trying to grab an eel.

"I think my friend here has had too much to drink," the man said. He slipped some coins onto the bar, paying for all her drinks. She became fixated on the coins, gleaming bright against the dark wood of the bar. The stranger stood her up and Asa didn't resist. She knew she needed to go back to her place anyway. She'd have to apologize to Suzo for not being here, but she was just so tired.

The man led her out of the bar. Asa needed to lean against him as they walked. Some part of her screamed, but she couldn't react. She didn't even think she had the strength to pull herself away from him.

They walked out into the cool night, the streets largely empty. She looked over at him. "Who are you?"

He just kept smiling, not replying. Then her world went black and she didn't remember any more.

oji woke up every morning feeling exhausted. Being on the road was never easy. Camp needed to be set up and broken down daily. Food had to be hunted and gathered, butchered and cooked. He needed to train, complete his missions, and cover leagues of ground day after day. He liked the challenge and the simplicity of life on the move, but they were all getting worn down like swords in need of sharpening.

Despite the sheer amount of work, Koji didn't think he'd ever been more content. His tiny force, small yet powerful, made a name for itself as they wandered through Katashi's lands. They'd fought in a few small skirmishes when local militia groups tracked them down, not realizing the force they were up against. More than once, after a storehouse burned or a noble died, a local commander and his troops took it upon themselves to exact vengeance. They never made that mistake twice. Koji's blades made certain of it.

Since they crossed the border, Koji had yet to lose a single blade. Twice he had come close, but twice the dayblades with them managed to save the lives of the injured.

Rumors of their group flew on the wind. They couldn't even approach villages safely any longer. Sometimes they would send in a pair to gather what information they could, but no one welcomed strangers anymore. The laws of hospitality, it seemed, were broken and discarded in Katashi's lands. When they were lucky enough to meet someone who would speak to them, they heard all about the demons terrifying the countryside. But everyone believed help was coming. They didn't know how or when, but they were certain it was on the way. Their faith in their leader was absolute.

Koji wasn't sure they were wrong. He suspected his blades had caused enough damage that they had attracted Katashi's attention. If they hadn't already drawn part of the army out of House Kita's lands, the time would be coming soon. They would soon face a challenge stronger than a local militia.

The fact that he was changing the course of the war was everything Koji could hope for. Maybe, if he killed enough nobles, he would be able to lure Katashi himself. The thought of driving a sword through that man brought him immense joy.

Koji also reveled in the continued companionship of those he fought beside. His blades trusted him, and he was willing to die for them. They still suffered through the occasional petty arguments, but the blades were united by a common purpose, and their particular style of training—relying so much on partners—helped build a measure of respect few other fighting systems could. Laughter echoed around the campfire at night, and even though their task was sometimes horrible, Koji couldn't think of a single place that he would rather be.

It was late in the day's march when one of their scouts approached. She'd come at a full run, and all eyes turned to her as she made straight for Koji. He raised his own eyebrow in anticipation. The woman had been scouting the land behind them, so it meant they were likely being pursued. Being as they hadn't seen a local militia in days, Koji suspected he had a good idea who was behind them.

The nightblade gave her report, gasping for breath. Koji held out his hand and encouraged her to take a few moments of rest. When she had gathered herself she started again.

"One of Lord Katashi's armies is behind us," she said.

Koji didn't believe they'd been that successful, despite his hopes. "An entire army?"

She blushed and hung her head. "No, sorry, but nearly as bad. I estimate maybe a hundred and fifty men, all mounted. They wear red uniforms and are making good time."

A hundred and fifty cavalry against his dozen blades? He wasn't sure how they'd win that fight. Even if they weren't tired, that was a difficult advantage to overcome. "How far behind are they?"

"About three leagues. When I left, they were dismounting and setting up camp for the evening, but I expect they'll be able to reach us by tomorrow."

Koji gave the woman a short bow. "Thank you. Get your rest. You may need it soon."

Everyone's eyes were on him. He ignored the questioning looks, staring off into the distance, thinking. Nothing came to him. There wasn't any terrain nearby that would allow him to negate the cavalry's advance, and while nightblades could be effective against horses, they wouldn't be at this scale. A single charge would wipe his small group out without problem. This was their first true challenge since coming across the river, and he wasn't sure how to solve it.

Fortunately, he wasn't alone. Everyone had heard the report, so he asked for ideas.

Several plans were suggested, but few appealed to them. The lands of House Amari were flat, at most suffering from the occasional rolling plain. There was no place to run to, no place to shelter them. On the open prairie, the mounted warriors had every advantage.

Sakura suggested an idea that brought all other conversation to a stop. "We could double back and attack them as they sleep tonight."

Koji fought against his instincts. There was no honor in the action, but it was the only way he could think of where they could possibly survive. He waited for someone else to speak up against it, but no one did. The truth, horrible as it was, couldn't be argued against.

He hated to even contemplate the idea, necessary as it might end up being. "Are there any other thoughts?"

A few other strategies were suggested, but none that had a realistic chance of success. The cavalry could move faster, stay out of sword range, and harass the blades until they died. At night, though, every advantage would be theirs. Blades didn't need to see to fight, so the darkness wasn't a problem. The cavalry wouldn't be mounted, negating the edge they had.

Koji took a big gulp of air before he spoke. The mission would still be dangerous, and he would almost certainly lose some of the friends he'd made among this group. But if they didn't act, they would all almost certainly die. "Get some rest. We move out when night falls."

KOJI HADN'T SLEPT MUCH, but he'd managed a short nap. Given their work tonight, he suspected it was all he'd be likely to get. No one else slept much more. Koji considered allowing the blades to sleep without any guard duty, but the risk was too great.

The night was dark when he gave the order to move out. They had a fair amount of distance to cover, and then they would have to fight. Koji allowed himself to slip into a trance as he ran at a steady pace, his awareness of his surroundings light. It wasn't rest, but it would have to do.

Like shadows, the blades followed, a soft rustling of robes the only indication they were still behind him. They were all in excellent condition, having trained since birth to run for long distances and fight at the end. That training, brutal as it was, rewarded them on nights like tonight.

Koji fought against his exhaustion. He'd been tired before this, and his eyes seemed to close of their own will, ignoring his repeated attempts to force them open. He stumbled and quickly recovered, the short burst of energy enough to keep his eyes open. He only had to last a while longer.

After Koji estimated they had covered a little over two leagues, he sent out scouts while the rest of the group slowed. Fortunately, the night was cloudy, and the moon was often obscured. Still, it was high in the sky when the scouts returned.

Their report was disheartening. The cavalry had made camp, but had done so on a small rise. Although it couldn't even be called a hill, it gave them the advantage of the upper ground and allowed them an uninterrupted view of the area around them. Koji and the other blades would have to crawl through the grass to avoid detection.

Koji didn't allow himself the luxury of despair. The path in front of them was their only one. The clouds would keep the moon from shining too much, which gave them a chance. Still, all it would take was one observant guard and one mistake from the blades to lose the element of surprise. If they lost that, the battle could be anyone's to win.

Koji figured they had jogged about another half a league when the scouts motioned for them to begin crawling. Off in the distance, Koji could see the fires of his targets, which looked far away, tiny flickering lights off in the distance. They were thousands of paces away at least. Still, there was no other way of sneaking up on their enemies, so they dropped to hands and knees, crawling as one large mass toward the encampment.

By the time Koji guessed they were halfway there, his limbs burned. Running was a challenge he could handle. That, he had trained for. But crawling was exhausting. More than once, Koji signaled for a stop. If the others felt as exhausted as he did, the rest would be necessary. They still needed to fight. One advantage, if it could be called that, was that there had been few rains lately, and the ground underneath them was firm. But while their hands and knees didn't sink into soft dirt or mud, he soon began to feel as though he had rubbed his knees and hands raw.

They drew close enough that Koji didn't dare raise his head above the level of the grass to explore the surroundings. He could sense the life of the soldiers in front of them, and he could sense the energy of the blades behind him. Crawling through the grass had separated his blades, the task testing even their physical abilities.

Making matters worse, the moon continued crawling toward the horizon, signaling the imminent break of dawn. Koji had to assume that the soldiers would be up early to continue the pursuit. The window of time they had to surprise their opponents closed with every torturous movement the blades made.

Soon he was within twenty paces of the nearest guards. He stopped, waiting for some of the stragglers to catch up. As they did, they all caught their breath. So far the alarm had not been raised, but they were quickly running out of time. Glancing over his shoulder, Koji could see the very first hints of light on the horizon. Before long the camp would come alive and their surprise would be wasted. At the same time, his people were exhausted. He was exhausted, and in battle, that could easily mean the difference between life and death.

Koji needed to find the balance between rest and action. He lay in the grass, breathing deeply, focusing on finding the moment they should strike. He felt the strength of the blades returning around him. They had pushed to the limit of their abilities, but the work wasn't yet over.

He didn't know why he made the decision when he did. Perhaps he'd heard the cough of a man waking up from sleep, or maybe he'd just grown tired of waiting. The tension before the battle could drive a warrior to madness. Acting almost on impulse, Koji closed most of the distance between him and the guards and leaped at them.

Their surprise was complete. He could only imagine it. All night, they had kept watch on what they had believed to be an empty prairie. And now a nightblade had risen from the grass like a ghost of vengeance.

Koji was between the first guards before they could even work their swords out of their scabbards. His own blade cut twice in the fading darkness, and the guards fell without a sound. All around the camp, blades came out of the grass, attacking the guards nearest them. There weren't many. In moments, the initial assault was over, and an eerie silence fell over the camp.

The blades had given no battle cry. For a moment, an alert warrior might have heard the sound of bodies falling limply to the ground, but then a breeze came up and the only sound was the swishing of the grass in the wind.

Koji gave the signal to the rest of the blades and they began working their way through the camp. He tried not to think about what he did. Steel pierced the hearts of sleeping enemies, or was drawn over exposed necks. Death came as silently and softly as the summer breeze.

With every kill, Koji felt himself falling, a little piece of himself left in each tent he entered. This wasn't battle, but murder. How long could it last?

His answer came about the time he'd worked his way halfway to the center of the camp. He supposed it was only a matter of time before someone awoke to discover what was happening. A yell came from the other side of the camp. "Attack!"

The shout was quickly silenced, but the damage was done. Around the camp, the soldiers who still lived roused to wakefulness, and several other shouts joined the first. The orderly slaughter became chaotic battle in moments.

Koji moved faster, trying to end the battle as quickly as possible. He moved surely, not a single cut wasted. When he sensed life inside a tent he stabbed his sword in through the canvas. His aim wasn't always true, and not every thrust was a kill, but every stab at least wounded the occupant inside. Those who managed to stumble out of the tents, bleary-eyed and unclothed, met a cleaner end.

Koji was surrounded by death, blood, and screams. One man came out of a tent with his hands up, and Koji cut through him, only realizing after the deed was done the man had surrendered. Dawn was still a little ways away, and the soldiers who did make it out of their tents were cut down by shadows they could barely see.

Near the center of the camp, one man stepped out of his tent, his sword already in a high guard position. There was something different about this man, and it took Koji a few moments to figure out what it was. A second glance revealed that the man held himself well but was also dressed in finer clothes than the other soldiers. Perhaps he was a noble. Eager for an actual fight, Koji passed by several occupied tents to duel the swordsman.

He let Koji make the first cut, reacting with practiced ease, countering and moving into a strike of his own. Even though the risk to Koji was greater than just moments ago, he found himself relaxing into the fight. This was combat, something he understood.

He let the fight go on longer than he should have. Fighting the noble centered him in his body again, and he didn't want to let the feeling go. He knew the other blades approached the center of the camp and their work was almost done. Finishing this fight meant confronting what he had just done.

Koji won the centerline and almost struck, but then allowed the man a wild flurry of strikes. With Koji's sense, he felt the attacks coming before they arrived and had no problem parrying or dodging each one. Finally, realizing how foolish he was being, Koji dodged a cut, slipped inside the man's guard, and killed him. That kill, at least, had been honorable.

As the noble fell lifeless to the ground, the enormity of

what they had done sunk into Koji's heart. His blades wandered throughout the camp, killing the last survivors with little difficulty. The rout was complete, but as Koji looked around he felt no sense of satisfaction. This was no battle, no contest he would ever be proud of.

Blood trickled throughout the camp, and eventually the final sounds of the dying were silenced to nothing. The only sounds were those of songbirds chirping in the distance and the fire crackling in the center of the camp, almost burned out. Koji looked around again, torn between imprinting this scene on his memory to guide him forever, or to close his eyes and pretend like it had never happened.

He didn't even give the orders to loot what supplies they could. He simply wiped his sword clean, sheathed it, and walked away.

15

Mari experienced a strange mix of emotions as she looked out over the walls of Stonekeep at the procession moving up the narrow road. Lord Isamu's banners snapped in the wind, the symbol of his house making her feel ill. Those banners hadn't been seen anywhere near Stonekeep for many cycles, as the southern lord preferred to have the others come to him in times of peace.

Those banners also flew over the armies that invaded her lands. The armies that, thanks to Hajimi's timely information, sought to destroy her even as their leader met to discuss the terms of peace.

Part of her wanted to call out to her archers, to shout the order to rain down death and destruction on the small party. It would be easy. They'd been certain to withhold all other traffic from the road during the procession. Attacking Isamu wouldn't risk a single soldier, and it would kill a man who worked to destroy her lands.

Unfortunately, killing Isamu did no good other than sating her own anger. If Isamu died while under her protection, not only would the opposing armies have a new cause to rally behind, but her enemies within the house would have reason to doubt her ability to lead. Perversely, Isamu's well-being was crucial to Mari's own.

Besides that, of the other lords, Isamu was the most likely to be amenable to a deal. He was a coward and an opportunist. He was the only lord who had served under a king, and he had weathered the storms of the past two cycles by keeping himself out of the middle of the battle. But if she could convince him to cease his attacks, the balance of power in the Kingdom would shift.

Mari wondered what the lord was thinking as he approached. Did he expect her to surrender? She wouldn't be surprised. By most accounts, Mari and House Kita were losing this war. If not surrender, Isamu at least expected an alliance with major concessions.

Whatever he expected, he would not be pleased by the time he left. Although this meeting had been forced by the other nobles of her house, their reasoning was sound. Mari would support Isamu's claim to the throne, but she would demand more than he might be willing to give. Lacking that, she had other ideas, which he also might detest. But he would not receive her surrender. Her people would not suffer the oversight of a different house that would only take advantage of them.

Mari felt a slight shiver pass through her body as the first ranks of Isamu's honor guard crossed underneath the gates and into the narrow alleys. The group would be vulnerable to attacks for hundreds of paces, even when they reached the first courtyard, which was also designed as a killing ground in case of attack. The temptation to order one almost overwhelmed her. With one command, she could cut off the head of another house. Denying herself tested her will nearly to its limit.

She shook her head. Isamu's line was strong, and given the chaos of the past cycles, she no doubt his successor was prepared, unlike in the other houses. Killing him would only turn them more firmly against her.

Mari came down from the walls to the courtyard where Isamu and his honor guard waited. Although this was a routine greeting, Mari could feel the tension in the air. She brought with her only four of her closest guards, no more than she'd take if she was taking a trip to the outhouse. Asa, for some reason, hadn't shown up, but that was a problem for Mari to solve later. Against the hundred soldiers that made up Isamu's guard, they stood no chance. Mari offered the same chance to Isamu he'd offered by coming into Stonekeep. What better way to prove her trust?

With an unseen signal, the guards, dressed in the green of Isamu's house, split apart, giving Mari an open passage to Isamu. She stepped forward, leaving her guards behind.

Isamu slid down from his horse, and their eyes met for the first time in many cycles. Mari kept her face carefully neutral as she bowed towards him slightly. He returned the bow to the same depth, a small token of respect at least. Perhaps there was a chance for peace. She almost dared to hope.

"I welcome you to Stonekeep, Lord Isamu. It has been many cycles since you last visited, and I am honored that you accepted my request."

Isamu looked around warily, as though still expecting some sort of trap. His reply was rote, not displaying a hint of his true feelings. "I am honored by the invitation. Thank you for your hospitality."

Mari gestured towards the path that led to the main

center of the city. "In your most recent letter, you indicated a desire to visit the shrines dedicated to my father and brother. I would be pleased to escort you. Any men who don't join us will be shown to their lodging by my chief adviser, Takahiro."

Isamu agreed to the idea and selected four of his own guards. Mari made note of the number, pleased that Isamu didn't disrespect her hospitality. The signs were small, but the other lord gave every indication of being willing to work together.

Mari led the way toward the shrines for her departed family. The journey was a considerable distance, and out of respect for her guest, she deliberately slowed her pace. Stonekeep's steep roads exhausted most visitors, and Isamu was hardly in peak condition. As a consequence, it took them no insignificant amount of time to get to the shrines, and by the time they did, the heavyset lord panted constantly and wiped his brow every few moments, even though they never moved much faster than a slow walk. As a polite host, Mari made no mention of it.

With all the duties requiring her attention, Mari hadn't visited the shrines nearly as often as she would have liked. She was the one who'd ordered them made, and their design reflected her own simple beliefs. There were small symbols representing each of the family members she had lost. The shrine was guarded day and night by a few members of the previous honor guard, and Mari had made it known that any attempt to dishonor the shrine would be met with the harshest consequences.

She was surprised to see the genuine emotion on Isamu's face as he knelt slowly and bowed his head towards the shrines. When she'd received the note, she had expected the request was some sort of political maneuver designed to influence the way she felt about the lord. But seeing the small contortions on his face and the grief that he wore, Mari revised her original assumption. She paid her own respects, then waited until Isamu finished. When he stood back up, she was surprised to see that his eyes were bloodshot.

She spoke softly. "I did not know how strongly you felt about my family."

Isamu's lips compressed into a tight line. When he spoke, it sounded as though he was still fighting for control. "I miss your father dearly. We were both rulers in a time of stability, and in the chaos that surrounds us now, his wisdom is greatly missed. However, it is Juro that I miss the most. Did you know that I was with him just a day before he died?"

Mari gave a small nod. Thanks to her own research, plus her acquaintance with Asa and Koji, she knew the story of Juro's last days better than almost anyone else.

Isamu continued, his eyes focused on some point far in the distance. "I've thought often about those days, and if something could've been done differently. I do not have many answers, but I can tell you this: Juro always behaved honorably, no matter how desperate the situation became. He was a good man, and in many ways, when I look back upon my behavior in the time of crisis, I am ashamed. Your brother, young as he was, taught me to hold myself to a higher standard. You should be proud of him."

The words touched Mari. She bowed, more deeply, to Isamu. "I am."

Isamu's posture shifted, and Mari received the impression that they were about to move to the reason of Isamu's visit. He spoke with a sudden firmness. "I also know from your father's letters that Juro only accepted the head of his household with great complaint. He did not seek to rule. Unfortunately, he was born a warrior, but he died before the war arrived."

He gave Mari a meaningful glance. "But here you are, claiming the head of your house in the midst of the war. From the reports I've heard, you've clawed and scratched your way to the top and barely hold your house."

The pride and warmth that Mari had felt vanished instantly. There was no respect for Mari's rule in that statement. Isamu acted as though she only played at ruling the house and clearly did not take her authority seriously. But she wouldn't meet his disrespect with her own. "Like all of us, I only do what I'm called to. My people need protection in these chaotic times, and that is my sole concern."

Something she said must have resonated with Isamu, because he nodded as though she had said something worthy. "I think by inviting me here, you've taken the appropriate first steps. This war could destroy us all."

Mari didn't want to begin this conversation quite yet. Isamu had arrived more quickly than she'd anticipated, and to have the strongest bargaining position, she needed another day. Fortunately, as host to this gathering, there were many tricks at her disposal. "Lord Isamu, we do have much to discuss, but I would not take advantage of one who has spent all day traveling. As you may recall, here in Stonekeep the sun sets early. You and your men will be provided for, and tomorrow at noon we will hold a feast to celebrate your arrival. Afterward, we can discuss the future of our two houses."

Her last line had been carefully crafted. If he did suspect surrender, it would lull him into a false sense of security. Regardless, she dangled a carrot out in front of him, making it in his best interests to be agreeable. A brief look of frustration passed over Isamu's face, but he hid it quickly. If Mari hadn't been looking for it, she probably wouldn't have seen it.

Isamu's interests would be better served by moving faster. Every day that passed was another day where his army's plot to the south might be discovered. But Mari had her own reasons for delaying. The two of them played a complex game, and they had just made the opening moves.

MARI FORCED herself to stop tapping her foot. Soon she would meet with Isamu for the first time that day, and the true negotiations for the future of her house would begin. Her mind sprinted from idea to idea, never pausing long on any one. Concerns threatened to overwhelm her.

Foremost in her mind was the future of her lands. She'd scripted, rehearsed, and practiced for this meeting. Takahiro had spent most of his time the past few days pretending to be Isamu. How he'd gotten anything else done, Mari had no idea. Mari knew she was prepared, but the stakes were impossibly high. Mistakes today could doom everyone in her lands.

Beyond that, she still hadn't seen Asa. The last time she'd seen the nightblade had been the day before Isamu's arrival. Everything had seemed normal then. But Mari knew Asa detested her role as head of Mari's guards. Had the woman finally decided to leave? Mari considered the idea to be out of character for Asa, although knowing the nightblade hated her position kept that seed of doubt alive.

But right now, she couldn't worry about Asa. Her guards functioned well even in Asa's absence, so the nightblade was a problem for when Isamu left. Still, Mari's mind kept returning to the problem she couldn't solve.

Finally, it was time for the feast to begin. Mari took a few deep breaths before leaving her small office and walking toward the chambers.

When she arrived, Isamu and his key advisers were already in place. The wine cups stood full, with attentive staff ready to refill any empty cup. Mari had spared no expense to throw this feast. Like every part of this visit, the feast was a piece of theater. She showed Isamu that her people were still happy and well fed, and the feast accomplished both tasks without her having to say a single word. She shuddered at the cost and the better uses the food could be put toward, but she told herself that she could save more lives than if she spread the food around.

Mari herself was dressed in decadent blue robes that she had argued against for days. She had wanted to present herself as a serious ruler, dressed in somber clothing. Eventually she had acquiesced to Takahiro's arguments. The wealth of the house needed to be on display, no matter how uncomfortable she found the robes or the message they sent.

Mari didn't know how influenced Isamu would be by any of her preparations. He was a veteran of the political battles that had raged since she was a child, but she suspected he underestimated her. Men always seemed to.

Her attention was focused entirely on the scene before her. Several of her own nobles were present, of course. Yoshinori and Arata stood on opposite sides of the room, like two separate pillars. Mari noted who talked to whom, and what the various expressions around the room gave away. No detail was too small.

She felt a sudden pang of sorrow as memory washed

over her. This was the first official reception in the halls of Stonekeep for over a cycle, and it brought back memories of receptions much like it that she had suffered through as a younger woman. Back then, Juro or Hiromi had always been there to keep her company. They would never do so again.

When she found Takahiro in the crowd, she made straight for him. She felt her shoulders relax as she neared. He looked as though he was the only one present more uncomfortable than her.

Most of the guests looked relaxed, like they belonged. Takahiro looked as though he was heading into battle. She was sure he didn't realize what he was doing, but he tugged at the robes of his dress uniform as though they didn't quite fit him.

"Didn't you have to attend these growing up?" she asked him.

He glanced at her. "Occasionally. Typically, my behavior was so poor my parents made excuses for me and left me at home. It made both of us happier. When I renounced my claim to the family lands, I was no longer invited."

Mari nodded. "Sorry to ruin that."

Takahiro chuckled softly, barely loud enough for her to hear. "We all must make sacrifices for our duty," he said.

They conversed for a bit before separating. After spending even a few moments with him, Mari felt refreshed, more ready to tackle the problem of Lord Isamu. It was just as well, as there was suddenly no end to the stream of people who wanted to speak to her.

The feast went longer than Mari had anticipated. By the time it finished, the sun was well on its way toward settling over the peaks behind Stonekeep.

Mari and a handful of her advisers retired to a small room with Isamu and his entourage. As they sat down, there was a knock at the door, and Takahiro allowed a messenger to enter. The messenger handed a short, sealed note to Takahiro, and Mari's heart started to race. She'd been waiting for this note. She stood up and he handed it to her.

She opened the missive with trembling fingers, wondering if a note had ever held a message of such import. The message was longer than it needed to be, General Masaaki verbose as always, but Mari breathed a sigh of relief.

Good news in hand, Mari sat back down at the negotiating table, feeling the first semblance of control. Some pleasantries passed back and forth, but thanks to the feast, they were blissfully short for a meeting of this importance.

Mari, as host, turned the discussion to the matter at hand. "Lord Isamu, I've invited you here today to discuss the terms of a peace treaty between your house and my own."

Isamu was a seasoned politician, but Mari's sharp eyes still saw the quick flicker of surprise. He really had thought she was going to surrender.

"Lady Mari," he replied, recovering quickly, "I'm honored to discuss such terms with you. What proposals do you suggest?"

With the note in hand, she opened with bold moves. "First, all your invading units must retreat back to your house lands. Once the retreat is complete, I propose a greater amount of trade between our houses. We have a surplus of gold and iron, and while we have enough food to survive the year, I desire more to build our reserves. Finally, I will support your bid for the throne of our Kingdom. I believe you are best suited to guide us in this time."

She wasn't sure of that at all. Isamu was a talented administrator and a political survivor. But he didn't often make the hard choices that would be all too common for the next king. Regardless, he was a far better choice than Katashi in her mind, and she didn't think the Kingdom would accept her. Her own house barely did.

This time, Isamu couldn't hide his shock. He certainly hadn't been expecting such aggressive opening terms. In Mari's mind, the offer was as tempting as she could make it. Anything less wasn't good enough for her people. But would it be enough? When Isamu answered quickly, Mari's heart sank.

"Lady Mari, I respect the courage that it must have required to come before me today and make this proposal. But you know as well as I that you and your house have very little bargaining power. You are outnumbered and on the retreat. Why should I retreat when victory is at hand? I am happy and more than willing to discuss the terms of your surrender, but make no mistake: that is why I'm here. The Kingdom's peace comes through your abdication."

Mari wasn't surprised Isamu felt that way. She'd hoped, maybe, that this might be resolved peacefully, but it had always been a long shot. She could take her next steps confidently, though.

After a brief pause, Isamu launched directly into his demands for her surrender. "Each of your generals will be brought forth for a trial regarding their conduct. I would suggest you also be brought to trial for your role in this war, but as a distraught young woman, you cannot be held responsible. Out of deference to your brother and father, I would not see you suffer so. Rather, it would be best if there was a stronger, more reasonable ruler for these lands. Lord Katashi and I would be pleased to find you a suitable suitor, someone worthy of the role of lord. If you refuse this opportunity, I will be forced to insist that you also turn yourself in to face trial. Your lands will be split between the two remaining houses, and you will acknowledge Lord Katashi as the rightful king of the Kingdom."

Mari couldn't help but be surprised by the extent of the demands. She had expected House Kita to go to someone like Yoshinori. She'd never guessed they'd destroy it completely if she didn't cooperate.

"You see no chance for a more equitable arrangement?"

Isamu's voice was cold. "If you resist, your house will be destroyed, and any noble who does not swear fealty to Lord Katashi will be killed. Your forces will be routed."

Mari finally let out a hint of a grin. "You mean, of course, by the heavy cavalry you're trying to sneak through my western pass?"

Isamu's face froze in surprise.

"They've been defeated by a large force of nightblades. My armies will continue to retreat in an orderly manner, and your advance is about to become much more bloody." She passed him the missive and gave him a moment to read it. "No doubt, you will receive word yourself in a few days when they fail to report."

The other lord read the message quickly, his face hardening with every passing moment. In terms of numbers, the force Hajimi and his blades had killed hadn't been that large, but they had been trying to flank General Fumio, who would have been caught between Isamu's heavy cavalry behind him and Katashi's well-trained forces in front. Even with the blades, Fumio wouldn't have had a chance. The war would have been over in a fortnight or less.

Now, there was no end in sight, and once Mari's forces were embedded in the mountains of their land, the price for every league of land was going to become much steeper. Isamu knew it.

"Lord Isamu," she said. "My house will not fall. You still have one chance to prevent more bloodshed."

Mari wasn't sure what the lord would do, but his reaction shocked her. He stood up, slammed his fists against the table, and stormed out without another word. She had never seen anything like it from a lord. He looked like a young boy whose play sword had been taken from him.

For the moment, she decided not to press the matter. Hopefully, when he was calmer, they could resume discussions. She didn't hold out hope, but any chance was better than none. And though her house could resist, she still didn't see the path to victory. She retired to her rooms, but before she could relax there was a knock at her door. There were only a few reasons why she'd be disturbed now, and none of them were pleasant.

As she expected, it was Takahiro. His voice was grave. "Lord Isamu is here to see you."

"Let him in." If he'd been interested in peace talks, they would have met more formally. This only meant that he was planning on letting his displeasure be known personally.

She wasn't surprised, then, when he came tearing into her office. "Your father would be ashamed."

His face was dark red, and Mari wondered for a moment if he meant to attack her right there, inside her own office. But then her own anger rose against him. "Nonsense. My father was an honorable man, and he would've wanted me to do everything in my power to keep my people safe. Katashi is not fit to be their king."

Isamu's rage was only stoked further by her defiance. "You continue to hide behind the blades, having them save your lands time and time again. But there is no place left for them here." He enunciated each word sharply, each a verbal sword hacking at her shields. "They will all die, and your house will wither and collapse because you didn't have the sense or the honor to act in a way befitting a lord of this realm."

Before she could muster a reply, he turned on his heel and stormed out the door, leaving her alone with her failure.

THAT NIGHT, a summer storm worked its way from the valley below to the mountains surrounding Stonekeep. Lightning cracked against the dark sky, and thunder boomed against the stone that surrounded Mari's home. Already unable to sleep, Mari finally gave up and dressed.

Possessing only a vague purpose, Mari made her way to Juro's shrine. In life, she'd leaned on her brother more times than she could count, his warrior's ethos a solid support in all her troubles. Those troubles seemed nearly meaningless compared to the challenges she currently faced. But perhaps Juro's spirit could still offer her some guidance.

She made her way through her city with her head bowed, lost in thought, escorted by her usual complement of guards. Asa still hadn't made an appearance, and Mari was becoming increasingly certain the nightblade had broken her word. Why else would she go missing for days?

The rain drove most citizens into the warm shelter of their homes, leaving only a few brave and hardy souls to bear the brunt of the storm. One of Mari's guards managed an umbrella over her head, fighting a losing battle against the rain. Mari continued on, heedless of the water soaking her clothes or splashing over her feet. She wasn't one to get cold easily, and the wet didn't bother her.

When she stopped, she stood directly in front of the shrine. Her first disjointed thought was that the shrine was too small. What her family really deserved was a large monument, a work of stone that would inspire awe in all who saw it. She wanted to leave something that would last beyond her life and her reign, both of which looked to be growing shorter by the day.

She shook her head to clear her thoughts and gave herself a small, sad smile. None of her family had ever been interested in the legacy that came with ruling. She suspected it was due to the influence of their father, a man who viewed their position as a responsibility and a duty. They'd been raised to believe the same, and that foundational belief continued to support Mari.

She stared at the shrine, her mind almost completely blank. The man she'd hired as the architect for the project had had the good sense to protect the shrine from the elements, and as the rain soaked through all of her clothes, the only thought that occupied Mari's mind was that she was grateful that the relics of her family remained dry.

A sudden wave of sorrow crashed over her, unexpected in its ferocity. She lost control of her legs and dropped down to her knees, her guard unable to move the umbrella quickly enough to protect her against the storm. Her tears mixed with the rain, and Mari was grateful that anyone walking by wouldn't see the extent of her distress.

As though her thoughts had summoned him, Takahiro suddenly appeared at her side. For once, he didn't look prepared. He looked like a man who had just been woken from a deep slumber.

He didn't speak, but dropped down next to her, his support silent and unwavering. He reached out and took the umbrella from the guard, who looked grateful not to have that duty any longer.

"Thank you," he said. "You may stand guard. I'll do my best to keep Lady Mari dry." He nodded toward the stone archway behind them, the only entrance to the shrine, which also gave some small protection from the storm. The other guards huddled beneath it. The guard nodded her appreciation and left to join the others.

Mari was grateful that he didn't ask her any questions. He simply knelt by her, protecting her from the elements and sharing in her grief. He remained as silent as the ghosts of her ancestors, and at that moment, she'd never been more thankful for the presence of a single person.

"Do you think they would be proud?" she asked. "Or would they be as ashamed as everyone seems to think they would be?"

A lesser friend would have consoled her, told her that of course they would be proud. Not Takahiro, though. "I do not know. I think Juro would've been proud. He always liked you best when you were antagonizing your father and pushing against the expectations of others."

Memories of childhood brought a thin smile to her face. "Juro would think that I'm foolish for grieving at his shrine in this way."

"Yes, he would."

Mari couldn't help herself. She laughed, loud and long, sorrow and absurdity blending into one. Takahiro didn't join her, but he had a slight grin, which was as much as she ever saw from him these days.

"I don't think I can put the Kingdom back together," she admitted.

"I don't know if people expect you to," Takahiro replied.

"They do," she said as she stood up. "People hate change. They want life to be the way that it was, even when returning to the past is clearly impossible. That is what my people want from me. No matter what I do, I cannot give that to them."

"So what are you going to do?"

Mari stood up. Something inside her had shifted, some last fading concern over what others expected sliding away. Even though the sky was overcast and the rain was pounding against the umbrella, she felt almost like a child on a summer day with the sun burning her skin.

"I can't bring back the past, but I can predict the future. Our people need to be safe." Her voice trailed off, as something Takahiro had said came back to her.

A seed of an idea sprouted in her mind, soon taking all her attention. Perhaps it could work. She tried building arguments against it, not even willing to speak of it until she was certain it wasn't foolish.

She knew it *could* work. She remembered her father once saying that the best compromise was one in which every party thought they'd been wronged. That was the mark of a true middle ground. Mari's idea certainly qualified.

The other lords would have to think there was no reasonable chance of ending the war. The cost of continuing the war had to be greater than the costs associated with agreeing to Mari's idea. Her mind started to race.

She needed to talk to Lord Isamu in the morning. After their disagreement today, it might prove challenging, but he was here, and she had to take the opportunity. Now, more than ever, he had to see what the war would cost to maintain. Together, they could bring the proposal to Katashi.

She was just about to tell Takahiro her proposal when a messenger ran up to the gate. He handed his note to a guard, who rushed to bring it to Mari. Takahiro took the note and flipped it over. Mari saw the black seal, indicative of an urgent message.

Takahiro took the note and read it, then passed it to Mari. His expression was unreadable.

Immediately, Mari saw the note had been written by General Fumio. His short, terse handwriting was unmistakable. She read it twice, just to be certain that she wasn't hallucinating.

"Katashi has stopped his advance."

Takahiro nodded. "If Fumio's scout reports are accurate, it means that a fair portion of Katashi's army is returning home."

For them, the connection was obvious. Koji's mission was doing everything it was supposed to. Katashi had to dedicate some of his forces to return home to stop the relentless nightblade.

Mari suddenly realized what this meant and how it could help her convince the other lords that pursuing the war was costly. Hopefully, she could make Isamu see reason in the morning, before he left the city. Katashi now knew how much the war was costing him. There would never be a better time to pursue her idea.

For the first time in moons, she felt a glimmer of hope. Perhaps she could find the way out of this. Perhaps she couldn't save the Kingdom itself, but she could save its people.

Then another thought occurred to her, dampening her spirits. If Katashi was moving as many troops as Fumio suspected, it meant that there was almost an entire army between Koji and the safety of her house lands, and they were out for blood.

16

***

Asa came to awareness slowly. She thought her eyes were open, but couldn't see anything. She squeezed them shut again, only then realizing that a blindfold had been tied around her face. She groaned, but couldn't move her jaw. An enormous wad of cloth had been stuffed in her mouth and tied tightly. As soon as she realized that, a host of sensations suddenly struck at once.

Her hands were above her head. She tried to move them, disoriented by the lack of feeling in her arms. She heard the rattle of chain and felt the sharp bite of steel against her wrists. Manacles, then, secured somewhere above her. Given the lack of feeling in her arms, she'd been in such a position for at least the better part of a day.

She tried to move her feet and found them chained as well. The chain had some give, and she could shuffle her feet around, but the chain felt as though it had been secured somewhere between her legs. She wouldn't be able to kick out very far if she wanted to.

Panic rose in her throat, making her want to vomit. But

nothing came up, and she took a few deep breaths to control her reaction. Fear offered her nothing useful in a situation like this. After a bit, she reasserted a semblance of control.

With control came anger. Anger at herself and anger at the man who'd done this to her. How foolish had she been, falling into such a predictable routine? She'd made herself a target through sheer laziness.

In hindsight, what happened was blindingly obvious. She'd been drugged and carried away from the inn, probably in full view of everyone there. Given that she was a regular who drank often, she suspected no one had even been curious about the incident.

Questions flooded her thoughts. Was anyone looking for her? How long had she been missing? Why had someone come after her? Did Mari have any idea what was happening?

The thought of Mari froze her thoughts solid. Whatever was happening to Asa, it had to be a plot to get at Mari somehow. Asa had failed in the one promise she'd made. Pure, white-hot rage shot through her body and she jerked against the chains, trying to scream.

There wasn't anywhere for her to go. The chains were all well-secured, and while a nightblade enjoyed plenty of gifts, the ability to bend steel was not one of them. After a few heartbeats, her rage burned out as quickly as it had flared up. Her sudden emptiness filled with sorrow, and she felt tears trickle down her face, to be absorbed by her gag.

A voice spoke, closer than Asa expected. She jumped, and she heard laughter. She'd been so focused on her own suffering, she hadn't even stopped to check her surroundings. Her old masters would have been disappointed in her. For more reasons than one, it seemed.

"So, she's finally awake," the voice said. Asa couldn't see the man who spoke, but his voice was low and gruff. She imagined a larger man, leering at her, closer than he should have been. Her heart raced, but this time she managed to control her reaction. She refused to show them fear. Were they going to torture her? Did she know some piece of information they sought?

"There's no point antagonizing her," a second voice responded. The voice, while still masculine, was higher and more refined. Asa imagined the situation. The first voice was the muscle, and the second voice was the brains. "He told us not to harm her."

So, there was a third. These two weren't even in charge, then. The comment also helped her relax. She'd been imagining possibilities, but if they weren't going to harm her, many of those were no longer relevant.

The first voice was now a few steps away. "But when he's done with her, what then?"

"I don't know. But don't get your hopes up."

"Fine."

Asa heard the shuffling of a man sitting on the floor. "She's a pretty one, though."

There were more sounds, and Asa remembered that sight wasn't her only way of getting information. She focused her sense, reassured that her gifts hadn't been harmed by the drug. There were two men, and only two men, with her. Strangely, there wasn't anyone else nearby. In Stonekeep, that was an impressive feat. What if she wasn't in Stonekeep? How long had she been unconscious?

The second man came close to her. "I'm going to remove your gag," he said. "Before I do, you need to know there's really no point in screaming. You're a nightblade, so you will know this is true. I will provide water and a little food, so long as you don't cause trouble. If you do, I'll just soak your gag in water and give you no food. You'll survive long enough without it. Do you understand?"

Asa nodded. The man wasn't lying about their situation. If she screamed, she didn't think anyone would hear her.

Gentle fingers removed the gag and paused. Asa didn't scream. She sensed the man nodding. He brought a cup to her lips and Asa forced herself to drink slowly. For a moment she considered spitting at him, but there was no point. It would only make her captivity more difficult.

Following the water, he gave her some spoonfuls of rice. Then he replaced the gag, ensuring it was as tight as ever. Asa hadn't even had time to ask a question. Then the man returned to his partner, leaving Asa trapped with no rescue to hope for.

TIME BECAME MEANINGLESS. At first, she tried to judge the passing of time by when the second man gave her water, but there didn't seem to be any order to it. Sometimes he did so frequently. Other times, it seemed as though enormous stretches of time had passed. Asa wondered if her perception was accurate, or if her understanding of time was distorted.

She became convinced that she was in a cave of some sort. The air felt damp and cold, and no matter how much time passed, there never seemed to be anybody nearby. If she wasn't still in Stonekeep, a cave was one of the only places that seemed reasonable.

She'd spent a little bit of time exploring her captivity. She'd confirmed that both her wrists and ankles were manacled. The chains were both well secured, as she'd proven when she tried to put her full weight on her arms. She'd almost certainly torn something in her left shoulder when she tried, her muscles unable to take the strain after the enforced position. The men who'd captured her had ensured she would have no escape.

They were so confident in their work, they didn't even seem to mind when she tested her bonds. They only cared when she made too much noise, and she suspected that was more because the noise annoyed them rather than put them in any danger of discovery. She'd felt no one else since she'd awakened. There hadn't even been a hint of the mysterious third person.

As time passed, Asa sank deeper into depression. She was angry at herself for being captured, but her captivity revealed something more frightening: she didn't know anyone who would come for her. Mari, knowing Asa's feelings about her role, would assume Asa had left without saying goodbye. Koji was focused on saving Mari's house in distant lands. She hadn't really befriended anyone else. Suzo was the closest she had to a friend, but even she knew Asa detested being head of the guards. She'd probably assume the same as Mari.

Asa had never felt as alone as she did in that cave. She'd pushed everyone who might care for her out of her life, and there was no one to lean on in her time of need. She was increasingly certain these men were careful enough that she'd never escape on her own.

She fell deeper into sorrow, self-pity overwhelming even her anger at herself.

At some point in time, the second man left. Asa worried that the first man might try something without the second man present, but he seemed to have thought better of his desires. Or at least, he was waiting until Asa's unknown purpose was fulfilled.

When the second man returned, Asa could hear the sound of water dripping off of him.

"How bad is it?" the first man asked.

"It was like walking in daylight, there was so much lightning," the second man replied.

The first man grunted.

So, Asa knew it was night. That was something, at least. It didn't really narrow down how long she'd been out, but any piece of information might be important later.

"Any word?" asked the first man.

There was no verbal reply, and Asa cursed herself for not being focused enough to pick up on the second man's motion. The cave lapsed back into silence, and time resumed its glacial pace.

In the distance, Asa felt another life. It was a ways away, but as the first change she'd felt in who knew how long, it was exciting all the same. She tracked the new life. It advanced slowly toward them, much more slowly than the second man had approached. It was almost as though the person didn't know the way. They backtracked a few times, but worked their way steadily toward Asa's location.

As the energy got closer, Asa recognized the person. Suzo. Her heart surged with excitement. A rescue!

The excitement gave way to fear. Suzo was good, but she was untested. The first man, at least, would know how to fight. Could Suzo win against men who knew what they were doing, men who had seen combat?

"Hey," the first man said, and Asa knew Suzo had been seen. There was a quick shuffling, and Asa could sense the two men standing and facing the intruder. "Who are you?"

The second man laughed, disdain in his voice. "One of

the women this nightblade has been training to be a guard for Mari. Pathetic."

More than ever, Asa wanted Suzo to kill those men. She wished she could help, but any action on her part was more likely to distract Suzo than the men. She forced herself to stillness.

Asa felt the entire battle. The second man came in with a lazy swing. He was playing with Suzo, but Asa hadn't taught her warriors to fight without sincerity. There were some battles where testing your opponent could reveal important details. But more often, it was far more reasonable to attack only with the intent to kill.

Suzo had learned that lesson well. She deflected the weak attack with ease, turning the sword and stepping inside the second man's guard in a heartbeat. Her sword stabbed into the man with a decisive, simple strike. Asa approved. Suzo gave away little of her own skill, but still killed one of her opponents. The woman was one of her best students for a reason, and Asa was reassured by the lack of hesitation in Suzo's movements. Hesitation could easily mean death.

The first man drew his blade, his surprise evident in the way he shuffled backward, away from Suzo. Once he had a little more space, he relaxed into a stance.

Asa mentally cursed. If she'd been instructing, she would have told Suzo to seize the advantage after the first kill. She'd had a few precious heartbeats to put the first man on the defensive. But it was Suzo's first kill, and momentary disorientation had taken her. Asa remembered her own. Even the best took a moment to recover from the effect.

Fortunately, Suzo turned to the final opponent within a few moments. She wasn't dazed from her first combat, or at least not enough to affect her.

She'd won her first battle easily, which would lend her confidence. But overconfidence was as dangerous as fear. For the first time, Asa was grateful she was gagged. If she hadn't been, she probably would have shouted out to Suzo time and time again, distracting the woman to death.

The man attacked, as Asa expected. As she feared, the man had seen combat before. But all the same, his movements were rough, and Asa realized he was an untrained fighter. He'd only survived by a combination of reflexes and innate skill.

Asa tensed with every cut, her body soon a mess of nerves and knotted muscles. Suzo moved out of the man's attacks with ease, and her training kept her safe. But whenever she tried to counter, the man's reactions were too quick. Neither of them did any damage to the other. The battle wasn't about who was the best, but who would make a mistake first.

It was Suzo, unfortunately. The man managed to make a cut through her leg, and Asa could sense the way Suzo's stance suddenly changed. Asa cursed. Now the man had every advantage. Not only had Asa's foolishness gotten herself captured, but it would also cause the death of a woman who deserved far better. She raged at herself.

The man came in for the killing blow, a strong swing designed to knock Suzo off her feet. The battle was over.

But Suzo didn't block. She recognized the blow for what it was and dodged low, letting the cut pass overhead. The two warriors stumbled toward one another, one because of her injured leg and the other because of the uncontrolled force of his strike. But Suzo still had complete control of her sword. She cut at the man. The cut was poor, slicing deeply through his stomach, but it would do.

Both fighters fell, but Suzo was quickly back on her feet.

She wasn't moving well, but she was moving. The other man seemed as though he was trying to shove his internal organs back in his body. Asa wanted to watch, and was disappointed the blindfold remained firmly in place.

The man wasn't dead, but he would be soon. Suzo approached to finish him off.

Asa screamed, the sound coming out severely muffled by the gag. She shook her head wildly, and fortunately, it was enough to get Suzo's attention. An opponent alive was a failure, but a man like this, knowing he was dying but not dead yet, was the most dangerous to approach. They had nothing to lose. Better to stay away and let him die slowly.

Fortunately, Suzo seemed to understand. She stepped away, placing herself firmly between Asa and the dying man. The kidnapper died slowly, and near the end he tried throwing his sword at Suzo, confirming Asa's guess that he'd been plenty dangerous.

But it finally ended. The man breathed his last, and after a bit more waiting, Suzo turned to Asa. Asa nodded confirmation. She couldn't feel the man's energy any longer.

Suzo cleaned and sheathed her sword after pulling off the blindfold and the gag. Asa gingerly closed her mouth, feeling the ache from having it forced open for so long. "Thank you."

Suzo nodded, taking a look at the manacles. As Asa slowly stretched her jaw around, Suzo went back to the dead men, and for the first time, Asa got a look at the cave she'd been in.

There wasn't much to look at. A small table held a deck of cards and some assorted supplies, and two torches burned on opposite ends of the rock, but otherwise, all Asa could tell was that they were underground. Behind her was the end of the tunnel, and the torches didn't light very far in front of her.

Suzo searched the bodies and quickly found a key on the second man. She returned to Asa and began unlocking the manacles. As soon as she did, Asa's arms fell to her side. She could move the right one a little, but the injuries to her left shoulder made it too tender to move. Every time her arm swung she almost cried in pain.

"How did you find me?"

Suzo looked up as she unlocked Asa's ankles. "It wasn't easy. When I showed up at the inn, I heard that you'd gotten really drunk and been escorted away by a man no one knew. That seemed odd to me, but no one knew any more."

Asa took a halting step forward, her legs immediately cramping up. Suzo went to get the water from the table. "The next day, you missed your duty, and I thought for sure something was wrong. But I had my own duty, and I couldn't be sure. I thought perhaps you'd maybe had enough. But when my watch ended, I went back to the inn and started inquiring. The story didn't quite sound true. The bartender didn't remember serving you enough to make you drunk, and I had a hard time believing you'd leave your duty without at least telling us."

She paused, and Asa got the impression there was a part of the story Suzo wasn't telling. "Anyway, I'd heard a rumor about old abandoned caves behind Stonekeep. They'd been built originally to provide a secret exit in case the city fell, and to store goods, but they eventually fell into disuse. People around the inn remembered you stumbling deeper into Stonekeep, so I figured the caves were the only place that made sense to hide a nightblade. I waited outside until someone came out. Then I followed them in."

Asa didn't quite believe the story, but she didn't question it. Not after Suzo had helped her escape. The woman deserved that much trust, at least. Asa found her weapons. Working with one hand, she started replacing them. Suzo, without word, helped.

"How are you?" Asa asked. "The first kill is always hard."

Suzo looked behind her with disgust. "They had it coming."

Asa finished replacing her weapons, then realized something. One of her swords was missing. She looked around, wondering if it lay somewhere else. She didn't see it anywhere. Suzo saw her looking. "What are you searching for?"

"My other sword."

Suddenly, realization clicked into place. She knew why they hadn't been allowed to harm her, and why she had been left in this cave. Asa cursed out loud, and her legs almost gave out on her again. "We need to move. They're going to kill Mari with my sword."

The two of them half-stumbled, half-ran out of the caves. Suzo remembered the way out of the labyrinthine tunnels without problem, and soon they were back in Stonekeep proper. Thunder rumbled and lightning flashed overhead, but they paid the storm no mind. Their clothes were soaked through, but they kept pushing. Asa noticed that Suzo's leg kept bleeding, and she worried the woman would collapse before they found help.

Fortunately, they made it to the gate of Mari's castle. They were let in, and they stumbled toward Mari's quarters. Other guards joined them, as the women's presence and injuries caused an uproar among the group. Asa felt that most of them thought she'd abandoned them. What a fool she'd been. If not for Suzo, a house would have been lost to her aloofness.

They made it to Mari's quarters, but the lady wasn't there. Asa looked around the empty room, wishing the walls could speak and tell her where she'd gone. "Where's Lady Mari?"

"She went for a walk," one of the guards replied.

Asa cursed. Why tonight, of all nights?

"I need every guard. Wake everyone! Find Lady Mari and bring her back immediately, no matter her orders. Everyone stands guard tonight!"

There was a moment of stunned silence.

"NOW!"

The group burst into action, and Asa saw Suzo's leg again. It still bled freely. She couldn't believe the woman had been able to walk. She wouldn't be standing for much longer. Asa grabbed another guard scurrying about. "Fetch a dayblade, now!"

For a few moments, her life quieted. She was too weak to find Mari herself. She had no choice but to trust the guards.

The scheme against them was brilliant, and she'd played right into it. Asa's swords were well known. If one of them ended up embedded in Lady Mari, House Kita would be taken over by Yoshinori, and the blades would be accused of treason yet again. There would be no haven in the Kingdom for them. Asa only hoped Suzo had rescued her in time for them to make a difference.

After a while, Jun came into the room. Asa nodded at him gratefully. He came to her, but Asa shook her head. "Her first." She gestured to Suzo.

Jun nodded and went to Suzo. Suzo's eyes went wide.

She'd probably never been healed before. The process was painful, but often blissfully short.

When Jun was finished, he came to Asa. "Your injuries?"

"Something is torn in my left shoulder, and all the pain associated from being chained with my hands above me for a few days."

Jun made no comment, but he started by healing her shoulder. Asa grimaced and fought back the involuntary tears.

The healing wasn't as painful as she'd expected. She'd suffered from discomfort during her captivity, but she hadn't been otherwise mistreated. When she stood, she felt tired but capable.

Not long after, there was a flurry of activity as Lady Mari and Takahiro were rushed into the room. The hallways immediately filled with guards following Asa's orders. When she saw the lady, Asa felt shame well up inside her. How close had they come to disaster because of her actions? Asa breathed a deep sigh of relief. They hadn't been too late, after all.

Mari looked at the head of her guards. "Where have you been?"

Asa related the story quickly. Mari's eyes went wide at times, but she didn't comment. When Asa finished, Mari turned to Suzo. "Thank you. Your actions tonight might have saved us all."

Suzo bowed, flush with pride, but didn't say anything.

Together, they all sat and waited. Asa knew who the third man would be, and they were all on guard. The plan was sure to fail now. If nothing else, Asa now had an alibi. Dozens of people had seen her. The more time passed, the more Asa felt certain that they'd triumphed. By the time the sun rose, she was beginning to feel ready to sleep, finally.

A shuffling of feet in the hallway beyond perked them all up. After a small commotion, a messenger came into the room, his face ashen. Asa's heart sank. What could possibly have happened?

"It's Lord Isamu," the messenger said. "He was murdered last night in his sleep."

17

Another estate stood in front of Koji and his blades. The sun was beginning to set on the horizon and Koji used the last light to observe the area.

The estate stood alone, well-designed buildings interrupting the otherwise endless plains. Koji could see a handful of guards, but there wasn't even a wall around the property. Perhaps the noble had never worried about being attacked, but Koji assumed the noble house was so small it wasn't worth spending the resources to protect it.

Koji felt trapped in a loop. This was the fifth—or was it the sixth?—estate that they'd raided. His warriors were becoming old hands at this, and that complacency could lead to mistakes.

Ever since the slaughter of the heavy cavalry unit, Koji had wondered if they should begin their return to the lands of House Kita. Summer was coming to a close, and while the days were still hot, in the evening cold breezes cut down from the north, signaling the change of seasons. Koji believed they had made a difference. He had to. Otherwise, what had their sacrifices been for?

But they couldn't do this forever. He'd been fortunate enough not to lose a blade yet, but the only true challenge they'd faced was the cavalry, and their surprise in that instance had been complete. Soon, blades would fall, and they were already a small group.

Worse, he couldn't get the scenes of this past summer out of his mind. He had nightmares about wading through rivers of blood, scenes of the slaughter of the cavalry replaying nearly every night. When he trained, he noticed that he was getting slower. He'd been bested a few times even in the past few days. The blades who'd beaten him thought it was because they were getting stronger. He didn't want to disabuse them of the notion, but he alone knew the truth. He was getting weaker.

Below him, the estate settled into its evening routine. The guard patrol was regular and small. Koji didn't see that many people, but considering the size of the estate, he wasn't terribly surprised.

The blades gathered as night fell. Koji ran through the plan quickly, but there wasn't much to say. They'd approach from a few different directions and kill the guards at once. Then they'd raid the estate, burn what they couldn't carry, and kill the noble. Koji didn't see any reason to alter the approach that so far had worked so well.

They split up into their normal groups and made their way toward the estate. Thanks to their gift, they could keep track of each other even in the dark. As they approached the estates, though, Koji began feeling a sense of unease. His hair stood up on the back of his neck, but he didn't know why.

He paused, pushing out with his sense to understand why he worried. Then he realized his mistake. From their observation at a distance, the estate hadn't been very crowded. To his sense, though, as he got closer, he could feel the energy of the lives inside. There were a number of people there, far more than he would have expected.

Did it change his plans? He could think of a few reasons for the difference. Perhaps the nobles were hosting another family, and they'd all been indoors for their meal. Perhaps the family was much larger than he'd guessed. But he couldn't quite get the pieces to fit with his intuition. This was wrong.

Just as soon as he'd come to that decision, he heard a soft *whoomp* off in the distance, and a red, burning ball of light hung in the sky. There were several more of the deep sounds, and soon the entire ground was bathed in an eerie red light. They were like fireworks, but not exactly.

Koji sensed a trap, even if he didn't know what exactly it was. Before he could react, archers stepped out of the main buildings in orderly lines. The guards who had walked the perimeter must have been acting as spotters, because they pointed out where a group of blades stood, visible to a watchful eye. Koji's people had gotten complacent.

Bows came up in unison, and Koji just barely had time to yell, "Shields!" before the first wave came at them.

Koji brought his shield up just in time to feel the solid *thunk* of an arrow. Several others went wide. His small group hadn't been injured, but he didn't have time to check on the others.

They'd only been about thirty paces from the estate perimeter when the fire, now slowly drifting down, had shot into the sky. Koji didn't dare turn his back on the archers. "Charge!"

His group of blades ran forward. Koji sensed the other two groups doing the same. A small part of him recognized the groups were smaller than they should have been, but he was in the thick of battle and didn't have time to think.

Some of the archers had switched to swords. Others were trying to fire their bows at close range. Koji could tell the group had some training, but not enough. His blades fell into them, tearing them apart now that they were inside effective bow range. Koji attacked with the others, losing himself blissfully in the battle.

He felt slow, like all his limbs were weighted. He could still sense his opponents, and they were still slower than him, but Koji knew he was capable of more.

As soon as they reached the archers, the battle was over. The trap had been sprung, but the archers still hadn't been prepared to fight the blades. The group worked their way through the house, and Koji stepped into the main room just in time to see Sakura cut through an older man's neck.

The man had been on his knees, pleading, and from the quality of his clothing Koji guessed he was the head of this family.

Koji froze as he saw the scene. Not because it was unusual; their orders were to kill the nobles and leave the land in chaos. But something about the scene suddenly struck Koji as wrong. The man had been on his knees, and Sakura's face was devoid of expression. It didn't affect her in the least. She might as well have been harvesting rice as killing a man.

Koji shook his head, trying to straighten out his thoughts. Another noble family had fallen, helping Mari reclaim her land and heal the Kingdom. He just had to keep that in the front of his mind.

Reports came to him quickly. First was the news that the storerooms of the estate were almost entirely empty. Somehow, Koji didn't find that surprising. They'd been ready for the blades. Either the food was all gone, or it had already been sent off to the armies.

Then came the word he'd been dreading. They'd lost two blades in the initial attack. Koji ordered pyres built so they could be sent to the Great Cycle, as befitted a blade. He knew the sorrow would come, but for now, he simply felt empty inside.

He wanted to go home.

AFTER THE RAID on the last estate, Koji decided to begin heading northeast. The path would take them back in the direction of House Kita lands, and would hopefully take them out of the way of enemies chasing them. As far as Koji knew, the far north was quieter than the south, where all the armies and supply routes were focused.

They traveled for two days without incident, but on the morning of the third, disaster found them.

One of their scouts came running toward the main group, a look of fear on her face. Before she even spoke, Koji knew something horrible approached.

Koji didn't even have time to ask what happened. The scout shouted as she approached. "There's a large regiment in front of us!"

She stopped in front of Koji, out of breath, hands on her knees.

"Tell me what you saw," Koji demanded. He'd worried that this would be a consequence of their success. Eventually, Katashi had to devote forces to stopping them. It had been part of the plan all along.

"I got as close as I dared, but even that wasn't close. I'd estimate five hundred soldiers, all well-trained. They are marching in good order. Although I couldn't be sure, I'd say we're looking at a frontline unit."

Koji didn't waste time questioning the scout's assessment. In the time his group had been together, he'd learned to trust the other blades completely. Although part of him didn't want to believe it, he suspected the time had finally come. Katashi was coming for him.

The blades only needed to discuss their actions for a few moments. The scout reported that the force was moving west. If Koji and the blades moved further north, the force would pass behind them and the blades could keep moving toward home.

Koji redeployed his scouts and they turned north. He would've liked to hurt Katashi's army in some way, but they didn't have a chance against a force that size. Fortunately, there wouldn't be any need to fight.

When Sakura, who had been scouting to the north, came running back, Koji felt a stirring of fear. Running into one force was unfortunate. Running into two wasn't a coincidence. His group was being hunted, and by no small number of people.

When the blades reconvened, the tone of the conversation had shifted. All of them felt the same as Koji. No one was naive enough to believe that running into two strong forces was chance. Their conversation, by necessity, was brief.

"Are we sure these are frontline units?"

Sakura nodded. "I'm almost certain of what I saw."

"So we think all this pressure is coming from the invading armies?"

There were nods around the circle. They all knew what that meant. If the armies were coming from the east and north, the safest direction was west, farther into enemy territory.

"Do we chance going deeper into Katashi's lands?" Koji hated the idea. He wanted to be home, not chased endlessly through hostile plains.

The group stood silent. No one knew the answer. Going west might only prolong the inevitable.

"The only other idea I can think of is to sneak through the gaps before the groups converge. Do we risk it all in one attempt, or do we make them chase us?"

"That's assuming they don't have forces coming from the west, too," Sakura said softly.

She had a point. They didn't know if they were surrounded. If they chose to go west and ran into another force, the noose would already be tight around their necks.

"I'd rather try to sneak between the forces while we have a chance," Koji decided. Some of Mari's leadership style had rubbed off on him. He didn't want to move unless most of the blades agreed with him. Fortunately, they all seemed to share a mind regarding this.

The decision made, everyone secured their gear tightly and began running. Koji pushed them as hard as he dared. He needed to balance the need for speed with the awareness that they had to keep some energy in reserve in case they needed to fight. They kept together as a group, with some of the faster runners a few hundred paces ahead to act as scouts.

The sun was high in the sky when the scouts returned to the rest of the group, chased by mounted archers. When the scouts reached the main group, the archers rode in circles around the blades, lazily shooting arrows at them. The horses never came close enough to counterattack, and Koji was forced to gather all the blades into a circle, forming a wall with their shields. Arrows thudded into the protection, but the archers didn't seem particularly ambitious. They never neared, and eventually rode back to their lines. But for that entire time, Koji and his group had been pinned down.

Koji felt a knot forming in the pit of his stomach. He'd never quite seen tactics like these before, and they made him uneasy. This opponent they faced knew they were blades, and he had no desire to risk his people. A single cavalry charge might be enough to destroy Koji's group, but it would come at a cost of lives this commander didn't see fit to sacrifice.

Koji didn't see any other way forward, though. As a single group, they resumed running, trying to squeeze between the quickly closing gap between Katashi's forces. Twice more they were found and harried by mounted archers. The archers never came closer than fifty paces, and both times Koji and the blades were forced to stop while they acted as targets. Fortunately, none of them were killed during either attack. By the time the attacks finished, Koji's shield was almost filled with arrows. Every rider seemed to continue firing until his quiver was empty.

They ran again, and when they crested a small rise, they stopped completely. The gap had closed. Instead, they faced over a thousand cavalry and archers. Koji closed his eyes, tasting death on the air. He felt the knot in his stomach release. Having the opportunity to survive had been terrifying, but a certain peace came upon him once he knew they were trapped and done for. Behind them, cavalry encircled them, cutting off any hope of retreat, small as it had been.

Koji ordered a charge. His blades were tired, but they deserved to die with a sword in hand. Legs burning, they ran toward the enemy lines, their swords and voices raised.

Out of the corner of his eye, Koji saw two units of mounted archers spur themselves to action. Koji cursed. They'd be in range before the blades even reached the enemy lines. "Shields!" he yelled.

The blades slid to a stop, forming a circle of shields. The archers galloped around the circle, again never coming close enough to attack. But they didn't fire on the group, either.

Koji recognized it for what it was. The enemy commander was sending him a message.

Koji looked around the circle. These were the blades who had followed him most closely. The faces he saw were determined. Everyone knew they weren't going to survive this battle, but that didn't frighten them. They wanted to die with honor.

Koji knew the enemy commander wasn't going to allow such a battle. Mounted, they had every advantage, and the commander would take every one. If Koji and the blades charged, they'd be shot down by mounted archers. If they sat still, eventually enough arrows would fall to kill them. Either way, not a single one of his warriors would die with a bloodied blade.

He nodded to himself, his decision made. He stood up, breaking the wall. As he expected, though, no one attacked him. He pulled his scabbard from his hip and held it in his right hand, above his head. He heard the gasps and mutters behind him.

"We won't be given the chance to fight," Koji told them.

He advanced slowly, not making any sudden moves. He knelt in the middle of the field that would have marked the deaths of the warriors who followed him, laying his sword down on his right side, where it would be almost impossible for him to draw it quickly.

The enemy lines fell silent, the only sound the creak of leather and the occasional shuffling and snorts of horses. Eventually the lines opened and a single, older man came forward. Unlike Koji, he wore his swords, ready to draw in an instant. Such was the right of the victor.

The man approached and knelt across from Koji. Koji bowed, introducing himself. The man's eyes widened just slightly at the mention of the name. "So, you really are him."

Koji nodded slightly, but noticed the man did not bow to him. "I am General Emon. You come to discuss terms?"

"I will surrender to you if you promise safe conduct for the warriors who serve me."

Emon shook his head. "You are not warriors, but murderers."

Koji was angered by the accusation, but pressed forward. "Will safe conduct be granted?"

"No. You will all suffer very painful deaths for the crimes you've committed."

Koji narrowed his eyes. "That's not much of an offer for our surrender."

"And you're not in a position to bargain. I only came because I wanted to see face-to-face the man who has terrified so many. You'll never even get to my lines."

The statement was true, but Koji had hoped to see some shred of honor from the enemy commander. But, Koji realized, if Emon actually viewed them as criminals, his actions were honorable. Criminals didn't deserve the same rights as warriors.

Were they criminals?

Koji couldn't answer the question now. He needed to

save his people, but Emon was right, he had no reason to offer anything.

"You don't know what I'm capable of," he said, putting as much menace into his voice as he could.

A flicker of doubt passed over the general's face. Then he shook his head. "You can't win."

"No, but I can make the price higher than what you wish to pay."

Emon considered the threat, briefly. "You lie."

"Then I'll see you on the battlefield," Koji said. He moved to grab his sword.

His confidence must have done the trick. Emon held out his hand. "Wait."

Koji paused, his hand hovering over the scabbard.

"You'll surrender to me, asking only that your warriors go free?"

Koji nodded, hoping his reputation had grown fierce enough that the bargain seemed like a deal.

Emon thought in silence for some time. Finally, he made a decision. "Very well. I accept your surrender."

18

Mari sat at her desk, her eyes staring at nothing in particular. For the life of her she could not force her mind to make coherent thoughts. She felt as though she was living in a never-ending nightmare from which there was no escape.

The diplomatic envoy, which had become a funeral procession, had left just that morning. They had already sent birds back to their lands and Mari figured she would be dealing with a new ruler in the next few days. Worse, the ruler would believe that she had assassinated his predecessor. Any hope of a diplomatic solution had disappeared.

Her military wasn't prepared to deal with the threat they now faced. Although filled with brave and courageous souls, and well-equipped in terms of supplies, their lack of numbers would be their eventual doom.

The blades were another problem. Much of the strength she had used to obtain her position came from them, but now that very association threatened everything she had worked for. Mari did not believe that Asa killed Isamu, but there was precious little evidence. The sword that was found buried deep in Isamu's heart had been Asa's. Being as no one knew exactly when Isamu was killed, it was possible that Asa had killed Isamu and then sounded the alarm on Mari's life to provide an alibi.

Asa was many things, but Mari didn't believe—she refused to believe—that the woman she knew was capable of such an act. Besides, Suzo supported Asa's story, which was all the verification that Mari needed.

But what Mari knew to be true was not the same as what her people believed. No doubt, as she sat there, stunned, other nobles were already spreading the false story of what had happened. Combined with the pressures she already faced, Mari wasn't certain that her rule would survive.

She had no idea how to proceed. She had already leaned on every alliance she'd created, pulled in all the favors she'd ever been owed. Perhaps she could figure out how to survive one crisis, but when they just kept coming she felt like she was buried under an avalanche of disaster. Not for the first time, she considered the possibility of just giving in. Yes, she was certain that her people would suffer if she made that choice, but there was a limit to what she could do.

A knock on her door startled her from her reverie. "Come in."

A messenger came into the room, carrying a note that was sealed with black wax. Mari's heart, already close to broken, cried out in fear. What else could have possibly happened? She supposed the note could contain good news, but given the trend in her life as of late, she ruled such a chance slim.

With fingers trembling, she opened the letter. The message was from General Fumio. In his clipped, terse handwriting he let her know that he had just received news that Koji and the blades with him had been captured. According to Fumio, Koji had surrendered and was being rushed to the front, where a public trial and execution would be held. Fumio didn't say anything else in his note, but he didn't need to, the implications silently condemning her. Like Mari, he knew what Koji's tasks had been for the past few moons. In a trial, Mari had no doubt that the truth of her orders would come to light. Under other circumstances, she might not have been concerned. But with her position weakened as it was, and the blades already under suspicion for the death of another lord, Koji's capture was the final event that would end her rule. She knew that as certainly as she knew the sun was going to rise the next day.

Mari set the note down gingerly, as though treating it with respect would somehow change the contents of its message.

Mari sighed and rubbed her palms against her temples, trying to force new life into her tired mind. There had to be a way to fix what was broken. But no matter how hard she thought, she found no answers.

MORNING TURNED INTO AFTERNOON, and Mari still had no idea how to solve any of the problems that faced her. Trying to find a solution felt like banging her head against the thick walls of her castle. No matter how hard she worked, it made absolutely no difference.

Her stomach twisted into knots when there was another knock at her door. A messenger entered, bearing a request from Arata for a meeting. The knot in Mari's stomach tightened, and she was suddenly grateful that she had forgotten to eat lunch. Even though she did not know the details of what Arata would say, she could guess at the general tone of the meeting. Putting it off would make it no easier, though, so she accepted his request and ordered tea to be prepared.

When Arata entered, Mari saw that he looked even older than before. She reminded herself that the problems she faced did not only affect her. In times like this it was all too easy to think only of oneself, forgetting that a crisis rarely affected only one person. Her problems were the problems of her land, even if she sometimes found herself slipping into only thinking about herself and how she could stay in power. That was a path that led to poor decisions, and she needed to be careful to always put her people first and herself second.

Arata sat down across from her and she poured tea for both of them. Arata picked up his cup and gave her a grateful look. With a sigh, he immediately addressed the issue that had brought him there. "I just received word this morning that a nightblade has been caught in Lord Katashi's house lands. It is said that he has been assassinating nobles and burning food, and that he does so on your orders."

Mari wondered at that. She had just gotten the bird from Fumio, and she doubted that anyone else in the army was sending messages back to the capital. The news had arrived far too quickly for it to be rumor that had spread. Someone inside the capital was actively working with Katashi. Mari suspected Yoshinori, but she still had no evidence. The more important problem was right in front of her. She wasn't sure how to respond to Arata, so she remained silent, waiting for him to ask a question.

"Is it true?"

She nodded, not trusting herself to speak. Suddenly, in

front of this man she respected so much, the decision to send Koji seemed like a terrible mistake. But it had done its job. It had moved a substantial part of Katashi's army away from the front. No doubt, his forces were suffering from a lack of supplies that at least gave her army a sliver of hope.

The look of disgust on Arata's face stopped any rationalizations running through her mind. But he was too honorable to shout at her. He spoke softly, but every word felt as though she was being stabbed. "Do you know why I supported you when you brought your claim?"

Mari shook her head. She always assumed it had been loyalty to her family and the fact she controlled the strongest military forces.

"I supported you because I am old enough to remember a time when the blades were practically venerated among our people. They healed injuries and illnesses and they kept the peace better than any lord or militia ever has. I know that they have made mistakes, but they do not deserve the fate that they have been given. You, and you alone, seemed to share that view. I looked at you and I saw a leader who could envision a future where the blades and our people lived in harmony."

Mari had an idea now where Arata was heading, and she felt tears trickling down the side of her face.

"The mistake that the blades made was searching for more power when they had already been given enough. It caused them to make foolish decisions, and led to the distrust of the people. I see the same in you. Sending this young man to perform such a horrible task is exactly the reason why the blades will always struggle to find a home in the Kingdom. You've destroyed not only your own reputation, but any chance the blades had at a peaceful existence."

Mari began to weep. Every word Arata spoke was true. Every doubt she had about herself as a ruler suddenly became truth.

She bowed down all the way until her forehead touched the floor. "I'm sorry. I always thought that I had the best interests of our land at heart, but you are right."

There was so much more that she wanted to say, so many versions of an apology that felt necessary, but she held onto whatever dignity she had left. Words would never be enough, and they both knew it.

When she lifted her forehead off the floor, she saw that Arata's eyes were also damp. "I forgive you, Mari. I believe that everything you did was because you felt it was right. But that has been true of both good and horrible rulers in the past. Out of respect for you and for your family, I will not say anything in public for the time being. But I will no longer support you as the head of the house."

Mari had known it was coming. She had known from the moment she received the request to meet. But to hear one of her family's oldest allies and closest friends withdraw his support crushed her. She hated that she could not stop crying, but she managed to keep her voice even. "I understand, and I thank you for your wisdom and for your support, not just for me, but for my entire family."

Arata gave a stiff bow, barely keeping his own emotions in check. He stood up and left, leaving his tea unfinished. As the door closed behind him, Mari felt a sense of finality. Any chance that she might've had for holding her throne relied on his support. Without it, her hopes seemed more impossible than ever.

MARI TURNED to one of the only places she knew where she

would feel any sense of solace. She made the long walk from the castle to the shrine built in honor of her family. Her guards had secured the route ahead of time and made sure the shrine was empty of all well-wishers.

Word of the dramatic events was just beginning to trickle through the city, but for now the city rested, quieting as evening came. Like the calm before the fiercest winds of the storm, the streets of Stonekeep stood quiet. Mari was grateful not to fight her way through streets filled with people. At that moment, all she wanted was to be left alone.

The shrine was an oasis of peace. Mari felt the relaxation as soon as she stepped into the area. Her shoulders relaxed and her breath came more easily. Perhaps it was the beauty of the shrine, or perhaps it was the souls of her family, but there was something special about this place, something she would almost describe as sacred.

She knelt down in front of the shrine, not trusting herself to put her worries and fears into words. She simply sat, her mind curiously empty after the chaos that had battered it for the past few days.

She had no idea how long she'd been sitting there, but eventually she felt some small measure of peace. Perhaps intent didn't matter much to the living, by perhaps for those who had rejoined the Great Cycle, it carried more weight. She stood up and exited the shrine, walking back toward the castle.

On the way she stopped at an overlook, looking out at the valley that was a small sliver of the land and people she was responsible for. She stood there, lost in thought, until she felt a presence behind her. She turned and saw that Takahiro was standing there, a concerned look on his face.

He didn't speak, but stood beside her. She gave him a

small nod of appreciation and then returned to her contemplative state.

After a time, thoughts started to return to her. As wonderful as the relaxation had felt, the world demanded more of her and she could not escape forever. She turned slightly toward Takahiro. "You heard?"

"Yes. He came to see me after the two of you spoke. He was heartbroken."

"He deserves to be. My decisions were wrong."

"Perhaps. But it's easy to say that in hindsight. If you begin to doubt every decision, you will be no use to anyone."

"I will not be able to continue to rule."

Takahiro shifted so that he was facing her. "It should never matter whether you rule or not. You have always tried to serve the people. How will you do that next?"

The question felt like a verbal slap. Just earlier that day she had thought about how she needed to stop thinking about herself, but her mind kept leading her down the same paths. She needed to think differently.

If she could not be the ruler of her house, it was her responsibility to find somebody who would do the job well. Her first thought was Arata. He contained an incredible amount of wisdom and he'd always cared for his own lands well. He would make an excellent choice, except for his age and the fact that Mari had no idea how she could secure the position for him. Yoshinori had played his cards well, and Mari hadn't done nearly enough to stop him.

A sudden curiosity seized her. "Why do you continue to serve, even when you know the mistakes I've made? Why are you still here?"

Takahiro looked pained that she'd even asked the question. "I've not always agreed with you," he began, "but you've proven me wrong several times, and you've inspired me. We all make mistakes, but I know that you are focused on serving your lands, not just ruling them. I will always serve you."

The last line was uttered with a conviction that surprised Mari. She'd always known that Takahiro was loyal. But the emotion behind that statement went deeper than mere loyalty. When she recognized it, she suddenly understood and considered herself a fool for not realizing earlier.

The sudden understanding led to others. She saw new opportunities that hadn't been there before. A new idea blossomed in her mind, and for the first time in what seemed like ages she had hope once again.

Takahiro seemed to notice the difference as well. "What?"

She smiled. "I know what I'm going to do. I am going to give up the leadership of my house."

19

A sa knocked on the door to Mari's office. Even though the guards outside didn't stop her, she could see the way they tensed as she approached. Whether others believed her or not, the rumors had done their work, perhaps too well. Even the women Asa herself had trained didn't completely trust her.

A moon ago, that might have made her angry. She might have raged against the unfairness of it all and made plans to leave the Kingdom. She still felt frustrated, but not in the same way. She recognized that she had brought some of this on herself. No one stood alone in life, no matter what they thought. Had her behavior been different, she might be facing overt shows of support instead of suspicion.

The door opened and Mari stood there, looking more energetic than Asa had seen her in some time. Mari's posture had changed, no longer carrying the burdens of her people by herself, as she had for so long. In a way, they'd had to learn the same lessons. Perhaps that was why Mari had always interested and frustrated her so much.

Mari's smile made Asa's complaints disappear. Here, at

least, was one woman who had never doubted her. That trust meant more than any amount of gold. Never again would she take it for granted.

Asa bowed and entered the room, taking in the familiar office with a glance. Papers were scattered everywhere, even more so than usual. She'd heard that Mari had been busy these past few days, but it looked like the rumors didn't go quite far enough.

Of course, the whole castle was abuzz with news, as was most of Stonekeep. A person could hardly turn a corner without hearing something about the upcoming event. From what Asa had heard, most people were overjoyed. The average citizen of Stonekeep could barely keep up with all that had happened this summer, and most were excited by the stability that a marriage would bring to the land.

Mari didn't look like a woman whose wedding was the next day. She looked like an overworked but cheerful administrator.

"So, you're really going through with it?" Asa asked.

Mari nodded, an even wider grin breaking out on her face. Asa had never considered Mari to be the type who would marry. Of course, as a noble lady, especially one of House Kita, she would marry eventually, but Asa had never put much thought into it.

"Congratulations," she offered.

"Thank you. But there's much to be done before tomorrow."

"I can only imagine."

Mari's face fell. "The first is something I don't want to do, but I must."

Asa interrupted her. "I'm no longer the head of your guards?"

Mari shook her head. "I know you never loved the position, but I didn't want it to end like this."

Asa was surprised how disappointed she was. Of course, she'd known the move was coming. Mari didn't have any other choice. But even though she had never wanted to guard Mari, she felt a pang of sorrow at not having the opportunity anymore.

"We don't always get to choose our endings. It's been an honor to serve you."

Mari's eyes narrowed at Asa's attitude. "We haven't had much time together since Isamu was murdered. What's changed?"

Asa shrugged, and Mari let the question go after a long heartbeat.

"Who would you recommend to head my guards now?"

"Suzo. She's talented and makes strong decisions. She'll help you more than I ever could. And she wants the position."

Mari nodded, and a short silence broke their conversation. "I imagine you'll go after Koji now?"

"Is it that obvious?"

"Probably only to me. If anyone can save him, it's you." Mari stood up. "Will you stay, at least until the wedding?"

Asa hesitated. "You know I can't be there."

"I'm sure we can find a place where you can watch. It would mean a lot to me, knowing you were there."

It would mean delaying her departure by a day, but that wasn't much. It would take Koji several days to arrive at the front in captivity. She needed to procure supplies anyway. She nodded, and Mari stepped forward and swept Asa into an embrace. "I don't know if I'll see you for some time. I know you've been wanting to join one of the expeditions and leave the Kingdom. If I don't see you again..."

Mari's voice trailed off. Awkwardly, Asa returned the lady's embrace. She wanted to say everything to Mari, but nothing seemed adequate. Finally, she stepped away. "Thank you, Mari. It's been an honor." She took another step back and bowed deeply.

Mari returned the bow. "And thank you, Asa. I've also been honored to know you."

With that, Asa turned and left, not wanting to prolong the moment. As the door closed behind her she took one last look at Mari, trying to imprint the vision on her memory.

ASA HADN'T GONE FAR when she sensed a presence chasing her. She turned around to see Suzo. Just the sight of the woman was enough to put a smile on Asa's face. Suzo caught up and matched Asa's leisurely pace around the castle.

"May I speak to you in private?"

Asa led Suzo to her private quarters in the castle, which she assumed she'd have to give up soon. Despite the sadness of leaving Mari, she didn't much mind. She'd never liked being in one place for too long.

As soon as the door closed, Suzo stepped closer, her voice low. "What happened? The guards on duty told me Lady Mari summoned you."

"It looks as though you'll be moving up in the world soon," Asa replied.

Asa wasn't expecting the anger in Suzo's voice. "She took away your position? I thought she, of all people, would stand next to you!"

Asa shook her head. "It has nothing to do with standing next to me. Most of the Kingdom believes that I murdered

Isamu. Mari might have been willing to keep me close as evidence of my innocence, but when she gets married, they need a new start, and they can't be associated with me. I have nothing but respect for her, and you'll make a better guard captain than I ever did."

Suzo calmed down. "Thank you. It just hurts, knowing what you went through, and knowing that you'll be punished for that."

"Anyone who thinks life is fair is a fool. Anyway, it frees me to perform other duties."

Suzo shifted, looking suddenly awkward. "That's actually what I wanted to talk to you about, if I could."

Asa waited for the guard to find her courage. It seemed unusual for this strong and determined woman to hesitate like this.

"Well," Suzo began, "I should probably start by saying that I'm not exactly who I said I was."

"What do you mean?" Asa's heart raced, wondering if Suzo was another traitor. She couldn't be, not after rescuing Asa.

"The story I told you about my family being poor, and about almost being sold? That wasn't true." She paused, taking a deep breath before continuing. "I actually lost both my parents at a young age. I ended up falling into smuggling. That's what I did before Lady Mari's offer to women. I left my smuggling crew to try out. I already knew I was pretty decent with a sword, and I knew that I wanted something different for my life."

Asa was stunned. She'd never suspected, but the story helped her understand some of the questions she'd had about Suzo. It explained why she'd taken to the sword so quickly. She'd already had some training, rough as it was.

And it explained why she'd known about the tunnels. No doubt they were popular with smugglers.

In Asa's mind, though, little of that mattered. If Suzo wasn't allowed to put her past behind her, then any good Asa had done since killing Kiyoshi was meaningless. Suzo deserved the chance.

"Will you protect Lady Mari with your life?"

"With all my lives, if I could."

Asa believed her. The woman had put herself completely in Asa's hands. "Then it doesn't matter. Was there something else you wanted to tell me?"

"I think I know where the man who killed Isamu is. At least, I know what area of town he's in."

She quickly related her efforts. After getting a description of the man from Asa, she'd spent the time after Isamu's death trying to find him. She'd disguised herself and visited some of her old haunts. She'd spent almost every waking moment that she wasn't guarding Mari trying to track the man down. Suzo's story made Asa feel ashamed of her own efforts. In contrast, Asa had spent the last few days moping around the castle. She'd never even thought of trying to track the assassin down.

Suzo was uncertain. Asa's description hadn't been too detailed, but she believed she'd seen the man a few times in the same areas of town.

"I wasn't certain enough to take action, but if you saw him, you could be sure," Suzo said. "And, if it is him, I think you should have the opportunity to speak to him first." The menace in her voice was unmistakable.

Asa was liking Suzo more and more these days.

Suzo led Asa to a part of Stonekeep that Asa hadn't

explored before. Asa found it fascinating that after all her time in the small city there were places she hadn't been. Her routine had been a cage in more ways than one.

They didn't have much of a plan. Suzo had never been able to track the man without arousing suspicion, but she'd seen him twice in the same area since the assassination. Given a lack of options, they chose to wander the area, stepping into a few of the more well-known taverns. The strategy relied on chance, but the section of town was small, and if Suzo was right, they had a decent chance of encountering the assassin.

The two wandered all afternoon, talking and occasionally stopping in taverns for a single drink. Now that Suzo's secret history was out in the open, they talked freely about their pasts. Asa found herself fascinated by smuggling routes, by ways to hide people and goods, and the culture of those who did so for a living.

Suzo found Asa's life interesting, but not in the way most people did, which turned out to be surprisingly refreshing. Most people wanted to know what it was like to be a nightblade, to have the sense. But trying to describe the sense to someone who didn't possess the gift was like trying to describe color to a blind man. Asa had always had it and didn't know what life was like without it. As such, she couldn't describe it well at all.

Suzo was more interested in the lifestyle of a nightblade. How did they train? Who decided where they traveled? How free were they to act? Asa enjoyed answering the questions, and from Suzo's sharp attention, she had no doubt the guard was memorizing useful information.

Evening fell, and the two still hadn't come across the man in question. They'd just left another tavern and Asa figured it would have to be the last for a while. She could feel the drink on the edge of her awareness. If they did find the assassin, she couldn't risk losing her edge. Whoever the man was, he at least had the courage to take on a nightblade, even if he didn't have the gift himself. That alone made him a rare breed.

Then they turned a corner and he was there. He looked up, and Asa saw that same half-smile on his face. If she hadn't been certain before, she was now. He froze, realizing instantly that he'd been recognized. That smile never left his face, though. He looked at Suzo, then at Asa.

"I wondered how you'd escaped," he said.

He looked behind him, as though he considered running. Then he shrugged and planted his feet in a warrior's stance, facing Asa.

"I've always wanted to fight a nightblade," he said. He drew his sword and Asa noticed that the blade glinted unnaturally in the light. She guessed a poison coated some or perhaps all of the weapon. She couldn't allow herself to get cut.

Killing the man was important, but she needed answers, too. "Who hired you, and why?"

"Now, now," the man said, "a gentleman never tells. As far as why, why do anything at all? It sounded like a challenge, something actually worth attempting."

He leaped forward, his cut well executed. Asa sensed the attack and was already moving, her own swords clearing their scabbards with ease. She slid around his cut, and his timing was thrown just a little off by her sudden movement. She sliced once as they passed, then turned and snapped off a cut with the other sword once she was behind him.

The man fell, dead before he even hit the ground.

Asa cleaned her swords and sheathed them. She glanced over at Suzo, who watched the whole scene appreciatively.

"I'd always figured you were good," Suzo said, "but I never realized you were that fast. He never had a chance."

Asa nudged the assassin's fallen sword with her boot, making sure not to touch the blade itself. "He'd coated his weapon with poison. A single nick probably would have been enough to kill."

Suzo approached and stared. "It would have been nice to know who he was working for."

Asa nodded. "Yes, but he never would have told us. Lady Mari will always have enemies. Now, finding them will be your responsibility."

Suzo looked at the corpse. "It certainly won't be a boring life, will it?"

Asa shook her head. "No, I don't think it will."

"Drink?" Suzo asked.

Asa smiled. "Yes, please."

ASA STOOD high above the dining room, in a small alcove protected by a dark sheet. Takahiro had shown it to her that morning. Mari had really wanted her to be part of the ceremony, and this was the closest she could get, given the political situation.

While most of the guests remained outside, Takahiro and Mari joined hands in the dining hall. Arata had been asked to perform the ceremony. They each took a turn reciting the words that would legally bind them together. Then they took three sips of wine. The first sip was offered by Arata, officially finalizing the ceremony. The second sip was taken alone, with each participant sipping from their own cup. Finally, the third sip was first offered by Mari to Takahiro, and then from Takahiro to Mari.

With that, the ceremony was complete. Arata moved to

the door to invite in the guests. As he crossed the hall, Mari looked up to where Asa stood. Asa bowed, and a small smile appeared on Mari's face. Asa knew Lady's Mari's struggles were far from over, but her marriage to Takahiro solved or delayed most of them. The decision had overjoyed her allies and frustrated her rivals. Officially, Mari had no power anymore. In reality, Asa expected the two of them would rule the house together. Takahiro knew Mari's worth, unlike those who constantly underestimated her.

The guests came in, each bowing deeply to the new lord and lady. Even this gathering was small. Most weddings of this magnitude would draw hundreds, if not thousands. But the land was in crisis, and the couple had desired a small, quiet ceremony. Asa didn't doubt the crowds on the streets were taking the opportunity to join in the revelry in their own way, but they hadn't been allowed into the castle.

Various nobles sat down to enjoy the feast. Asa noticed that some of Mari's most vehement enemies weren't present. Idly, she wondered if they hadn't been invited, or if they'd declined to attend. Before she could think too much about it, she stopped herself. This wasn't her world, and she didn't care why they weren't present. After so long in Mari's company, she'd started to develop her own political understandings. She'd be happy to lose them and return to a world where right action was far more obvious.

Thinking of that reminded her that she should be going. Her plan had been to leave before the evening fell and possibly make it down to the blade encampment below. She could get more information, then be on her way. As disappointed as she was to leave Lady Mari's side, the idea of being out on the open road, on her own again, was powerfully appealing.

Below, the feast went well. For a single afternoon, the

worries and cares of the house were put aside. They would still be there in the morning. For now, friends and allies mingled, sharing food, wine, and laughter. Part of Asa wanted to be down there, too. Had she not been such a dividing presence, she probably would have been invited.

But such was not her lot in life. She stood above the gathering, watching but not partaking. She was removed from the flow of this world, and she keenly felt like the outsider she was.

Asa focused her sense on the couple. Not being nightblades, their energy was weak, but she could still pick them out. As she shut out the other noise, focusing only on them, she could sense their hands touching. Perhaps it was only her imagination, but she thought she could sense a trickle of energy passing between them.

Asa waited until Lady Mari looked up one more time. Their eyes met across the room, and Asa bowed one final time, saying her goodbye. She wasn't sure she'd see Mari for a long time, if ever again. Mari seemed to understand, dipping her head just a little.

It was enough.

Asa turned and left, leaving the sounds of merrymaking behind her without a second glance.

20

The trip to the front was uneventful. General Emon might have hated Koji, but he was a man of his word. As soon as Koji was in chains, the rest of the blades were allowed to return to the lands of House Kita without injury. A small group of cavalry followed them to ensure they kept their word, but they were otherwise left alone.

As a prisoner of war, Koji wasn't treated with much respect, but he also wasn't harmed in any way. He rode in a cart surrounded by Emon's troops at all times. His wrists and ankles were manacled and chained to a bolt in the cart. While he had some freedom of movement and wasn't uncomfortable, he wouldn't be running or fighting anytime soon.

They didn't take any chances with him. He was never allowed to take his chains off, his weapons were never near, and a minimum of twenty men constantly surrounded him.

Recognizing his inability to escape, Koji quickly gave up thinking about it. He kept alert for mistakes, but stopped trying to create elaborate plans.

Sometimes General Emon came to speak to him, to ask

what knowledge Koji possessed, but he continued to be disappointed. Koji had no secret intelligence, and couldn't really give Emon the answers he wanted. He didn't know where the blades were or what they planned on doing next. He didn't know when Mari would launch her next offensive. He didn't even know who was in charge of House Kita at the moment. Apparently there some disagreement even about that.

Koji worried for Mari, and for Asa, but there was nothing he could do at the moment.

Beyond the occasional conversations with the general, Koji remained silent. He could see the looks of hate and disgust on the faces of his captors, hostility deeper than he was used to. These men didn't just hate him for being a nightblade. They hated him for being a monster.

Koji wallowed in self-doubt, the same he'd had since attacking the sleeping cavalry group. He'd always thought himself a warrior, but his actions, seen at a distance and through the eyes of others, certainly didn't seem like those of an honorable man. He'd killed nobles and men at sleep, and while it had been to serve another, he wasn't so sure that it justified his actions.

The guilt, which he'd managed to bury under his devotion to Lady Mari, had returned with a vengeance. He had killed a lord and a king, and if any one person was responsible for the suffering seen throughout the Kingdom, it was him. And instead of fixing the problem, he had become a demon. Perhaps he deserved his death.

He didn't have answers, but the questions that consumed him tore at him, demanding a resolution he couldn't give.

At some point he stopped asking, and his mind slipped into numb observation of the world around him. He didn't have much longer to sit with the questions, anyway. He breathed deeply and tried to take in as much of the world through all his senses, while he still could.

WHEN THEY REACHED THE FRONT, Koji was transferred from the cart to a tent. At first, he thought he would have a chance to escape. But once there, Koji encountered his first real surprise in some time: he had nightblades guarding him. As near as he could tell, there were at least five nightblades working with Katashi. During the day, one would guard his tent with a few cavalry officers. At night, when they seemed most worried, two guarded his tent at all times. Any thought of escape disappeared. Worse, the other nightblades slept just next to his tent. Even if he did somehow manage to kill the two guarding him, the other three would immediately wake up to their friends dying. Katashi took no chances with his prize captive.

Koji considered talking to the blades, but their occasional jeering comments made it clear no conversation would be possible. He kept his silence until Katashi himself showed up, escorted by two more blades.

Katashi looked as though he'd never had a hair out of place in his life. From the way he dressed, it would be easy to assume he'd never held a sword, but Koji saw the calloses on his hands and watched the way he moved. Katashi might not be as strong as Koji, but Koji knew he could defend himself. His manicured appearance, like everything else he did, was contrived. Everything was a calculation in his games, and he stood alone as a master of them.

Katashi looked Koji up and down, then knelt in front of him, outside of easy range. Koji's manacles were now attached by a longer chain to a heavy rock in the center of his tent. He had free range of the tent and a little outside, but beyond that he'd have to carry the rock. He could, but between the weight and his reduced stride, he wouldn't make it very far if he tried to escape. He figured if he was lucky he could run for three or four tent-lengths before someone caught him or cut him down.

The two blades stood directly behind Katashi, hands on the hilts of their swords, ready to draw the instant they sensed Koji trying to move. Even encumbered, the sight of the nightblades stoked his desire to fight. Could he kill Katashi before they killed him? He saw them tense, even as he had the thought. No, he didn't think he could, especially as slow as he felt these days.

"You've caused me no end of trouble."

Koji wasn't sure how to respond. In the past, he might have enjoyed antagonizing Katashi, but the gesture seemed empty now. Katashi would put him to death, and Koji could do nothing to stop it. Others might have felt courage, knowing their options were limited. Koji only felt resignation.

Katashi moved closer, and Koji suddenly realized he was being tested. Katashi was trying to push him. With the distance suddenly reduced, Koji wondered again if he could kill Katashi before he died. Now, the chance was better. Was it worth taking?

"Thinking about killing me? Why not? You killed my brother."

Sometimes Koji forgot that Katashi was Shin's younger brother. Now that it had been mentioned, the resemblance was remarkable.

Koji relaxed backward. He wouldn't kill Katashi, not like this. The man deserved death; of that, Koji had little doubt.

This was the man who had ordered Starfall burned to the ground. He'd killed countless blades and caused thousands to suffer. The crimes he'd committed against Mari alone were worth the most severe punishments.

But today, that punishment wasn't Koji's to dispense. "No. I will not kill you."

That seemed to take the wind out of Katashi's sails for a moment. He hadn't expected Koji to act reasonably. It made Katashi seem ridiculous in comparison.

Even if Koji had gone against his expectations, it only sent him off track for a moment. Katashi would always have plans within plans. "What if I told you that everything you fought for is falling apart?"

Koji simply looked at the lord, trying to stare the man down.

"Mari is no longer the head of House Kita. She married Takahiro, making him the new lord. And Takahiro will fall, soon. Lady Mari has been a true delight to plot against, but she doesn't know when to acknowledge that she's been beaten. As we speak, I have an assassin hiding in Starfall, ready to move against Mari the moment I tell him to. You two have quite a bit in common, killing lords. He's already killed Lord Isamu."

Koji could feel the anger building within. His muscles tensed, and he forced himself to relax. He knew Katashi was trying to get him to react. Koji would never think fast enough to outsmart Katashi, but attacking the lord somehow played right into his hands. He forced his muscles to relax.

Katashi upped the stakes, getting right into Koji's face. Koji couldn't fight his emotions any longer. He snarled and leaned forward, and in an instant, two blades were at his throat. Koji blinked. He'd sensed the moves, but those nightblades were fast. Of course, they'd been expecting it.

Katashi leaned back and laughed. "You like them? So many of your kind are busy killing themselves for noble causes, but you've shown them a new way, Koji. They don't have to be bound by tradition anymore, or by the laws our ancestors put into place. Thanks to you, they don't have to be neutral judges any longer. They can fight and be rewarded as their talents dictate."

Koji fought the guilt he felt. As much as he hated Katashi, he also knew the man spoke the truth. This was his doing. Perhaps the fault wasn't his alone, but his actions had made it far more likely for nightblades to act in such a way. Koji hated himself.

"You know," Katashi said. "I give my nightblades the best in everything. Plenty of money. The best food. The finest women. Perhaps you'd be interested in joining? With your skills, I have no doubt you'd live a life of leisure and enjoyment."

Koji glared at him. He knew the man couldn't be serious, but his seeming sincerity made Koji doubt.

Katashi broke out into another grin. "I don't think so. You don't quite have the qualifications I'm looking for, do you? You believe so deeply in Lady Mari, you just won't know what to do when she dies and House Kita is mine, will you? Fortunately for you, you won't live to see that day. In fact, you'll be a part of her downfall."

Koji finally found his voice. "Katashi, why are you here?" The lord had enjoyed tormenting him, but that couldn't have been his only purpose. Katashi always had an ulterior motive.

Katashi stopped smiling, and Koji thought for the first time he was seeing the man as he was. His voice changed, becoming steady. "I'm here because you and your kind need to be humbled. I wanted to ensure that you know what you've become. You've killed nobles in cold blood, and while you accuse me of evil deeds, you don't see your own. I've had to do horrible things to become a lord, but at least I know they're horrible. I commit my crimes with wide-open eyes, knowing that I will unify the Kingdom and bring an era of peace unlike any before it. But you are a demon who doesn't realize how black your own heart is. Your actions have plunged this Kingdom into chaos and cost thousands upon thousands of lives. You have abused your strength and torn families apart, mine included. I will end you and all those who put their hope in you."

Katashi paused, then made sure Koji met his gaze. "By the time I am done, I will be king. Lady Mari will be dead or exiled, and a friendly noble from House Kita established, ending her line. Every blade who stands against me will die. And tomorrow, your death will be the start of it all."

With that, Katashi stood and left, the traitorous nightblades following him out.

Koji wasn't sure he'd ever been in a darker mood. As much as he hated to give Katashi the victory, his words had cut Koji deep. Combined with the doubt he already felt, he was beginning to look forward to his execution the following day. Although no one knew exactly what happened after death, Koji had been around enough fighting to sense the energy in a person returning to the Great Cycle. He didn't believe death was the end, but simply an ending.

Lacking options, he tried to make peace with his upcoming end. He had made many mistakes in life, and the least he could do was die with dignity. He would miss some things, like the time spent with Asa, but perhaps even she would be better off without him. If he did get another chance at life someday, perhaps he would have the wisdom to see farther ahead.

He sensed one of the nightblades from the tent get up and leave, called away by some duty. He shook his head, trying to clear it of distractions. If this was his last night alive, he could spend it in meditation.

For a while he managed to focus on his breath, but it didn't last long. His mind refused to be controlled. In the past, he'd always had some feeling of purpose he could cling to, something to guide him. Now, at the end of his life, he found he had nothing left.

The blade headed back to the tent beside them. Or at least, that was how it seemed at first. Before the nightblade got to the tent, he detoured and came toward Koji's tent. Koji ignored the information his sense provided, cutting himself off from the world.

That only lasted a few minutes as he heard the soft sounds of a scuffle outside. Koji frowned and embraced his sense once again. Now that he was trying to pay attention, he felt foolish for not having noticed earlier.

Asa.

As soon as he thought of her, she stepped into the tent, wearing the red uniform of Katashi's soldiers. He had always found her attractive, but at that moment, he thought she was the most beautiful person he'd ever seen. She gave him a look. "So, it seems that Katashi has some nightblades on his side."

Koji realized she hadn't killed the guards outside. He was only confused for a moment. If she had killed the blades, the other blades sleeping in the tent nearby would have noticed. Turning his mind to the present, he nodded. "He does."

"Anything else I should know before trying to get you out of here?" She dumped a red uniform in front of him and went to work unlocking his manacles.

Even as she brushed against him, freeing him from captivity, he realized how much he'd missed her. He shook his head. "Not that I know of, but I'm probably not the best source of information at the moment."

They worked quickly, and it didn't take them long to drag the unconscious guards into the tent and get Koji changed.

He glanced at her. "How did you find me?"

"It wasn't too hard. Everyone's been talking about the execution, so I figured you were with the main army. I simply disguised myself and wandered toward the middle of the camp. Before long I sensed the other blades. I didn't know how to approach without giving myself away, but Katashi also has a few guarding him. When the nightblades rotated their watch, I ambushed one, so my approach wouldn't be remarked on."

Koji nodded. No one was better at infiltrating enemy encampments than Asa. Her training with Daisuke had given her some enviable talents. "How much of a problem will we have getting out?"

Asa shrugged. "The guard patrols are focused to the east, where Katashi's forces face Lady Mari's. I approached from the south, but had to kill two guards. I don't think the bodies have been found yet, but I'd suggest leaving to the north. Then we can work our away around the army and make our way to the nightblade encampment. I assume Hajimi will want to meet with you."

Koji thought back to his conversation with Katashi. "I've

learned things I need to tell Mari, too. Perhaps he will let me send a bird."

Asa nodded and gave Koji one last appraising look. Seemingly satisfied, she turned and slipped out of the tent, Koji following close behind her. Soon the darkness of the night swallowed them up.

BACK IN THE BLADE CAMP, Koji and Asa relaxed together in a small tent found for them. Koji rested his head on Asa's lap, enjoying the feeling of her hands running through his hair. Upon his arrival, they'd been whisked to Hajimi, where Koji had written Lady Mari a letter while suffering Hajimi's relentless stream of questions.

In return, Koji hadn't received much, if any, information at all. His presence in the camp was being kept quiet, and he'd been asked to remain mostly indoors for the next few days. Koji had the feeling that important events were unfolding around him, but for now, his only duty was to wait.

In the past, he would have fought against the lack of activity. Today, though, he didn't find it much of a problem. For the first time in as long as he could remember, he had no desire to rush out and take part in the world's problems. He was content, here with the woman he cared for.

"Is this how you feel?" he asked.

She gave him a confused look.

"I know that a storm is coming, but for now, I'm happy just to be here. I don't care as much about what happens outside this tent."

She nodded. "Sometimes. Perhaps it is selfish, but sometimes I think we are so concerned with trying to create a better world we forget to stop and enjoy the one we're in."

He glanced up at her. "You've changed, too."

She just continued playing with his hair, not responding. Once they'd gotten beyond the patrol lines, they'd spoken softly as they made their way toward the blades' encampment. She'd caught him up on her adventures, but he noticed that she didn't say much about her own captivity. Koji knew her well enough to know that she'd tell him in time, if she ever desired.

"What's next?" he asked, thinking aloud.

"I would like to join one of the next groups out of the Kingdom," Asa replied.

Koji surprised himself by not being upset about the decision. After his own experiences, the idea of leaving it all behind sounded more tempting than ever. But hope still died hard. "You don't think Hajimi will be able to work out an agreement?"

She shook her head sadly. "No. I think, after the events of the past few cycles, there won't be a home for us in the Kingdom anymore. Especially not with Lady Mari ceding her throne to Takahiro. There are so many rumors surrounding us that no one knows what is true or not. And I don't think many people care anymore. They believe we burned Haven to the ground, that we've killed kings and lords, and that we now massacre nobles in their homes." She gave Koji a pointed look.

He held up his hands in surrender. He'd been involved in far too many of the beginnings of those rumors.

"Yes, there's truth to some of the stories," Asa continued. "But the truth doesn't matter. I think we've gone too far. People believe we've destroyed the Kingdom, and I don't think that trust can be repaired. I think if we stay we either get wiped out in one big push, or we get slowly hunted to extinction. Our only hope is to leave."

Koji found himself agreeing with Asa. For once, their views aligned. He couldn't shake the way Katashi's soldiers had looked at him as they'd transported him. He was used to hints of fear and sideways glances, but he'd never seen such disgust before. If those soldiers were indicative of the rest of the Kingdom, Koji couldn't imagine enough acts of goodwill to repair the damage.

"If you're going," Koji decided, "then I'll come with."

She looked at him with surprise. "Did they hit you on the head when they captured you?"

He grinned ruefully. "Sometimes I wished they would have. But no, I simply understand your reasoning better than before, and I'm not sure what we can do to make it better. At the very least, we need to protect our people."

Saying the words still made him shudder. "Our people," in his mind, should be everyone. But when the rest of the world didn't agree, what good did his idealistic view do? Koji didn't see blades as being particularly different than anyone else, but he stood alone in that decision.

Asa leaned down and kissed his forehead. "Thank you. I didn't want to leave you again."

He reached up and pulled her closer. "And you'll never have to."

21

Mari sat across from Hajimi in her private receiving chambers. Ideally, she would have liked to meet him in the office space she used to use so often, but the space had become Takahiro's. He labored in there now, meeting with various nobles and advisers, trying to plan for the seasons ahead. Summer drew to a close, and the harvest this cycle had been particularly poor. Mari didn't know if it would be hunger or war that killed more of her people over the next six moons.

Takahiro complained, but he settled into the role of lord well. He'd been a guard for many cycles, intimately involved with the day-to-day happenings of Mari's family, so he knew every noble family already. He'd been chief adviser for Mari, so there'd been almost nothing he hadn't known when rising to the head of the house. All in all, it had been an incredibly smooth transition.

They enjoyed a brief respite from the chaos of the summer. Mari knew it wasn't real. The world would explode within the next half-moon. The forces of both houses marched against them as Fumio and Masaaki retreated. The best that could be said for the situation was that Fumio would at least be able to pick the battleground. Beyond that, there seemed little hope. Takahiro's forces would be outnumbered at least two to one, and possibly by three to one, if some scouting reports could be believed.

The question wasn't if there would be a final battle, but when it would happen. In theory, Fumio could retreat his forces all the way to Stonekeep, but then his army would die a slow death instead of a quick one. Katashi didn't need Stonekeep to rule the land. All he had to do was cut it off, which he was already only days away from doing. Takahiro could feed the people already inside Stonekeep, but he'd never keep all the soldiers fed if they settled in for a long siege.

No, they had to fight, and that deciding conflict would probably come in the next fortnight.

And now another problem sat in front of her. Hajimi, strangely enough, hadn't come to visit Takahiro. He'd requested Lady Mari specifically, and that made Mari very curious. She'd seen no reason to deny the request, so she'd had her private reception room made ready and the old blade had entered.

The stress of leading the blades had definitely aged Hajimi. Mari had known the man for many cycles, but he'd never seemed so old to her. His hair was almost completely white, and while he still moved with the deadly grace of a blade, he had lost too much weight to be healthy. They chatted about meaningless things for a while, Hajimi particularly interested in Mari's new marriage.

It wasn't like him to make small talk. In all her memories, he'd often shunned convention and driven straight to the point. But something in his bearing caused her not to mention her observation. This meeting, like so many things in her life, seemed to be an ending.

Finally, after a lull in the conversation, Hajimi handed a letter to Mari. "This is from Koji."

"He's alive?" Mari couldn't hide her surprise, and Hajimi hadn't said anything yet. They'd heard rumors that Katashi had killed the nightblade and placed his head on a pole that led his army. No one had been able to confirm the rumor, but Mari had accepted it as true.

"He's fine. Asa rescued him from Katashi's camp the evening before his execution. He would have come on his own, but given the attitude of many toward the blades in general, and the feelings toward him specifically, we decided it wise that he not make an appearance today."

As much as Mari would have liked to see the blade again, she knew the decision was correct. She opened the letter and read it, and more pieces fell into place. This letter was confirmation that Katashi had been the architect of most of her problems over the course of the past few moons. If she ever had the chance to sit in judgment of him, he would regret crossing her.

She lay the letter to the side. "Why come to me instead of Takahiro?"

"Because what I have to say, I think only you would understand."

She waited for him to continue.

"The blades are going to leave the Kingdom. They march within the next few days."

Mari frowned. In that time, enemy forces would cover the entire opening in the valley. A few lone warriors or travelers might be able to sneak through, but the whole of the blades would never have a chance. Although, even if they left today, they still probably wouldn't make it out of the valley before the jaws of the enemy closed on them. The battle was too close.

Hajimi saw the expression on her face and read it without problem. "Yes, we'll have to fight, but we need the time to gather food and supplies. We've been preparing as fast as possible, but given how difficult it is to feed people right now, it wasn't as fast as we would have liked."

"Where will you go?"

Hajimi shook his head. "You've been the strongest ally the blades have had in at least a generation, Lady Mari, but this I cannot tell you. The Kingdom will not have us anymore, and while many of us still desire to serve the Kingdom, the greatest service we can provide now is to leave. My only hope is that you'll be able to take advantage of our departure. We will punch a hole in the enemy lines. It will be your responsibility from there."

Mari's eyes narrowed. Even for the blades, attacking the enemy lines seemed foolish. Katashi had trained huge numbers of archers to fight against the blades, felling them from a distance. Against the sheer number of archers and soldiers, Mari didn't see how the blades could survive. "What are you planning?"

"Three nights from tonight, on the evening of the new moon, we will leave. We will move in the shadows, and we will attack them as they camp. I have no doubt we will kill many, but we won't seek to destroy them. Our goal is simply to escape. But if we can do this as a gift to you, as our final gift, we will."

Mari contemplated the horror of what was being discussed. The nightblades didn't need torches or light to fight by. They wouldn't be able to mask their movements, but in the new moon the archers wouldn't see well. It would be a devastating battle, on both sides. Perhaps the blades could sow enough confusion to give House Kita a chance to survive. If Takahiro could launch his attack at dawn, they might just have a chance.

The effort would be bloody, though. Very bloody. But did they have a better opportunity to win the war? Mari had considered the problem for a long time and hadn't found any better solutions.

"You'll do this, regardless of the actions of my house?"

Hajimi nodded.

"You know that this will finish the blades. Even as it is, I'm not sure I see a way to restore your power, but this will poison the people against you for generations."

"We understand. But we hold no hope for ourselves any longer. You alone have the foresight to take our sacrifice and forge peace with it. Even if we are hated, we can give this one last gift. It will be your responsibility to ensure the peace lasts."

With that, Hajimi stood. He offered Mari one last bow. "It has been an honor fighting by your side, Lady Mari."

Before she could even reply in kind, he left. She watched him go, and Mari wondered if she would ever see any of the blades again.

TWO DAYS LATER, the deadline for action approached. The casual observer wouldn't have noticed any preparations, or at least Mari hoped that was the case. But behind the scenes, both she and Takahiro had been busy. Hajimi's intuition had guided him well. Takahiro had been furious at the news, both because he felt betrayed by the blades abandoning his house, and also because as a soldier he saw this sort of action as entirely dishonorable.

But what could they do? They couldn't turn on the

blades, and they couldn't sacrifice the opportunity the blades would give them. Takahiro hated the blades, and hated himself for the decisions he'd been forced to make, but he'd still made them. Everyone understood the stakes.

There was one part of Koji's letter that Mari hadn't shared with Takahiro. Now, just before it became too late, she was beginning to understand how Katashi's devious mind worked. And although they still had a battle down in the valley below to fight, they had their own here in the castle.

Mari sat in her private reception room, trying not to fidget nervously. She looked around again, making sure that everything appeared just so. She could have used the office for this task, but she didn't want to. She wanted to look weak and beaten. Having the meeting here would promote that idea. She glanced back at the door that led to her bedchamber. The door stood open, but the room looked empty inside. She walked around the reception area, her eyes always on that door.

Finally satisfied, she returned to sitting. Eventually there was a knock on the door, and Suzo opened it slowly to admit Yoshinori.

Even the sight of the noble made Mari's skin crawl, but she controlled her revulsion. She asked Suzo to bring in tea, and the guard nodded silently, her face betraying nothing. She'd been an excellent choice to replace Asa.

Yoshinori's eyes swept over the room, as though looking for a trap. Mari motioned for him to sit, and he did. The tea came in moments later and they sat there in silence, each studying the other. Mari gave him long enough to become comfortable with the environment, then proceeded. "Thank you for coming."

Yoshinori didn't even bother with proper manners. "What do you want, Lady Mari?"

Mari pulled out a letter. She held it up, then tossed it casually between them. "I received a message from one of my spies not long ago, a serving woman who's been in Katashi's employ now for cycles. She claimed to have overheard a discussion in which you figured prominently. Katashi claimed that he had an assassin in our city. One who killed Isau, and who killed Lord Isamu while making it look like a nightblade's fault. He claims that the assassin's next target is me."

"And what does any of that have to do with me?" Yoshinori wasn't even flustered.

"Well," said Mari, "Katashi also claimed you knew all about this. That you were a conspirator with him. Yoshinori, how could you?"

The letter in front of them did say that, but it was based on Koji's letter to her, which hadn't painted nearly so complete a picture. Koji only knew that Katashi was coordinating with a noble inside Stonekeep. But Mari was confident in her deductions. She only needed Yoshinori to believe that she had evidence.

"How could I?" Yoshinori shook his head, glancing around the room one last time. "I could because I believe you are destroying this house. Anyone with reason should see it. I regret the loss of life, but a leader must be able to make the hard decisions. Thanks to my work, this house will survive."

Mari didn't think she'd get any closer to a confession from him. "If you really believe in saving these lands, Yoshinori, throw your unconditional support behind my husband. I will never show him this letter. You have my word."

The statement had been carefully crafted. Mari assumed Yoshinori saw her as idealistic and naïve, and that if she was going to attempt blackmail, it would look something like this.

Yoshinori chuckled. "Lady Mari, you believe in your own lies, don't you?"

Mari tried to appear shaken.

"I don't care if you share that with your husband. What will he do? In less than three days Lord Katashi will be here, and Takahiro will step down or be killed. And finally, I'll lead this house. We both know you don't have the support of enough nobles to execute me. If you tried, half your house would revolt."

"Is there no way we can come together and unify our people?"

Yoshinori stood up, apparently tired of this thread of conversation. "In a few days, Lady Mari, you may come to me begging for mercy. Until then, do not bother me again. There is much work to be done."

He turned and left the room, and Mari waited a few moments after the door was closed to allow herself to smile.

Takahiro and a select group of nobles stepped out of the bedchamber, where they'd hidden far out of sight, but where they'd been able to hear the entire discussion. Arata was present, of course, but more important, several of Yoshinori's supporters stood there, too. They'd been selected carefully. Some of Yoshinori's supporters would stand behind him regardless of his actions, but there were several who supported him only because they believed he was the best choice to lead their house lands. Like her, they supported dissent, but could never condone treason.

All it took was one glance at the faces around the room

to know that it had worked. Yoshinori had underestimated her for the last time, and had hung himself cleanly.

The nobles spoke softly for a few moments, gathered around Takahiro. As tempted as Mari was to join the conversation, it would be better if Takahiro alone handled this challenge. She waited demurely, off to the side, as Takahiro gave his guidance to the other nobles.

In short order the meeting finished, and Takahiro escorted all the nobles to the door. Once they were alone, he turned back to Mari. "You're sure it was wise to allow him to leave? He deserves death, but at least we could have captured him."

Mari shook her head. "Better the enemy you know than the one you don't. Now that Yoshinori's treason is known, we can feed him false information. If that is relayed to Katashi, that's another advantage we have. He can watch all his plans crumble around him, and then we can arrest him and execute him."

Takahiro nodded. The whole setup had been Mari's idea, but he saw the wisdom in it. Takahiro wasn't a subtle person by nature. When he saw a problem, he attacked it head on. Mari wasn't sure he'd have survived the political infighting of House Kita on his own. But he was a leader they could look up to in troubled times, and Mari was happy to work with him to rule the house. They'd taken care of one problem, and now there was only one left. They needed to survive the next few days and force the other houses to sign a new treaty.

22

The sun fell below the mountains behind Stonekeep, and Asa and Koji packed up their tent and supplies. As usual, torches had been lit as night fell, and combined with the fading light of the sun, there was just enough light to work by. The torches would remain lit and in place even as the blades began moving out, supporting the illusion that the camp was still present.

The past few days had been filled with preparation. Carts were acquired, food was prepared and stored, and organization was determined. The blades had always had a home, but that home was no longer theirs. When they left the encampment, they would be a nomadic people, at least for a while.

Asa and Koji had learned the news with the rest of the blades. The council had decided on a new land beyond the Kingdom, a place where they were certain the blades could live in peace. Hajimi didn't say more, not wanting to give away anything to the lords. As Koji's experience had so well proven, not all the blades were loyal. Some had loyalties to a lord, or only to themselves. Only Hajimi and a few others knew where they would go. The other blades were asked to take the journey on trust alone.

Asa didn't think Hajimi would have much trouble with most of the blades. As she'd walked among the camp the last few days, she'd seen enough to know that the blades were near the edge of their limit. Hajimi had recalled the blades fighting with Lady Mari's forces, and Asa saw their exhaustion-lined faces, the empty stares that indicated warriors who had pushed too hard.

Even those who had lived in the camp all summer looked ready for a new start. Their homes had been destroyed, and now they lived in a tent city with the constant awareness that they were surrounded by enemies. That inability to relax, to enjoy life without worry even for a few days, took a toll on a person. Asa had never imagined she'd see the blades in such horrible conditions.

Hajimi held out hope, though. He shone a light at the end of their darkness. Like miners trapped in a tunnel, the blades scrabbled furiously toward that last glimmer of light.

Hajimi's plan was simple. As night fell and it became harder to observe the camp, they were to finish packing and storing their supplies. Carts had been left throughout the camp, and all packing that could reasonably be done beforehand had been. But as soon as night fell, the tents and final supplies would be loaded onto the carts. The carts would then move out, with most of the remaining nightblades leading them out the valley and eventually to the north. Dayblades and those too weak to fight would stay close to the carts.

The mouth of the valley that led to Stonekeep was well over a league wide, but Katashi's forces had joined with those of the new Lord Satoru, Isamu's successor. They had filled most of the valley. The blades were going to drive straight through the heart of Katashi's forces. Koji had observed, when he heard the plan, that when the blades left the Kingdom, they would destroy most of the lords' ability to make war as well. Asa wondered how intentional that decision was.

Asa helped Koji finish packing the cart that he would be escorting. Even though there wasn't anything physically wrong with him, Koji had decided not to take part in the upcoming battle. He would escort a cart himself, following the other nightblades as they cleared a path.

The two of them had talked late into several nights about Koji's challenges. At one time, his energy had been almost blinding, even at rest. Now, he felt almost like a regular citizen, his skills as a blade almost useless. Asa firmly believed that Koji had lost his center. Koji wasn't Koji unless he was fighting for something he believed in, but he'd seen the directions that blind belief could lead him in. Because of that, he didn't believe in much at all, and the source of his strength had waned.

She hated to see him like this, but he was finding his way. Choosing not to take part in this battle was part of it. He'd told her that their night raid on Katashi's forces was far too similar to a choice he'd made over the summer, and he didn't want to be involved in anything like that again. He'd help the blades by escorting the cart, but he wouldn't repeat his mistakes. Asa wished he would lend them his strength, but she respected the decision he'd made.

"Are you ready?" he asked her as she loaded up the last of their goods. She turned and looked over the empty patch where their temporary home had been. When they stopped again, they could build a real home. She looked at him, eager for the opportunity. Sometimes she struggled to believe that they'd only known each other for a few cycles.

Sometimes, she felt as though they'd known each other since the days of their birth.

"I am."

"Be safe," he said.

"You too." Asa wanted to say more, but the words couldn't quite form on her lips. She approached the cart, pulled Koji down to her, and gave him a kiss.

She could feel his initial surprise, then his pleasure as he relaxed. Asa had never been much for public affection, but it was the best she could express herself at the moment.

She broke the kiss off, giving him a playful shove. She didn't say anything else as she strode forward into the formation of nightblades gathering at the head of the column.

ASA WAS among the last of the blades to form up. She took direction from another blade, finding a place near the middle of the formation. The blades with battle experience formed the front ranks, paired up with partners they had trained with and trusted. Asa, not being a part of Koji's new tactics, was relegated to the main body.

There had been some discussion about attempting to train all the nightblades in the tactics Koji had used in his battles. Some training sessions had been held, and many new partners had learned to work together, but there simply hadn't been enough time to train everyone.

As they began their march, Asa felt a vaguely familiar presence sidle up next to her. She looked down and saw Junko, the young nightblade she'd rescued from Starfall, walking next to her. She hadn't seen Junko in well over a moon, locked up in palace intrigue as she had been. Junko met her gaze, and Asa realized the girl had grown up since they'd last met. The girl who'd been terrified of soldiers was gone, replaced by a young warrior, a blood feud burning in her eyes.

Asa considered telling the girl to go back, to join the carts where she should be safer. But she reconsidered. There were many warriors among their ranks who were too young. But if they could handle a sword and were willing, they'd been allowed to join the ranks of the fighting nightblades. Junko wasn't even the smallest that she could see in the immediate area.

When Asa looked at the girl, she saw more of herself than she was comfortable with. Like Junko, she'd lost her family too early, and from the way the girl moved and the determination in her eyes, Junko had thrown herself into training the same way Asa had.

"It's good to see you," Asa said.

The girl, who looked as though she'd been nervous, suddenly brightened. "Thank you. I've been training hard."

"I can tell." Asa debated her next words, finally deciding they were right. "Shall we fight together?"

Junko nodded, and although she didn't speak, Asa could see the way she set her jaw. Ever since Starfall, the girl had looked up to Asa. Now she'd finally earned the chance to fight next to her. If Junko wasn't foolish, Asa didn't mind having another blade nearby keeping an eye on her, either. Between the two of them, their swords would make quick work of unsuspecting enemies.

"Just listen to whatever I tell you to do," Asa said. It wouldn't be as good as having trained together, but if Junko trusted Asa's sense in the midst of battle, they could work well together.

Junko agreed, and the two of them walked toward their final fight.

"I never did thank you for rescuing me," Junko said.

"You don't have to," Asa replied.

"I do," Junko disagreed. "I trained in combat my entire life, but none of it meant anything until you came. Now, I know what it means to fight for a purpose."

Asa looked at the girl, surprised. Junko kept her face forward, not meeting Asa's eyes.

After a few moments, Asa followed suit.

They all walked as quietly as they were able, but over a thousand blades couldn't move without making a sound. From the creak of the carts to a man coughing viciously a few paces away, their advance would hardly be a surprise to anyone. Junko noticed the problem first.

"Aren't we supposed to be closer to those mountains?"

Asa looked to the dim outlines of the peaks to the north. In the darkness of night they stood like silent giants, barely illuminated by the stars above. Junko was right, though. If the blades were marching to the heart of Katashi's camp, they needed to be closer to the mountains.

Asa's confusion only lasted for a moment until she figured it out. "We're not heading straight for Katashi's camp. Hajimi lied to us all in case there were spies among us."

Asa jumped up, trying to see over the mass of blades in front of her. She felt foolish, and it took her a few attempts, but eventually she was able to get an idea of where they were going. In front of them were two distinct camps of light. One had to be Katashi's, and the other Satoru's. They were heading roughly between the camps.

Hajimi's true strategy struck Asa as being much more sensible. Had they attacked the heart of Katashi's camp, the carts would have struggled among the tents, no matter how much damage their attack created. By trying to split the forces, the blades could hopefully create confusion between the opposing armies. With luck, Katashi and Satoru might even attack each other for a while.

Asa figured the night was half over by the time they neared the enemy. Every step heightened her anticipation, and she saw no small number of blades holding onto their hilts nervously.

Off in the distance, to the north, a sudden burst of red light hung in the sky. Asa took a short glance at it, just as several more lights joined the first. The lights drifted slowly to the ground, like a firework that refused to burn out. With a start, Asa realized the enemy was attempting to light the battlefield.

In the flickering red light, she saw that Katashi's camp was up and prepared for battle. Koji had worried that they'd be attacking a sleeping army, but someone within the ranks of the blades had warned Katashi. However, they'd expected a charge through their camp. As a result, Katashi had lined his forces up against an empty field.

Suddenly, the mass of blades shifted as though through some unspoken command. Perhaps orders had been given at the front and Asa hadn't heard. Regardless, the blades changed direction, heading more to the north now, deeper into Katashi's camps.

The red light didn't illuminate the enemy like Katashi's men had expected, but they cast enough light that they could see the columns of blades. Lines attempted to re-form just as the blades hit them, and chaos erupted everywhere.

For a few surreal moments, Asa felt as though she stood in the heart of a battle without any of the danger. In front of her, as the lines clashed, the sounds of battle echoed. But for the moment, she was surrounded only by fellow blades.

The moment didn't last long. Soon, soldiers in red

uniforms started streaming through the blades, and Asa's swords came out, her body already responding to the nearest threat.

With so many bodies in such a confined space, her sense couldn't travel far. She pushed it out to about five paces, then reined it in. The information was near the edge of what she could handle safely in combat, and her skills had never been put to the test like this. In a heartbeat she went from seeing a handful of soldiers to being nearly inundated with them.

For most encounters, her strategy was simple. She parried blows with one blade while cutting with the other. In the cramped press of bodies, the shorter length of her swords became an advantage, as did the additional steel. Asa felt Junko only a few paces away and moved in that direction, cutting down a young man who was about to strike at the nightblade.

The two women held their ground, clearing the space surrounding them. Asa allowed herself to leave her back exposed, trusting Junko to cover it, the same as she covered Junko's. The girl wasn't bad. Some of her strikes were a little wild, but she was fast and fearless, and in the dark, they possessed plenty of advantages.

The eerie red light diminished, but new ones were launched into the air. Asa guessed they were supposed to negate some of the nightblades' advantages, but the reality was almost the opposite. The flickering red light allowed Katashi's soldiers to think they should be able to see, but it wasn't bright or constant enough for combat. Katashi's soldiers trusted their eyes and were betrayed, while the nightblades trusted their sense and were rewarded.

Still, the difference in numbers was telling. All the advantages in the world counted for very little if you could be cut down from behind while focusing on the enemy in front of you.

Paired up, Asa and Junko managed to avoid the fate of many of the blades near them. Without someone to watch their back, too many blades fell to overwhelming numbers. But Asa and Junko kept their space clear, advancing one bloody step at a time.

Every once in a while, Asa had to yell at Junko to slow down. The girl's eagerness was almost the death of her, and she needed to fight her desire to wade constantly deeper into the battle. Fortunately, she listened to Asa's commands, and every time they almost split apart, she either returned or waited for Asa to catch up.

In the short breaks between individual fights, Asa sometimes risked looking up at the mountains, trying to pin their position down. The blades had started the march heading almost directly west, but after the lights had been lit, they shifted their direction northwest. Asa hoped that the carts remained safe from the worst of the fighting.

Time and place lost all meaning as the fighting continued. Most of the blades had tried to sleep the day before, knowing the long night that waited for them. But if most were like Asa, their rest had only been intermittent. All Asa could do was keep her sense focused tightly on the space immediately around her and hope for the best.

She barely noticed when the green uniforms started joining with the red uniforms. In the darkness, color was hard to make out, and enemies and friends looked much alike. Only to the sense was there a difference, the glowing energy of a nightblade brighter than the dull light of a house soldier.

Hajimi's plan, if that was what it was, seemed to be working. The red lights in the sky were becoming more intermittent, and Asa figured they were running out of whatever they were. With less light and more darkness, Asa reveled in the additional advantage. Without the flickering light, Katashi and Satoru's forces fought one another almost as often as they fought against nightblades.

Junko and Asa encountered a clump of soldiers, all fighting against one another. The two blades skirted around the conflict, only to find themselves in the heart of another battle. Junko attracted three opponents and Asa two. The soldier on Asa's left cut down, and Asa moved her left sword up to deflect the strike. As she did, the soldier on the right cut across, a vicious slice with more anger than technique behind it. Asa stepped backward, sensing the swing coming. The soldier's blade cut in front of her, missing by a narrow margin. Unable to control his cut, the soldier cut through his partner, who couldn't block as his own sword had been knocked out of the way by Asa's deflection. The man fell, a look of surprise and betrayal on his face.

The soldier on Asa's right looked shocked and numb as he realized what he'd just done. Asa didn't give him time to regret his decision, stabbing into his throat with one quick motion.

Behind her, Junko was hard pressed. Her sword moved quickly, but against three opponents, she needed to give ground that wasn't there to give. Asa sensed all the strikes. "Junko, down!"

Had Junko been fighting alone, the decision would have killed her. She listened, though, dropping into a low squat without hesitation. One cut passed just over her head, and Asa spun and slashed at the other two attacks, knocking them off their lines. Junko didn't waste the openings Asa had given her. She stabbed through one opponent as Asa twisted and cut at the other two.

Out of position, Asa's attacks didn't do much but force the other two to give up ground, but then Junko joined the counterattack, and the two men fell quickly against the combined might of the two women. Junko gave Asa a small nod of appreciation and they waded deeper into the battle.

ASA SAT, utterly exhausted, her muscles limp, as she watched the scene from the small rise she and Koji had climbed to.

The blades had broken through Katashi's lines a little before daybreak, and by the time the sun had risen, the blades were out of range of Katashi's archers. Too many had been lost to arrows after the worst of the fighting was over.

The fight had been brutal, a bloody mess of swords and hatred, and both sides had paid the price.

Katashi's forces had been broken, and for every blade that had fallen, Katashi had lost at least three men. Katashi was still a threat, but Asa was reasonably certain he now had the smallest force on the field, as well as the most disorganized. Satoru's forces had taken casualties as well, but they'd largely remained out of the fighting. The new lord of the southern lands now found himself with the largest fighting force. Unfortunately, unlike Katashi's troops, who had trained diligently both under Lord Shin and Lord Katashi, the southern troops were inexperienced. Isamu had never prepared for war.

Koji sat down next to Asa. His black robes were covered in blood that wasn't his own. The carts had been attacked, and Koji had been forced to defend them. By all accounts, some of the fiercest fighting had taken place back there. Asa wanted to ask about it, but Koji's attitude made it clear he didn't want to speak about the evening.

Together they looked over the battlefield they'd just left. Katashi's forces were trying to regroup, and Satoru's forces looked to be in disarray. Katashi hadn't shared his intelligence of the impending attack with his ally, and many of Satoru's men had been asleep when the battle began. They'd woken up to red lights in the sky and the sounds of battle, but had been completely disoriented.

Even now, this morning, from the movement of troops among the camp, it looked like Satoru wasn't sure if he would attack, camp, or retreat that day.

In contrast to the two opposing armies, the combined force of all of House Kita's troops rode down into the valley from the mountains they'd traveled through for many days now. They formed up in the valley below Stonekeep, lines orderly. Asa assumed the battle would begin soon.

Most of the blades continued to march north. Neither Asa nor Koji knew where Hajimi led them, but the blades followed without question. The price of breaking through Katashi's lines had been high. Asa estimated there weren't more than four hundred blades left in the group. Although many still certainly wandered the Kingdom, Asa was certain their total number was far less than a thousand now. So few of them were left.

Some blades had come with Asa and Koji, curious about the outcome of their actions. Maybe three dozen stood or sat on the hillside. Junko had wanted to join them, but Asa had insisted the girl remain with the others. She didn't need to see yet another battle.

Even after the nightblades' actions, Takahiro's forces still seemed to be outnumbered, although not by much anymore. They'd certainly never have a better opportunity to defend their land. Just as Asa had the thought, the House Kita troops started marching forward. Before long, archers were sending waves of arrows into the enemy troops.

Katashi's forces responded, though more sluggishly than Asa had seen them react in the past. They'd been up all night fighting and had taken heavy losses. Takahiro's troops were well rested and defending their homeland. Would it be enough?

It didn't take long for the lines to collide. They were far enough away that Asa couldn't pick out the details of the fight, but neither side seemed to be gaining an advantage. As the sun rose and heated the late summer day, the fight seemed to stall.

Few of the blades spoke, and when they did, it was usually in hushed whispers. Asa and Koji remained silent, watching as the fate of the Kingdom was decided without them.

As Asa's eyes drifted over the battlefield, her attention was drawn to Katashi's forces. They were hard pressed, and except for one pocket, seemed to be on the verge of collapse. Then Asa saw Katashi's flag, far back near the rear of the formation. The man rarely risked himself in combat. A hard decision occurred to her.

Katashi's men weren't paying any attention to their flank. Under normal circumstances, they wouldn't need to worry. The mountains protected them from forces trying to work their way around the battle. But they'd forgotten about the nightblades. She looked around. No one else had noticed, or if they had, they didn't care.

But they could go back. They all had more than enough reason to kill Katashi. He was the one who'd burned Starfall to the ground, who had murdered a fellow lord in cold blood.

Asa turned to see if she could see the column of blades

retreating to the north. They had moved out of her sight. They had already left everything behind.

Asa thought of the freedom that awaited her. A home where she wouldn't be judged for the skills she possessed. All she had to do was nothing.

And she thought of Mari, smiling up at her as she got married.

Asa stood up, attracting the attention of most of the blades. She pointed to Katashi's flag. "Katashi is undefended from the rear. I'm going to kill him. Anyone want to help?"

23

P art of Koji had simply stopped thinking. He was finding it easier to go as the wind tossed him, like a ship upon stormy seas. The best he could do was ride the waves.

He followed Asa and the almost two dozen nightblades. Like him, they hadn't seemed to need much convincing. He approved of Asa's decision even as he was surprised she'd made it. Seeing Katashi brought to justice for the crimes he'd committed would be satisfying. Having met the man in person, Koji was certain he should never be allowed to rule.

He felt a spark of something inside him as they ran toward Katashi's lines, something he hadn't felt in many days. He stood with Asa, running toward a battle with other blades at his side. His actions were entirely his own, and what they did was *right*. He felt so in his bones.

With every step, energy built within him. The closer Katashi came, the angrier Koji became at everything that had happened. His energy surged, like a wave cresting just before it crashed, and although he'd already fought for an entire evening, his steps were light and his focus sharp.

Those around him seemed to feel it, too. Koji ran faster, overtaking Asa. They shared a glance and she nodded. She had started the charge, but he would lead it. He felt as light as air, power welling up inside him. He increased his pace. Although the other nightblades were also tired, he could feel them keep up easily as well. Together, they shone brightly in his sense, almost blinding in their intensity.

Koji saw a few haphazard arrows being launched into the sky. Some of the archers had noticed them and were trying to pick them off. The blades hadn't come equipped with shields today. They had traveled lightly to break through Katashi's lines, and they hadn't thought they'd need them when they climbed the hill to observe the battle.

They couldn't sense the arrows, either. Their gift only worked with living objects, so sight was their only defense.

Fortunately, there was no organized resistance. Koji and the blades saw the arrows and were able to easily dodge the few that came close. The archers did warn the back lines, though, and by the time Koji and the other blades closed the remaining distance, they were facing organized lines.

Koji knew Katashi would surround himself with some of his best warriors. He wondered whether the lord would dare include the nightblade mercenaries under his command. Although his sense got confused if he sent it too far into the battlefield, Koji didn't sense any other blades.

Koji slapped a spear aside as he hit the lines. The spearman held on to his weapon, but the force of Koji's strike turned him slightly to the side. Koji cut and the man fell, opening the first gap in the line. Koji twisted as another spear point came at him, driving his elbow into a soldier's face. He let his momentum carry him into the middle of enemies, stopping only when he rammed his shoulder against a giant of a man in heavy armor.

The giant stood at least two heads above Koji, and his armor bulged over muscles. Moving more quickly than Koji expected, the man swung one of his meaty fists at Koji, the nightblade too close for the man's long, curved sword.

Koji sensed the blow coming from far away. He stepped back, letting the fist pass in front of him. Before the giant could respond, he brought his sword up to block another attack from another enemy, and then another.

Then the giant swung his sword in a deadly arc. Koji had seen such blades before, but not often. They were too big for the average warrior. This man, though, held it as well as Koji had ever seen. The blade cut almost horizontally, and Koji couldn't step far enough away to avoid it, the reach too long. He brought up his own sword, bracing it with his free hand. The huge sword clanged off Koji's, redirecting up and away from him.

Koji's arms quivered at the force of the impact, and he barely recovered in time to respond to the other soldiers around him. He needed to clear his space so he could focus on the giant, but he had too many attackers to deal with at once. He was fortunate not to have been skewered already.

Where were the other blades? He wished he had even a moment to pause and assess the situation. He could feel their presence several paces behind him, so close and yet unreachable. A spear snuck in between two enemy warriors and Koji had no place to dodge. He twisted and the spear cut along his upper left arm.

Koji ignored the pain, focused only on getting to Katashi. He cut down a soldier between defending against attackers, but another immediately stepped into his place. Koji wasn't sure how much longer he could avoid the sheer number of strikes coming at him.

Suddenly, Asa was beside him, her twin blades flashing

and blocking strikes. Koji flowed into an attack stance as she passed, his sword cutting down and then across. Soldiers started falling, and for the first time in several moments, Koji advanced against the enemy.

The giant warrior saw an opening and swung down at Asa. Koji couldn't react in time, but Asa dove out of the way. Koji attacked the soldiers around her as she returned to her feet. Then another nightblade plowed into the mix and the battle became more even. The giant took his sword and cut horizontally, forcing the blades back.

Koji stepped into the space behind the attack. The giant had the advantage of reach, and he was plenty quick for a man of his size. But Koji refused to feel intimidated. He gripped more tightly to the hilt of his sword, taking comfort in the cold, unbending steel. He'd taken on every difficult opponent he could find, and this man was no different.

The giant stepped forward and cut down, allowing gravity to do much of the work accelerating the sword. Koji's first impulse was to deflect the attack, but he remembered the opening he'd allowed the last time their swords had met. Even a glancing blow might give the man the time he needed to finish Koji.

Koji stepped to the side, his sword still in a high guard. Impossibly, the giant seemed to have predicted the move, and managed to halt the blade in the middle of the downstroke, cutting across with impossible quickness.

Koji couldn't bring his blade down fast enough, so he followed Asa's example and dove to the side. The ground rushed up to meet him, and he fell hard on his left shoulder. He grimaced in pain as he tore his spear wound open further, but got to his feet before the giant could land the killing cut.

The two of them stood there, judging each other. Koji

wondered if he was quick enough to get inside the long blade and deliver a fatal blow. The giant rarely overextended with the blade, displaying his comfort and expertise with the weapon. It was a lot of space to cover, and Koji wasn't sure he could step forward without getting cut.

He took a deep breath, feeling the tension drop from his muscles. He was here to fight and kill Katashi, to end the terror who'd haunted the blades. Koji felt a warmth flood through his body and down his limbs. The sounds of the battle faded around him, leaving only him and the giant. He felt the giant lower his sword for another horizontal cut.

This time, Koji went deeper into his state of relaxation, following unknown instincts. He felt the enemy's muscles contracting, could read the intention as the mighty warrior began his cut. The giant was prepared for Koji to either block or dive out of the way, and his counters were already prepared. Either move would only prolong the fight or bring about his death.

Koji saw the answer in his mind before he performed it. He bent forward, and the huge man expected that the nightblade was going to dive again. The enormous sword started cutting downward in a deadly, graceful arc. Then Koji leaped and twisted, bringing his arms in tight to his torso. Thanks to the man's reaction, the sword was low enough that Koji's leap took him over the dangerous steel. Koji landed on one foot, continued twisting, and sliced through the gap in the man's armor at his neck.

There was no time to celebrate. As the large man fell, two more warriors took his place and the battle continued. But now Koji and the blades had regained their momentum. Koji could feel the presence of the blades diminishing behind him. His kind were dying to bring an end to this war.

Koji found himself with a few heartbeats of time,

looking up to see where Katashi's flag was. The flag was close, only ten paces away. Koji could see Katashi, mounted on his horse, pressed in with soldiers on all sides.

Koji felt a surge of energy wash over him like water from a cool stream. He pushed forward, his weapon finding holes in the defenses of his enemies. He had eyes only for Katashi.

The lord's eyes met his, and Koji saw the abject terror of the man. Katashi had trained in the deadly arts, but he was no warrior. Koji cut through the last of the guards and Katashi tried to run him over with his steed. Before he could get the horse turned around, though, Koji cut through the animal without remorse, bringing it crashing down.

Katashi was either skilled or lucky enough to survive the horse's collapse, rolling away awkwardly and coming to his feet uninjured. He drew his sword, still polished even though his forces had been at battle all night and all day.

The lord came in with a cut, as perfect as any master swordsman could ask for. But the strike was slow and lacked conviction. Koji sensed it coming and stepped into Katashi's guard before the man could react. He thrust out, driving his sword with all his strength through the man's armor, cutting into his stomach. Koji could have hit the lungs, but a slower death seemed better suited to the man.

Katashi dropped his sword as soon as Koji's entered his body. His eyes went wide with disbelief and Koji thrust his blade all the way in, feeling Katashi's ragged, surprised breath on his own face. Koji glared at the lord, then stepped back and pulled his blade out, twisting and slicing as he did. He'd leave no chance for Katashi to survive.

A moment later Asa entered behind Koji, cutting down Katashi's standard-bearer.

One guard, blind with anger and rage, charged at Koji. Koji cut at him dismissively and the man fell.

He heard mad laughter below him, and he looked down to see Katashi with a gleam in his eye. When Katashi saw that Koji was looking, he laughed again. "You're too late," he sputtered, blood coming out the corners of his mouth.

Then Katashi, Lord of House Amari, breathed his last.

24

F rom her perch on the road that led up to Stonekeep, Mari watched the battle unfold with her untrained eyes. She'd already seen more battle in her life than she ever wanted, and even Takahiro had encouraged her to remain behind. But if anyone had to face their responsibility for this war, she had to. She had made the decisions that led to this moment, and she wouldn't hide behind the walls of her castle. She would watch what she had set in motion.

Doing so was far from easy. Every time the lines moved, she thought of the lives that movement cost. Off to the side, Takahiro conferred with Fumio, adding his suggestions as he saw fit. For the most part, though, the path was silent. Fumio was the best tactician among them, and the battle was his to win or lose.

Although she believed it was important for her to be present, Mari didn't have anything besides her presence to offer. She didn't know battle strategies, and she certainly didn't understand the nuanced clash of armies happening below her.

At times she thought she saw a glimmer of the battle happening underneath the battle. She saw how an infantry unit took a small rise in the land, then guarded it so archers could better strike at their enemies. She saw how cavalry remained mobile, crashing into the parts of the battle that looked to turn against them. Other times she saw actions she couldn't understand, but she refused to panic. She trusted Fumio and his orders. He'd always been a gifted general.

Mari did see Katashi's banner fall. Squinting her eyes, she thought she could make out a pool of black among all the red. Had some of the nightblades attacked from the rear? Hajimi had promised no such action. He'd made it clear that once the blades passed through Katashi's lines, their role in the war was over. Mari had seen the pitifully small remnant depart as the sun had risen, leaving a wide swath of destruction in its wake.

She couldn't be sure what she saw, but the loss of Katashi's banner had an immediate impact on his remaining soldiers. The line buckled, and although it would still be some time before the army was defeated, even Mari could see that the greatest single threat to her house lands had been conquered. Yoshinori, probably hiding somewhere up in Stonekeep, would be sorely disappointed to know that his benefactor had died.

Mari contained her pleasure at the knowledge. As tempting as it was, she never wanted to become the person who delighted in the suffering of another. Yoshinori might be a fiend, but he was still a member of her house. She needed to remember that.

She heard Takahiro walk up next to her. He reached down and grabbed her hand as they watched the battle.

"You saw Katashi's flag fall?"

She nodded.

"I believe it was Koji and Asa. I couldn't quite see clearly, but I'm fairly certain."

Mari wished that they had more of the looking glasses. Right now, every one Stonekeep possessed was being used by a commander or military officer. She would have loved to see Katashi's fall up close. What Takahiro said seemed reasonable, though. If anyone was going to turn around and attack Katashi from his flank, it would be those two. They had just as much cause to hate Katashi as she did.

The news was good, but she didn't allow herself hope, not yet. The winds blew from the west, filling her nose with the scent of death. The cost of this battle was already too high, and it wasn't yet over.

As Katashi's forces slowly collapsed, Mari turned the bulk of her attention to Satoru's forces. There, Kita's soldiers were outnumbered, but the southern soldiers fought poorly. Isamu had never focused much on his military forces, and that mistake was costing his house now. Mari watched their house lines hold easily against haphazard assaults.

Mari looked over at her husband, feeling warm even as she thought the word. "Can we win?"

Takahiro thought for a moment before answering. "We can, but this battle could still turn either way."

His hand felt solid in hers, something she could hold onto no matter how chaotic the world around her became. Mari clasped it tighter as they watched the battle for the fate of the Kingdom.

Her attention was suddenly attracted to a commotion below her. From their position, Mari, Takahiro, and Fumio could look down on the field from a position of relative safety. If the battle had gone poorly, it left them the option to retreat back to Stonekeep. However, they'd kept a large force of guards below them, and any enemy would have to break through their lines even to get that far.

Near the beginning of the road a battle was ongoing between their warriors and a large contingent of Katashi's warriors. But the group of soldiers in red was pushing through the blue. The battle was small compared to the larger fight below, but few of the commanders seemed focused on it. Their attention was on the greater battle.

As Mari watched, she saw men in red uniforms cut down her own warriors with ease. She'd seen that type of fighting before. She squeezed Takahiro's hand and pointed down the road. "Are those nightblades with Katashi's army?"

Takahiro turned and watched the battle himself, then cursed. "They are."

The nightblades pushed their way into the ranks of guards, cutting through them like grass. The fight was getting close enough that the commanders were noticing as well.

Suzo was the one who saw reason first. She stood a little below them on the road, between them and the fight. She turned to Lady Mari. "We need to get everyone back to Stonekeep, immediately."

Takahiro protested. "If we leave, morale is going to take a hit, and we'll lose communication with our commanders on the ground. We could lose the entire battle."

Suzo hesitated, caught between her duty to her lord and her duty to keep Lady Mari safe. A glance from Mari was enough for the head of the guards to realize that Mari wasn't going to leave her husband. She cursed, more colorfully than Mari would have expected. Even Takahiro's mouth gaped open for a moment before he reasserted his calm.

"Fine," Suzo said. "But I'm going to have horses ready. If we can't hold them, I'll expect you to retreat. You can't enjoy the victory if you're dead!"

25

A sa felt the exhaustion deep in her bones, like a weight she carried with every movement. Being near Koji helped, but even his gift, supporting them all, had limits.

She didn't have the language or the energy to describe what had happened. Something about Koji fed the rest of them. Looking from face to face, she saw the others were thinking it, but they too were shaken by what they'd experienced. Nothing like this existed even in legends.

After a night of fighting and running they should have been too tired to make that charge against Katashi. But Koji changed them, somehow deepened the reserve of strength they could draw on. Even now, Asa could feel it. When he came close, she felt more awake and aware, the weariness sloughing off her like dead skin. But when he turned to another and took a few steps away, she could feel the exhaustion settling over her again.

She didn't have a good explanation. She could sense the way energy flowed into Koji, lit with purpose again as he was. Some of that energy seemed to be flowing into them as well.

Their small group of nightblades, now less than twenty strong, stood in a strange place in the battlefield. They were almost entirely surrounded by Katashi's soldiers, but no one fought. A handful of soldiers had attacked immediately after Katashi's death, driven by grief and rage. They'd been quickly killed, and now the blades were left alone.

Something bothered Asa. Why had Katashi said it was too late? He'd sounded so confident, and it seemed unlikely that his last words were a bluff. So what was he referring to?

Asa struggled to her feet, looking around at the battle. Takahiro's forces were almost to where she and the blades stood, which meant Katashi's forces must almost be destroyed. From her position she couldn't see much of the battle between the other two houses, but that couldn't have been what Katashi spoke of.

Asa turned and looked to the road up to Stonekeep, where the flag of House Kita snapped proudly in the wind. Below the flag a skirmish raged, some last force of Katashi's making a final push. But they were outnumbered, so it shouldn't matter.

As Asa watched, though, she saw the way Katashi's forces sliced through their enemies. They might be outnumbered, but they were winning. Asa cursed as connections built in her mind. She couldn't confirm her guess. That particular battle was farther away, and in the mass of people, Asa's sense couldn't travel nearly far enough. But she felt confident she was right.

Asa called Koji over and pointed to the road. "Are those Katashi's nightblades?"

Koji only watched for a moment before reaching the same conclusion. "They must be."

Around them, Katashi's men began surrendering. The battle, at least here, was ending.

Asa looked over at Koji. "You want to save her." It was barely even a question.

He nodded, and although his expression remained calm, Asa could sense even more energy pouring into him. What kind of man was he? She could sense everything happening to him herself, but she could barely believe what her sense was telling her.

Asa looked back to the north, where the other blades had now disappeared. She felt a pang of jealousy for those who had gone on, for those who had already put all of this behind them.

And in that moment, she saw glimpses into the future. The blades were making her mistake, thinking they could leave life behind and strike out on their own. They didn't see the connections that tied them all together. Eventually, the blades would either have to return or would wither and stagnate on their own.

Asa felt some of Koji's excess energy seep into her, strengthening her limbs. "One last battle," she said.

"One last battle," Koji said.

THEY RAN, Asa's breath coming in short gasps.

Koji had gathered the remaining nightblades and told them what he planned. Asa didn't know if they simply followed Koji, or if they agreed that Mari needed to be protected, but every single person followed. Asa suspected it was Koji. He was the type of person others wanted to follow.

They had tried going through House Kita forces but quickly realized their error. Those soldiers didn't necessarily view them as friendly. They didn't attack as quickly as Katashi's forces had, but they also weren't just going to let nightblades through their ranks. After a few moments of hasty negotiation, Koji had given up and decided to run around the rest of the battlefield.

The confusion from the last remnants of battle helped them. Katashi's men were surrendering, and little attention was given to the blades as they ran on the outskirts of the field. Occasionally a unit would attempt to follow, but never for very long. They had other responsibilities, and no military unit wanted to take on a collection of nightblades.

Asa knew she shouldn't be able to keep running, but Koji kept them moving. Asa wondered, once this was all done, what the damage to her body would be.

They made it to the road and started the long climb. Katashi's forces, combined with the mercenary nightblades, had broken through the infantry units protecting the base of the road and were now engaged with the guard units above. Once the guards fell, nothing stood between Mari and her doom. Why didn't she leave?

The answer became apparent as Asa crested a small rise in the road. The horses that had been held in reserve for the nobles were riddled with arrows. Katashi's archers had focused on the beasts, forcing the nobility and command to stand their ground. They didn't have any hope of defeating the incoming mercenary blades in a footrace.

As they gained elevation, Asa glanced over at the last of the battle. The focus had turned entirely onto Satoru's forces, which looked to be gradually collapsing. The battle could be won, but Mari needed to be alive to reap the benefits of their costly victory.

Asa turned her attention back to the road as they neared the chaos.

The advance of the nightblades hadn't gone unnoticed. A rear guard of Katashi's soldiers turned and drew bows, and Asa cursed.

Arrows leaped from the bows, cutting into their ranks. They still didn't have shields, and with the narrow road and little time to react, there weren't many options. The only fact in their favor was that the archers only got off two volleys before the blades got too close.

The remaining nightblades crashed into Katashi's forces. Asa cut down an archer who hadn't had enough time to reach for his sword, then sliced into the leg of another warrior, dropping him to the ground.

Then she ran into her first enemy nightblade. Apparently, some of them had turned to meet the threat from below. The blade was a man she didn't recognize, his red uniform failing to disguise the energy pouring off him. He was strong.

The man stepped forward calmly, cutting down at Asa's head. Asa deflected the cut with her left sword, allowing his strike to glance off her weapon, then cut across at him with her right sword.

The man slid smoothly back. He'd kept his distance as he struck, remaining out of easy range of her shorter swords. With his ability to sense her attacks and his advantage in reach, she would have a hard time safely closing the gap between them.

They squared off. Asa tried to close the distance, but the other nightblade was having none of it. He kept the separation wider than Asa wanted. If she managed to back him into a tight space he'd launch himself forward, driving her back under a quick flurry.

She needed to fight her instinct to give ground against fierce attacks. The next time he attacked, Asa stepped forward and their blades met in a frenzied clash of steel. The other nightblade was even faster than she was, but her ability with two swords kept them evenly matched. He slid around another attack, then managed to push his own sword inside her guard. The bloody tip sliced toward her face and Asa found herself stepping back to avoid the cut. Her right foot slipped and she realized she was near the edge of the road, a long fall behind her.

Panicked, she stepped forward, right into his next attack. Asa barely dodged the cut at her neck, and the man's sword sliced a deep gash across her cheek. Lacking choices, she fell back, realizing too late she wasn't sure how far from the edge she was. Fortunately, she landed on her back, looking up as the man turned his sword to drive it into her.

She lashed out with her leg as she twisted away. The other nightblade, committed to his attack, couldn't shift his weight even though he sensed the blow coming. She caught his knee and felt it shatter under her foot. The nightblade's sword cut into the road where she'd just been. She continued the twist, bringing herself up to her knees, then used one of her own swords as a crutch to stand.

The other nightblade tried to stand, but his left leg wouldn't support any weight. Asa stepped close, deflecting his halfhearted attack, then drove her second sword deep into his lungs.

She turned and continued the fight.

Koji's fighting had reached a standstill. Only one nightblade stood against him, but she had support. The only explanation Koji could think of was that, somehow, Katashi had given the nightblade mercenaries the time to train with one of his units. Their coordination wasn't by chance, and Koji was close to giving up ground against them.

The nightblade stood side by side with two spearmen.

Working together, they formed an almost impenetrable wall. The spears forced Koji to keep at a distance from them. Individually, none of them would have posed much of a challenge. But whenever he got inside the guard of one of the spears, the nightblade was there, defending until the second spear could push Koji back again.

If they'd been foolish enough to attack, Koji might have had an opportunity. Attacks opened up opportunities for counterattack, but if he didn't attack them, they simply held their ground, preventing him from moving forward. Koji felt the frustration welling up inside him. As he stood there, stuck, the other enemy nightblades made more progress toward Lady Mari. This grouping in front of him knew they didn't need to beat him. They only needed to hold him back.

Koji raged, launching into a series of cuts that should have brought them all down. But the other nightblade, sensing his intent, stepped forward, blocking his cuts as the spears stabbed around her. Koji suffered two more gashes, one across his torso and one on his right leg. He retreated, cursing his impetuousness. Pride had brought down plenty of warriors before him. He couldn't let his name be added to the roster. Not yet, at least.

He paused and took a deep breath, calming himself. Doing so took an enormous effort, especially as he saw the progress the enemy nightblades were making. Mari needed his support one last time, and she needed it soon.

Rescuing Mari from the attack would probably cost him his life. There were still so many enemies, and although his allies fought valiantly, their time was running out. Koji couldn't allow harm to befall Mari, though. He'd made too many mistakes in his life, and he refused to live with that one. His life was a small price to pay.

He glanced at Asa, who'd just won a duel with another

nightblade near the edge of the road. He would have liked more time with her, but he had enjoyed the time they had. He hoped she would understand.

Koji didn't know how he brought the energy into himself, but as he settled into his stance, he felt alive and whole in a way he hadn't felt since he was a trainee, young and idealistic. He'd always been torn between the blades and the Kingdom, his own life and his duties. Now, for the first time in cycles, he felt complete. Everything felt like it had come to this.

He stepped forward and a new world opened up in front of him. He sensed attacks far before they occurred, so far in advance the extra information almost confused him. He saw his potential responses and sensed what the reaction to those responses would be. In moments, he knew how this particular battle would end.

Koji allowed one spear tip to pass less than a hand's width away from his neck. He twisted and stabbed, ready for and expecting the downward cut from the nightblade as she moved in to block his stab.

He responded by spinning, twisting all the way around with a strong horizontal cut. The second spear, seeing his back, stabbed at it, the strike true. The enemy nightblade, focused only on deflecting Koji's cut, didn't sense her partner's attack. As her own sword came up, she cut through her partner's attack, slicing his spear in two.

Not only did the attempted deflection save Koji from the spear, it also caused the blade to lose her focus, surprise shattering her rhythm. Koji cut through her and the first spearman in one smooth motion. The second spear fled before Koji even had a chance to focus on him.

The attack had been effortless. Koji waded deeper into the battle, attracting enemies to him with every step.

· · ·

FOR A MOMENT, Asa couldn't help but stare as Koji attacked
the remaining enemy forces. All her senses jumped alive,
the sights, sounds, and sense of him vivid. He moved like
lightning. Turning her sense toward him almost brought her
to her knees. One thought rose above all others as she saw
him tear through opponents. *What was he?*

No easy answers existed. She wasn't sure any of the
blades had encountered someone like him before.

Simply put, he was Koji.

No one was like him, and she wasn't sure anyone would
ever be like him again.

Her own body practically crackling with energy, she
threw herself into the fray, trailing about five paces behind
him. Katashi's soldiers didn't stand a chance against their
overwhelming strength and speed. Asa moved almost
casually from attack to attack, every cut true.

She didn't know where her skill ended and Koji's gift to
them began. It didn't matter, truly. Swords swung at her and
spears stabbed at her, but she sensed every strike with ease,
finding the paths that kept her safe. In response, her own
swords cut through necks, torsos, arms, and legs, attacking
every target of opportunity.

All that mattered was remaining close to Koji. So long as
she moved with him, she was safe.

They seemed to have broken through a wall. The unit
attacking Mari had left a few nightblades to cover their
flank, but Asa and the others had pushed through. In the
center were only soldiers. The last nightblades stood in
front of them, making their own way toward Mari.

For as strong as Koji and his allies were, there weren't
many left. Of the more than two dozen that had joined them

in their initial charge against Katashi, Asa figured there were less than six now. But those few fought like demons, leaving no enemy standing as they charged forward.

Only fifteen paces separated her from Mari, and for the first time, Asa could see details in front of her as she cut her way forward. Suzo was bloodied and fighting, standing side by side with Takahiro. The man might be a lord now, but Asa knew he could fight. Once, he'd even beaten a nightblade while sparring. Or so Asa had heard.

Suzo and Takahiro fought against a nightblade, but they were losing ground. A little higher, General Fumio was calmly giving orders. But if the signals of the flag men were any indication, Fumio had plenty to say. He alone acted as though there wasn't a battle just below him. He'd win this fight, even if it cost him his life.

And there was Mari. She too was calm, her face impassive as she watched the battles, proudly standing there as a symbol to her warriors below.

Asa cursed. It would be just like Mari to stand there, noble until the very end.

Asa caught up to Koji and passed him as he engaged with another one of the nightblade-and-spear combinations. She cut down one of the spears as she passed, making Koji's life simpler. The nightblade attacking Suzo and Takahiro felt her coming, and turned around in time to meet her attack. Their swords met overhead, but the blade had forgotten the enemies behind him. Two swords drove through his chest in unison, Suzo and Takahiro racing to be the one who killed him.

Off to the right, two nightblades in red uniforms broke through the last of Mari's guards and charged toward her. Asa sprinted after them, sensing Koji finishing the nightblade who'd held him up.

Suzo and Takahiro followed closely behind, but Asa's pace, even after all she'd been through, outstripped them. Being near Koji still filled her with power she didn't understand.

Swords met with resounding echoes. Asa fought the two nightblades, doing everything she could to keep both away from Mari. She lasted for one heartbeat, and then another, and then they broke through her guard.

Takahiro and Suzo were there then, just in time to keep Mari safe. Suzo fell almost instantly, a cut open across her back. Asa couldn't see how deep it was. Takahiro lasted for a few moments longer, but he too fell to a cut across the leg. Again, Asa fought against the two nightblades, unable to hold them for more than a few moments. Her mind was empty of thought, her entire world steel and desperation. She'd been pushed back until Mari was only a pace or two behind her.

Then Koji was there, pushing one of the enemies back toward the edge of the road. The final nightblade, knowing he didn't have much longer against the two of them combined, brought his sword back for one last desperate stab.

Asa could kill him. Her swords were high and ready to cut from above. He was wide open, dropping his guard completely for the attempt on Mari's life. But her attack wouldn't stop him. His attack had already started, and it would finish no matter the killing blow she executed. His sword was too low for her to reach in time.

She stepped in front of the blade, feeling the cold steel stab straight through her torso.

Grunting with the effort, fighting against the sudden weakness in her legs, she drove one of her swords into the nightblade's neck. His face went slack and he dropped to the ground. As he did, Asa saw Koji kick the last enemy nightblade off the road to tumble to his death on the rocks below.

Asa's legs gave out, and it took all her control to fall to her knees and remain upright. She looked down at the sword embedded deep within. Even though she knew it was there, it still seemed so unreal to her.

Blackness swam at the edges of her vision, but surprisingly, there was no pain.

Koji and Mari were both there, seemingly at the same moment. Asa allowed herself to fall against Koji, relaxing in his embrace. As always, he was strong, like a wall that wouldn't be moved. She'd always loved that about him, even if it had frustrated her endlessly.

She looked at them both, the two people who had come to mean the most to her in her life. She'd thought she'd have something to say, but she found she didn't. A deep weariness was coming over her, a sleep she knew she'd never wake from. It made it difficult to speak. But also, she knew that both Mari and Koji knew her heart. What else was there to say?

Asa felt Koji's tears falling against her hair. She was sorry that she'd have to hurt him one last time.

Beyond, she saw Suzo struggling to stand, helping Takahiro to his feet. Her heart was glad that they lived.

She reached up and touched Koji's face, pulling it down until she felt his lips against her forehead.

Asa smiled, and in that last moment, she felt the presence of all life, moving all around them in a cycle that defied their understanding. She knew then that she would see her family again soon.

She closed her eyes and exhaled her last breath.

She'd finally found peace.

26

Despite the political risks, Mari insisted that Koji stay inside Stonekeep castle. Only Koji and two other blades survived the final charge. After some discussion, Koji had sent the other two on their way. This battle was no longer theirs, and they seemed grateful to leave. Koji alone had gone up to Stonekeep with Asa's body.

He didn't have many memories of the next few days. Mari and Takahiro had been busy with the aftermath of the battle. They had won, but the cost had been enormous on all sides. Mari and Takahiro negotiated terms with the other lords. Katashi was replaced by Lord Tsuneo, a relatively minor noble who was thrust to the head of the house thanks to recent events. Koji heard all the rumors of changes, but couldn't bring himself to care.

He spent plenty of time with Asa's corpse, preparing her body for the pyre. As he worked, he couldn't help but think that she was even more beautiful in death than she had been in life. When she'd rejoined the Great Cycle, she'd been at ease, finally.

Beyond that, he felt empty. He'd been prepared to give

his life, but not Asa's. He ate and trained, but more often than not he simply sat there, staring at the stone walls, his mind blank. He wanted the world to stop and acknowledge what had happened to Asa, but the Great Cycle continued to turn, so much larger than any individual life.

Two nights after the battle of Stonekeep Valley, Koji, Mari, Takahiro, and Suzo gathered in a private courtyard of the castle, lighting the pyre together. As the flames consumed Asa's body, Koji finally broke down. He'd cried when she died, but hadn't since then. He fell to his knees, painful sobs wracking his body as he truly understood that he'd never see Asa again. All the pains he'd suffered paled in comparison.

The others didn't attempt to speak. Mari embraced him, and Takahiro laid a hand on Koji's shoulder. Suzo, not knowing Koji, simply bowed deeply. As the fire burned down to embers, they took their leave.

It took Koji almost half a moon to decide what to do. He wandered toward the rooms that had been remade as Mari's offices. She was alone when he was announced.

Koji entered and Mari greeted him with a smile and a bow. "You've reached a decision, then?"

Koji nodded. "That obvious?"

"It's the first time you've left your room on your own since the funeral."

"There are a few tasks I need to complete. Afterward, I will make my way to Highgate and find the rest of the blades."

Mari's spies had given them that information. Hajimi had led the blades to Highgate, a port town far to the north. From there, the blades had boarded ships and left. Mari's sources believed blades were still present in town, but nobody knew where the ships had gone.

Mari took a sip of tea at her desk. "I know you need to go, but I'll be sorry to see you leave."

Koji looked down at his traveling clothes. After the events of the battle, it had become clear that the blades weren't welcome anywhere. Fortunately, Koji's name was known more than his face. But if anyone else found out he was here, there was little doubt it would wreck the fragile truce.

"It's been an honor," he said.

She looked at him thoughtfully. "How long will your tasks take?"

Koji thought. "A few moons, perhaps. Why?"

"Will you come to the treaty signing in the spring? You are the only blade of stature I know left in the Kingdom, and although it can't be official, it seems wrong to have the treaty signed without at least one blade there to witness it."

Koji considered the offer. He didn't really have any strict plans. He nodded.

"You'll always be welcome here, Koji," Mari said. "Even if we can't see you officially."

Koji bowed. "Farewell, Lady Mari. May you and your husband reign in peace."

Mari returned the bow, even deeper, and Koji turned and left the room.

SUZO STOOD STILL, her weight balanced on her toes as she lightly held onto the rock wall outside of Yoshinori's house in Stonekeep. Below her, guards wandered the grounds, searching for intruders like her. Fortunately, it was night and no one ever bothered to look up. She'd gotten the idea from the assassination attempt on Lady Mari's life a few moons ago.

Despite her precarious position, Suzo didn't feel much fear. She'd climbed harder routes in more difficult conditions in her previous life as a smuggler. She could rest against this wall for as long as it took.

The window above her was open, Yoshinori's voice coming from inside. Suzo had no trouble picking out the words. The former noble was livid. Earlier in the day, the closed council had officially stripped him of his lands and title. He'd been found guilty of treason and Takahiro had sentenced him to exile. Suzo could hear him talking to an aide, already planning how to turn this setback to his advantage.

Yoshinori had no way of knowing that after the council, Suzo had met with Mari privately, suggesting that exile was too lenient a punishment. The man would always be a thorn in their side. Mari had met Suzo's gaze, understanding the head of her guard well enough. She had nodded, and that was all Suzo needed.

The aide left and the room fell silent above. Suzo climbed up through the window, as silent as a ghost. Yoshinori's back was to her, packing a trunk full of his silk robes.

Suzo stepped on a loose floorboard, intentionally letting Yoshinori know she was there. He snapped around, a look of wide-eyed panic plastered on his face. Then he saw who it was and the fear vanished instantly.

"Of course she'd send a woman after me." The tone in his voice was mocking, and he slowly brought his hand down to draw the sword hanging at his hip, as though he had all the time in the world.

Suzo dashed forward, the dagger punching him in the stomach. She punched again and again, ensuring no healing could save him. In a few moments it was done, and she stepped back.

She held his gaze as he died, content to let her face be the last sight he saw. Then she cleaned the dagger and began the journey back to the inn where she'd first spoken with Asa privately. She'd raise a cup for her fallen friend. She thought Asa would appreciate that.

KOJI SPENT the winter wandering the Kingdom. After leaving Stonekeep he slowly worked his way south, toward the lands where his adventure had begun. The winter was harsh, and starvation was every bit the problem that Mari had worried it would be. If there was a bright spot to be found in the war, it was that there were now far fewer mouths to feed.

There were still too many, though. Koji did what he could. He was an excellent hunter, and he often brought meat to villages as he passed. It was never much, but Koji had learned only to do what he could. He could spend his whole life in service to others and still not solve even a fraction of the world's problems.

Before long, he made it down to where Haven had burned to the ground. Memories ran through Koji, and he let them, remembering his service to Minori and the mistakes he'd made in that service. Although he hadn't burned Haven, he felt as though he'd had some part.

For almost a full moon he volunteered to help rebuild the city. They were going to call it New Haven, and it would be the new capital of Lord Satoru's lands. The city's completion was one of Lord Satoru's primary objectives, and Lady Mari, through Takahiro, had donated a substantial amount of gold to the cause, earning her no small amount of goodwill.

Koji experienced the joy of building something for the first time in his life. His entire childhood had been focused on learning how to use the sword, how to kill and destroy. Now he built, and while he ended every day hungry and tired, he felt a deep satisfaction he never had before. When the city wall was complete, they officially renamed the capital, and people started returning.

Eventually, though, he needed to complete the task he'd been putting off. He took to the road again, trying to find a location that had only been described to him in vague terms. When he finally found it, though, there was no question it was the right place.

The house sat on the edge of some old woods. The woods protected it on one side, and a large rise in the land protected it on the other. And it was the only house for at least a league in any direction.

Koji approached until he was close enough to sense the lives inside. Then he sat in the snow and waited. The sun was high in the sky, and although the air was cold, Koji felt plenty warm in his heavy traveling clothes.

He didn't have to wait long. Soon, the door opened and a man came out. He was armed with a sword and moved with the sort of grace that only came from being a nightblade. A nightblade with an awful lot of experience. Koji recognized a master when he saw one.

The man stopped about five paces away from Koji, giving Koji a hard stare.

Koji stood up and brushed himself off. He'd believed Asa, of course, but experiencing it was something else entirely. He could see the man in front of him, clear as day, but couldn't sense anything. "Now, that *is* disconcerting," he said.

The man frowned, not sure what Koji referred to. Koji realized he was looking at perhaps one of the only men in the Kingdom who could fight him on even terms. If Koji couldn't sense the man's movements, he lost one of his greatest advantages. Part of him itched to try, but that was far from the reason he was here.

"My name is Koji," he continued. "I'm here because of Asa."

The man looked him up and down, his gaze not missing any detail. Finally, he sighed, and his stance relaxed. "She's dead, isn't she?"

Koji nodded.

Daisuke looked around, as though he was expecting Asa to jump out of a clump of grass somewhere. He nodded to the woods. "Come, walk with me. You can tell me how she died."

They walked into the woods and Koji did just that, leaving out no detail that he thought was important. Daisuke listened to the entire story, and by the time Koji finished, they were deep in the woods. Koji, as always, was reminded of just how much life there was in places like this.

"Why are you here?" Daisuke asked.

"She looked up to you, and she once told me that if there was one place in the Kingdom where she felt welcome, it was here. I wanted you to know how her story ended. To let you know that I believe she found peace."

Daisuke nodded curtly. Koji could tell his words had affected the man.

Koji had a question for him. "Will you leave with us?"

Daisuke shook his head, the response Koji had expected. The man had lived in hiding almost his entire life, and he'd built a life beyond the blades. There was no reason for him to give that up. Koji reached up and pulled out Asa's swords. He'd cleaned and polished them. "Then I'd like to give you these."

Daisuke hesitated. "Why me?"

"Because you taught her how to truly use these. I have no need for them. And Asa told me that your daughter is also gifted. If you so choose, perhaps they could be hers."

"I'm not sure I will train her."

"Then they can be a symbol for you, a reminder of the girl whose life you changed for the better."

Daisuke frowned, then bowed and took the swords. "Thank you."

Koji could understand why the former nightblade had chosen this place. Here, in the deep woods, Koji felt a peace, separate from the concerns of the world. He was almost sad to leave. When they reached the edge of the woods, Daisuke stopped and turned to him.

"I'm sorry that I will not offer you shelter for the night. We came out here to escape the madness of the world, and I will not invite any in, even if it comes in the guise of a friend."

Koji didn't mind. He wanted to be on his way back toward the land of House Kita.

The two warriors bowed toward one another. "Thank you, Koji," Daisuke said. "May you find peace."

"And may the peace of this place remain with your family," Koji replied.

Daisuke returned to his house, and Koji wrapped himself up tightly in his robes and began the long trek back to House Kita's lands.

27

M ari wondered if she would ever be able to look down on the valley with the wonder she once had. Now, even though the battlefield had been cleared, she still saw only the bodies and blood of the battle that had shattered the Kingdom for good.

Her proposal, which had once been laughed at, was now becoming a reality. Even she didn't approve of the result, but she supposed that was the point. It was still better than any of the other options. It acknowledged the world as it was, not as they wished it would be.

The winter had been every bit as nightmarish as she had feared. Across the Kingdom, famine had ravaged an already-devastated population. Lord Satoru's land had probably fared best of all, but even his losses had been substantial. The war, combined with the weather, had devastated everything. Mari planned on taking a census this summer, but she suspected that only a quarter of her population had survived. Lord Tsuneo, replacing Katashi, had fared even more poorly.

Katashi had needed more resources, and he'd poured everything into his war effort. It was a gamble and he had lost. All in all, the Kingdom, in just a few short cycles, had fallen to a fraction of its former glory.

Mari knew the cost couldn't just be measured in lives. Those who had grown up with the time and leisure to advance philosophy and knowledge were gone. No longer could an artist make a living through painting or writing. Every hand would be bent toward survival.

The Kingdom was broken more deeply than most realized. It would take many cycles for them to return even to the types of lives they remembered.

They would have to find their own way forward now. A way without the strength of the blades to guide and protect them.

Thinking of the blades drew Mari's eyes to Koji, who had joined her party quietly as they left Stonekeep. No one paid him much attention, and his hood covered his face. She was glad he was here.

Below them, a large group of nobles were gathered. Lords Satoru and Tsuneo were present already, and Takahiro would complete the set of houses.

Before, Mari might have felt nervousness, but not today. She felt confident. There wasn't any other option. None of them could afford any other decision. And with Koji nearby, she couldn't help but feel secure in her personal safety.

They rode down to the gathering, Takahiro in the lead. Part of Mari felt a pang of jealousy. This whole treaty had been her idea, but it would be Takahiro who would go down in history as the one who'd made it happen. Only time would tell if he was viewed favorably or not.

The field was almost silent, a dramatic difference from

the last time Mari had looked over the valley. The only sounds were the flags snapping in the spring wind. As they reached the field, they dropped off their horses and walked into the tent where the other lords were gathered.

Mari worked over all the stipulations of the treaty in her mind, checking for the thousandth time that there wasn't a mistake they were making at the last moment. Over the course of the past few moons, there had been discussion back and forth between the lords, ironing out the final details of the agreement. Today wasn't about negotiating, it was about celebrating a new peace.

The first and most important stipulation of the treaty was that the old Kingdom would be no more. That, more than anything else, was what pained Mari. She'd fought long and hard, thinking that she could save the land. But after the damage of the past few cycles, she didn't think that was reasonable. Too many lives had been lost, too much history destroyed. None of the houses would willingly accept a separate ruler over them, and none of the houses had the military support to enforce peace throughout the land.

Her solution, then, was to not fight the fight in the first place. They'd been operating as separate houses for some time now, and continuing the pattern would be easier than trying to install a new king. The Kingdom would become the Three Kingdoms, each governed independently.

She'd left a clause in the treaty, a thread of hope for them all to cling to. Any of the lords, at any time, had the right to call a conclave that the others were required by law to attend. The intent, unwritten, was that it provided an opportunity for the lords to reunify the Three Kingdoms once again in the future. Mari didn't think it would be invoked in their lifetimes, and maybe not even their children's, but eventually they would put the hate of the past behind them and unify once again.

Dealing with the blades had been another thorny issue. While most of the blades had departed, new ones would be born. The gift tended to manifest in families where at least one of the parents was gifted, but sometimes one arose naturally. The best solution they'd come up with was a system of learning centers. Those discovered with the gift would be sent there, ideally to learn the skills of the dayblades. The Three Kingdoms could always use more healers. Unfortunately, without input from the blades, it was difficult to tell what was reasonable and what wasn't.

Any blade discovered who wasn't under the control of one of the learning centers would be killed. As soon as the lords signed the treaty, Koji would be killed if people knew who he was. Mari hated the lie inherent in their actions immediately after the signing of the treaty, but she still felt this was the best path.

For all that the treaty represented, the mood around the tent was somber. None of the lords gathered had been responsible for the war, but they were the ones there for the conclusion. They respected one another, at least, but there wasn't any love lost between them. This wasn't a treaty where they would give long speeches or celebrate with their people. It was a treaty that saved them all from absolute ruin.

By the time her mind wandered back to the signing, the lords were already gathered around a table. There were three copies, and the lords were looking through them to make sure they were the same. When they all looked up, they nodded to one another. Takahiro signed each of the treaties, then sent them over to Lord Satoru. Satoru signed them, then passed them to Tsuneo. Within a few moments, it was all over.

The Kingdom was no more, but the land would have peace.

EPILOGUE

He had tried to live on the island with the other blades, but Koji, as well as quite a few others, hadn't been able to take it for more than a few cycles. He'd tried. For Asa's sake, he had tried.

The island would have been paradise for her, he thought. The blades had built a home there, far away from the concerns of the Three Kingdoms. There were schools, and blades ran training sessions constantly. Not every person born to the blades was gifted, but many were, and after cycles of seeing their population diminish, their numbers crept upward once again.

Like the Three Kingdoms, they were slowly rebuilding. But the cuts had gone deep, and it would take an impressive amount of time for those wounds to heal.

Koji felt that most of the surviving blades fell into two camps. The first group, largest by far, was the group that felt no displeasure at leaving the problems of the Three Kingdoms in the past. They wanted to live lives of peace, wanted to embrace farming and training, with no real hope of ever needing their skills. Their island wasn't large, but for many blades, it was the first time they could live without fear of judgment from others. For most, the sacrifice of freedom was worth it. Asa would have loved it.

Koji didn't. He'd enjoyed constructing houses and planting the fields, but as soon as it was clear that they'd made a sustainable home for themselves, he found himself growing restless. He trained, and he taught new generations. No one quite understood how he managed to pull such energy into himself, and he wasn't quite sure either. He had his suspicions, but that was it.

But even daily sparring didn't satisfy him. Every day on the island he felt as though he was running in a circle, covering a lot of distance but going nowhere. He didn't have any particular goals, but he knew the island couldn't be his home.

He'd spoken with Hajimi, and the leader of the blades, now getting almost too old to lead, allowed him passage off the island.

Koji hadn't been the first, and he probably wouldn't be the last. So long as they swore never to discuss the island, Hajimi didn't attempt to force anyone to stay. They were returned to Highgate whenever a boat left, and abandoned. Hajimi's only rule was that if they left, they couldn't return. Other than the handful of navigators who knew how to find the island, the trip to and from the island was one-way.

When Koji left, there had been plenty of tears. For the first time since becoming a blade, he'd managed to make numerous friends, and if not for the deep discontent in his heart, he would have remained. Junko, for one, had become one of his best students, a sword master in her own right. But he needed more than this, even if it meant being hunted and an outcast for the rest of his life.

Koji crossed the sea to Highgate, then began heading

south. He had some idea that he wanted to see Lady Mari again, but he did not hurry. He had the rest of his life to spend in the land. He wandered from village to village, mostly just observing how life was progressing.

At Highgate, there was no evidence of the war. It had never gotten that far north. But after a moon of traveling south, the signs were still visible after five cycles. Buildings were burned out, as were some forests that were just starting to regrow.

Koji was also surprised by the number of people. Almost everywhere he went he heard the cry of babies, but there were so few citzens. The Three Kingdoms would take several generations to recover its population, and that was assuming no more disasters befell them.

Eventually, Koji made his way to Stonekeep. No one had bothered him for most of the trip. The only close call he'd had was when he passed one of the new learning centers. Some of the children had sensed him and told their elders. Fortunately, it was easy enough to escape them, but he made a note to himself. It would become harder for the gifted to live in the Three Kingdoms, harder than ever before.

He passed through the gates of Stonekeep without incident, renting a room at an inn and waiting until the next meeting of the open council. When the day arrived, he appeared early to claim a place where he could watch the lord and lady. When the sun reached its zenith, quite a crowd had gathered and the doors opened to admit Lord Takahiro and Lady Mari.

Koji hadn't expected the onslaught of emotions he felt when he saw the two of them. They walked hand in hand, and if possible, Lady Mari looked even lovelier than before. Her belly was round with child, and a very young girl walked behind the couple. Takahiro walked with a slight limp, evidence that his wound from the Battle of Stonekeep Valley had never healed completely.

The citizens brought forth their complaints, and Koji reveled in the experience. Takahiro and Mari listened to each complaint, judging it fairly. Takahiro gave the rulings, but Koji noticed that whenever a decision wasn't simple, he'd lean over and whisper with Mari. Only when they had reached some sort of agreement did Takahiro give his decision.

The citizens seemed content to Koji, pleased with their rulers. Some complaints were more severe, but each was handled with grace.

As the afternoon wore on, Mari's eyes finally traveled over Koji, stopping when she saw him. He gave a bit of a smile and a short bow. She didn't raise an alarm about him, and after the council finally concluded, excused herself from Takahiro's company. She came up to him, concern written on her face. "Is something wrong?"

He shook his head, and the little girl came up running behind her mother. "Walk with me?" Koji asked.

Mari nodded, and the three of them made their way to one of the viewpoints looking out over the valley.

Mari spoke first. "It's good to see you, Koji, but you know that it is death for both of us if you're discovered."

"I know. But I wanted to see you one more time."

"You never left?" Mari sounded skeptical.

"No, I did, right after the treaty was signed. But I couldn't leave the Three Kingdoms behind. I returned two moons ago."

"By yourself?"

Koji nodded. "You're doing well?"

Mari smiled. "Rebuilding has been a challenge, but we will become what we once were again. It will just take time."

The girl, who'd only been paying half-attention to her mother, began running all over the viewpoint. "Asa, stop that!" Mari snapped.

Koji gave Mari a look. She shrugged. "I couldn't think of any better way to honor her memory."

Koji nodded. "She would be pleased, I think."

They stood in silence for some time, looking out over the valley. "So, what will you do?" asked Mari.

"I'm not sure. Wander. Explore. Help however I can."

"You'll be hunted. Especially as the new students get older."

Koji nodded again. "I know."

Mari laughed. "It is good to see you again. But I should get going." She paused as she picked little Asa up. "Will I ever see you again?"

Koji shook his head sadly. "I don't think so."

It looked like she'd expected that answer. "Take care, Koji. Wherever life may lead you."

Koji bowed deeply. "It has, as always, been an honor, Lady Mari. Farewell."

Mari turned and left, and Koji returned to looking out over the Northern Kingdom, spread out before him. He could go anywhere, and eventually, he would. But for now he rested, enjoying the view, basking in the last rays of sunlight before evening fell.

He looked toward the north, where Highgate and the island of the blades stood. This land wasn't ready for them now, but someday, in the future, it would be.

Someday, the blades would return.

WANT MORE FANTASY?

As always, thank you so much for reading this book. I had a tremendous amount of fun returning to the world of *Nightblade*, and I hope you've enjoyed this journey as well.

This trilogy is a prequel to a series I wrote several years ago. If these books have been your first foray into the world of *Nightblade*, I'd recommend you check out the original trilogy, which starts with *Nightblade*.

Links to all of my books can be found at www.waterstonemedia.net

If you've already read the original series but are looking for some more fantasy, might I recommend a book I wrote called *Relentless Souls*? It's a standalone novel set in a new fantasy world, filled with fast-paced action.

THANK YOU

Before you take off, I really wanted to say thank you for taking the time to read my work. Being able to write stories for a living is one of the greatest gifts I've been given, and it wouldn't be possible without readers.

So thank you.

Also, it's almost impossible to overstate how important reviews are for authors in this age of internet bookstores. If you enjoyed this book, it would mean the world to me if you could take the time to leave a review wherever you purchased this book.

And finally, if you really enjoyed this book and want to hear more from me, I'd encourage you to sign up for my emails. I don't send them too often - usually only once or twice a month at most, but they are the best place to learn about free giveaways, contests, sales, and more.

I sometimes also send out surprise short stories, absolutely free, that expand the fantasy worlds I've built. If you're interested, please go to https://www.waterstonemedia.net/newsletter/.

With gratitude,

Ryan

ALSO BY RYAN KIRK

The Nightblade Series

Nightblade

World's Edge

The Wind and the Void

Blades of the Fallen

Nightblade's Vengeance

Nightblade's Honor

Nightblade's End

Standalone Novel

Relentless Souls

The Primal Series

Primal Dawn

Primal Darkness

Primal Destiny

Primal Trilogy

The Code Series

Code of Vengeance

Code of Pride

Code of Justice

ABOUT THE AUTHOR

Ryan Kirk is the bestselling author of the *Nightblade* series of books. When he isn't writing, you can probably find him playing disc golf or hiking through the woods.

www.waterstonemedia.net
contact@waterstonemedia.net